Praise fc

NIGHT OF THE LIVI

"Bringing new twists to old spine-tingling tropes, Shelly Page and Alex Brown have pulled together an all-star cast of both established and up-and-coming authors. *Night of the Living Queers* features tales that range from chilling to silly to downright gut-wrenching. This anthology is the perfect way to spend a blue moon Halloween!"

—Aiden Thomas, *New York Times* bestselling author of *Cemetery Boys*

"From delightful Halloween romps to gut-churning tales of rage, *Night of the Living Queers* has a story for every queer teen who loves the creepiest night of the year. Grab your flashlights, lock your doors, and dig in to this wonderfully chilling anthology!"

—Andrew Joseph White, *New York Times* bestselling author of *Hell Followed with Us*

"Full of thrilling scares, lovable characters, and riveting stories that get your heart racing, *Night of the Living Queers* is just as frightening as it is fun."

—Alexis Henderson, author of *The Year of the Witching*

"Filled with heart, haunts, and hit after hit, *Night of the Living Queers* will shock you in the best possible way. I actually fell out of my chair from sitting too far on the edge of it!"

—Sonora Reyes, author of *The Lesbiana's Guide to Catholic School*

"This anthology will have you watching over your shoulder and checking under your bed for monsters of the past come back to haunt you. Each author weaves an eerie tale set on the most chilling night of the year. Prepare to be spooked by queer horror that haunts you long after you've finished reading."

—Gabi Burton, author of *Sing Me to Sleep*

Night of the Living Queers

13 TALES OF TERROR & DELIGHT

Edited by
Shelly Page & Alex Brown

WEDNESDAY BOOKS
NEW YORK

This is a work of fiction. All of the characters, organizations, and events portrayed in these stories are either products of the authors' imaginations or are used fictitiously.

First published in the United States by Wednesday Books, an imprint of St. Martin's Publishing Group

NIGHT OF THE LIVING QUEERS: 13 TALES OF TERROR & DELIGHT. Copyright © 2023 by Michelle Page and Alessandra Brown. WELCOME TO THE HOTEL PARANOIA. Copyright © 2023 by Vanessa Montalban. THE VISITOR. Copyright © 2023 by Kalynn Bayron. A BRIEF INTERMISSION. Copyright © 2023 by Sara Farizan. GUESTED. Copyright © 2023 by Rebecca Kim Wells. ROCKY ROAD WITH CARAMEL DRIZZLE. Copyright © 2023 by Kosoko Jackson. THE THREE PHASES OF GHOST-HUNTING. Copyright © 2023 by Alessandra Brown. NINE STOPS. Copyright © 2023 by Trang Thanh Tran. LEYLA MENDOZA AND THE LAST HOUSE ON THE LANE. Copyright © 2023 by Maya Gittelman. IN YOU TO BURN. Copyright © 2023 by Em X. Liu. ANNA. Copyright © 2023 by Michelle Page. HEY THERE, DEMONS. Copyright © 2023 by Tara Sim. SAVE ME FROM MYSELF. Copyright © 2023 by Ayida Shonibar. KNICKKNACK. Copyright © 2023 by Ryan Douglass.

All rights reserved. Printed in the United States of America. For information, address St. Martin's Publishing Group, 120 Broadway, New York, NY 10271.

www.wednesdaybooks.com

Designed by Devan Norman

Moon art © Croisy/Shutterstock.com, Halloween icon art © DenysHolovatiuk/Shutterstock.com

The Library of Congress Cataloging-in-Publication Data is available upon request.

ISBN 978-1-250-89296-6 (trade paperback)
ISBN 978-1-250-89298-0 (hardcover)
ISBN 978-1-250-89297-3 (ebook)

Our books may be purchased in bulk for promotional, educational, or business use. Please contact your local bookseller or the Macmillan Corporate and Premium Sales Department at 1-800-221-7945, extension 5442, or by email at MacmillanSpecialMarkets@macmillan.com.

First Edition: 2023

D 10 9 8 7 6 5 4 3

To anyone who's had to pretend
to be someone you're not—
may you become the fabulous person
you were always meant to be.

CONTENTS

INTRODUCTION

Dear Reader,

If you're reading this, we're willing to bet that Halloween brings you joy. The leaves show off their color-changing skills, sweaters get dusted and donned, costumes are picked, and candy is bought. There's something inherently special about Halloween. It's a time for tricks and treats, scares and delights; but it's also a time for acceptance, remembrance, celebration, and rebirth. It encourages the exploration of the darker parts of humanity while offering a chance for many to be authentic without fear of judgment or reproach. It's when many people feel they no longer have to hide the best parts of themselves.

The idea for this anthology came to Shelly in the spring. As usual, she'd been thinking about horror and lamenting over the limited QPOC books in the genre. As queer women of color, we often feel overlooked and underrepresented—and we're not alone. The intersection of queerness and ethnic diversity is functionally invisible in most things, horror included. Queer people of color have been pushed to the margins and subjected to dehumanizing stereotypes, portrayed as "other," as "savage," and as "monsters." This warps the perception and authenticity of queer people of color, especially for young readers.

This anthology allows us to reclaim that narrative and celebrate the complexity of our long-denied humanity. It is meant to showcase our stories and is intentionally set during Halloween, a time when we are most visible.

All the stories take place during a blue moon, a common celestial event where an additional moon appears during the year. What's less common is for a blue moon to happen on Halloween night. That is a truly magical phenomenon and the perfect setting for this collection.

Inside, you'll find thirteen stories of love, loss, acceptance, bravery, adventure, and romance.

You'll find stories that will challenge, comfort, humor, and haunt. In all the stories, you will hear our voices.

Enjoy!

Shelly & Alex
Editors

"I have love in me the likes of which you can scarcely imagine and rage the likes of which you would not believe. If I cannot satisfy the one, I will indulge the other."

— Mary Shelley,
Frankenstein

WELCOME TO THE HOTEL PARANOIA

Vanessa Montalban

Her grandmother told her once that the sea gets what it wants. If you go against it, it'll show you who rules. So when her grandmother's hat had been carried off by the wind, touched its rim to the water, the hat belonged then to the sea. The earth was a lot like that too. You could take and take, build and build, but eventually, the land would take back.

Bathed under the garish tinge of a strange blue moon, Anabel knew for sure she was going to die tonight. From mortification. One glimpse through the hotel's double doors at the other costumes, and it was obvious she'd made a mistake. No one else was dressed like her. Their masks were ornate, dresses grand. The disguises were more Shakespearean and romantic literary than the polyester shit show she'd expected. These were *rich* kids—the foamy white cream of the crop, and they'd spent most of her adolescent life making sure she knew she was nothing but the grainy dregs.

She hovered on the gravel road—the never-completed roundabout to the hotel's entrance. A stiff wind cut across her collarbones through the rips of her tank. Everyone else was already inside, not a car in sight because the only way to get to the abandoned hotel was by a mile-long trek through the swampy forest littered with DO NOT ENTER signs.

She debated for the millionth time if this was a good idea.

The crumbly brick hotel looked like it was only a season away from growing teeth. At three stories tall, the hotel was built on land that had been dubbed Ghost City. The entire up-and-coming community had been deemed hazardous and abandoned due to a lawsuit over protected wetlands, grounds that had gone untouched for centuries. The bed-and-breakfast was the only structure ever completed on the acres of forested land, and it was rumored to be haunted by more than just unpaid contractor debts. She knew this because her father had told her stories. Like mostly everyone else in this shitty town, he'd been involved with the project in the '90s. He'd worked the land until his back gave out and his life boiled down to Percocets and beer.

People come back changed from that place, Anabel. It's bad soil. Sometimes you get so deep in the muck, there's no getting out.

But she was here for another reason. She was here for Chrys.

She pushed back her unruly hair again. From her pocket, she took out the note she'd found earlier today in her locker. The handwriting was so clearly Chrys's that she felt something sharp and parasitic take root behind her ribs.

Sinkhole Hotel. Ten o'clock.

So she was here, despite the warning bells clanging in her head. Despite Chrys's silence these past months since their kiss. Anabel had shown up.

She paused at the hotel's threshold. She could see the silhouette of a girl looking down at her from the ivy-covered balcony. She was dressed in a tattered brown dress and a skull mask that reminded Anabel of Santa Tierra—a sort of mother earth who dealt more in death than in growth. A long black veil crowned the girl's head with a stillness that set Anabel's teeth on edge. The costume was kind of messed up, considering their town had a long history surrounding Santa Tierra. An entire village who'd worshipped her centuries ago wiped out for their beliefs.

There was something familiar about the girl's silhouette, though, and the soft incline of her head, almost as if she were grinning from behind the mask. But she couldn't be sure, and by the time Anabel glanced away, toward the sound of a sharp laugh from inside, the veiled girl was gone.

Anabel had no idea the hotel would look like this. With all the rumors of it being deserted and haunted, she figured the walls would be stripped bare, the furniture absent, the interior a carved-out carcass eaten by time and neglect. But it must've been nearly ready for operations before they shut down. But that still didn't explain the electricity, the polished floors, or the full staff of servers. The split staircase wrapped the foyer in a homely circle, showcasing a small, intimate chandelier right in the center. The only sign of negligence were the sporadic plants, less a product of interior design and more a consequence of the encroaching wilderness outside, but the structure was unnervingly whole despite the trace of rotten wood in the air.

Still, between the open concept and her crappy costume, she'd never felt more exposed. Everyone in the entire lobby seemed to stop what they were doing as Anabel came in. She didn't recognize a soul. She was glued to the middle of the room under the sharp, precarious chandelier with nowhere to run.

"Anabel." The breathless voice was one she instantly recognized. She turned to see Chrys standing there in a full-length dress of white lace dusted with silver. She looked like a dream. "You're here."

Anabel's breath caught. It'd been so long since she'd seen Chrys this close. Seen the way her heavy bottom lip pinched in the center when she was stewing something over. The way her wood-grain-colored eyes pinned Anabel to the earth and made her forget her own name. The last time Chrys had said Anabel's name, she'd just kissed her. Chrys had taken the syllables of her name and framed them like a question. But Anabel had frozen up, and the surprise of something unexpected must've translated into something else. Something she could never take back or set straight, because right after, Chrys ran from Anabel's room and out of her life for good.

"I came because I saw your note."

"Right. My note." Chrys's expression looked pained for a moment before clearing. She tilted her head, studying Anabel's costume. She expected Chrys to say it was ridiculous and laugh, because it's what she would've said before. Back when they were brutally honest with each other and they were just two weirdos in a pod. Chrys looked over Anabel's makeup, the ripped tank and black jeans, the black jacket that used to be hers. "Superhuman undead female lead?" she asked, nailing it on her first guess because of course she did.

"Zombie Jessica Jones."

Chrys nodded at this. "No one ever considers the implications of an outbreak on the superpowered community."

"I know! That's what I keep saying." They laughed, and for a moment it felt like no time had passed.

"I like your hair this way," Chrys said, picking up a strip of Anabel's long, black wavy hair, like dipping her fingers into an oil spill. "Loose and wild."

Anabel's throat felt horribly dry. "I haven't unbraided it in so long." A last-minute decision. Chrys always liked when Anabel undid her braid that seemed permanently affixed to her head. Her large bounty of hair she hadn't cut since her mom died made Anabel's face look smaller, smaller than it already was.

Chrys smiled. "I know."

Anabel wanted desperately to keep the conversation going, tell her everything that had happened this past year without her, how much she needed her, but Chrys's expression suddenly cracked, a desperate panic leaching from her eyes that drew Anabel back. Like a holographic card turned to reveal someone else. "Why did you come here?"

Anabel felt struck. "W-what?"

A waiter showed up then, producing a tray of smoky drinks that smelled of burnt orange. "Spirits?" he asked. Anabel was about to say *No, thank you* when Chrys plucked two of the drinks and handed her one. The darkness in her expression was completely gone, almost as if Anabel had imagined it to begin with.

"Like I was saying, why don't you come with me? My friends are right over there—" And Chrys turned toward a dark corner of the room where an old-fashioned couch and pin-cushioned chairs were nestled in an alcove of mirrors. Anabel shook off the wave of shivers, the annoyance at the mention of *friends*, having no choice but to follow.

Luckily, conversation didn't halt when they approached. In one of the alcove's reflections, Anabel could see how weird she really looked. How out of place. Standing beside Chrys, she couldn't blame her friend for never having looked back.

Anabel swigged the orange drink, welcoming the burn down her throat.

Of course, Elisa was perched right in the center of the couch, her coven of followers glued to her sides like they'd been all through high school. Blair and Sasha, the twins, as they were called, though not related, made space so Chrys could settle in beside Elisa, their skirts like two bodies of water becoming one. Elisa's pretty face held a secretive grin that set Anabel's teeth on edge, and Chrys seemed like she was waiting for Anabel to say something or make an objection at the seating arrangements, but she didn't. How could she? This was Chrys's world now, not hers.

Chrys introduced them as if Anabel had never met them before. It was bizarre. They'd both known Elisa and her horde since elementary school. Everyone knew Elisa. Her father owned the town, including this plot of land and the hotel that was slowly sinking into the earth, that never should've been disturbed to begin with. But Anabel was just supposed to pretend like she'd never met these people at all? Like Elisa had never taunted her in middle school or the twins had never held her down in fifth grade while they rained tampons over her head?

"Isn't this place lovely?" Elisa asked, settling back. Her fingers played with the ends of Chrys's chestnut hair.

"Lovely," Anabel parroted.

From the love seat, someone spoke up. "Holy shit, what are you wearing?" The guy's name was Michael, another town founder baby—he was a senior who'd gotten suspended last year for painting all the urinals. "I fucking love it. Sit by me," he said, and she was immediately grateful. Michael didn't shut up about *The Walking Dead* or cult classic zombie movies. He barely took a breath between his rants, and she was honestly okay with it because the drone of his voice kept her from having to come up with something to talk about.

She wanted to ask about this place, though. Wanted to find out how they kept the hotel running and how they'd gotten permission to have so many people brought into a condemned building. But she'd downed her entire burnt orange drink and didn't think she could string a sentence together even if she tried, and besides, she knew money could buy anything.

But it wasn't easy watching Chrys with her new friends. She hardly recognized her. The held back laughs, the defeated hunch of her shoulders. Last Halloween, Anabel had lost her best friend. First when she fumbled the kiss, and then again when Chrys had been the only one invited to the annual Halloween party, crossing over the social gap she'd always wanted to. After that, Chrys made it clear she wanted nothing more to do with her, going as far as pretending they'd never even met. Erasing their years of history. Leaving Anabel alone in their shit town when their plan had always been to stick together. And now here she was like a glutton for punishment.

Because of the note. Her second chance.

Anabel's attention snagged back on the conversation.

"Looks the same as last year—"

She interrupted. "The party was here last year?"

The group went silent. Chrys leaned forward, her eyes strained. Urgent. "It was."

"But I thought—don't you all throw the Halloween party somewhere different every year? Wasn't that the big secret? The whole point?"

"Some things change," Elisa said, shrugging a thin shoulder.

Michael leaned back, crossing his feet. "And some things stay the same."

The mirrors—their reflections—were all looking at her differently. They looked . . . wrong. Anabel had to shut her eyes, rub them to shake the image. The lights were playing tricks on her.

Just then another waiter came by with more orange drinks, ending the conversation. "Spirits?"

As everyone got up to dance, Anabel stayed back, nursing her second cup. Michael tried pulling her after him, but she waved him away and he accepted this good-naturedly, taking the twins instead. He was the type of guy who pretended to get along with everyone, but she knew he had a mean streak. She'd seen him in the halls, lurking like a predator. She couldn't forget that this whole group was dangerous no matter how nice they were being now. She was here for only one reason.

There was a point when it was only Anabel and Chrys alone

in the alcove, an infinite version of them reflected in the mirrors. Anabel thought one of those versions of her had to be brave enough. Chrys kept cutting her a glance, inching her way closer, and Anabel found herself doing the same, blocked only by the armrests of their respective lounges. Anabel wanted to shake her awake, shake loose that dark fog that had settled over her friend for months.

If you would've just waited for me to tell you I felt the same, if you would've never come here, I'd be yours. We'd be ours.

Anabel swallowed down the sour taste of nerves, wanting to ask what was wrong, what had happened to them, but Elisa and Michael came barreling back.

Elisa hooked a slender arm over Chrys's shoulders. "Guess what just got here?" She wiggled her body in anticipation. By this time, Michael sat on the armrest, producing a tiny bag of little blue pills.

Dread dropped into Anabel's stomach. Parties, drinking, drugs. Duh. She wasn't sure why she was so surprised. She watched movies, she heard things—she wasn't *that* sheltered. But she'd been left out of these functions for so long, she hadn't expected to run into this choice now.

Elisa and Chrys took theirs. Chrys threw her neck back. She didn't even pause to debate it, as if the girl Anabel knew, the one who wouldn't eat anything with red dye or refused to take aspirin for headaches, never existed. As if, together, they'd never driven Chrys's mom to the hospital when she'd started foaming at the mouth.

Michael mimicked Elisa and dropped his heavy arm around Anabel, leaning too close. His breath hot and uncomfortable on her face. He was holding out a pill for her to put on her tongue. "Want to dream?"

Chrys's eyes already looked different. Or maybe it was the lights, or the fact she was wavering as if she were only a mirage. "You don't have to do anything, An. There's time now for everything."

What she said should've sounded hopeful, promising, but it only made Anabel's stomach turn. She declined Michael's offer to dream. Instead, they danced.

The lights cut across her sweaty skin. Her jacket was abandoned in some chair or consumed by the old walls.

What the sea wants, it takes. Like the earth.

The sense of abandon was contagious, even if she didn't take anything. It felt like she had. Like something was severed inside her, and she'd become untethered.

One second, they were all dancing. Chrys was in her arms. Smiling, laughing, and it did feel like a dream. But now Chrys was leaving. Elisa was tugging her away toward the top of the steps where other couples grappled for each other in the dark. Chrys turned back once, met Anabel's gaze, and disappeared. Again.

The twins were swaying their hands toward the ceiling, eyes closed as if they were wading through air. Michael held Anabel, pulling at her hips.

"I—" she started, but the music was too loud. Her voice too choked.

"Wait, baby zombie. Not yet."

She pulled away from him and he let go, eyes already shuttering as if he didn't care one way or another.

There were too many people crowding the front door, too many servers asking her if she wanted more spirits. She needed air. She stumbled upstairs, pushing past sweaty bodies, hearing snatches of strange conversation.

"This used to be her land, her people."

"They worshipped her. Then the village was desecrated."

Anabel couldn't meet anyone's glassy eyes. She made it down a dark hall, opening doors until she found an empty suite, relieved that no one seemed brave enough to venture into the privacy of the vacant rooms.

Again, she was surprised by how everything was so intact. The furniture hadn't been looted. Instead, it was charmingly arranged to welcome any weary traveler. A bed made with pristine white sheets. She didn't dare disturb it, though. She opened the balcony doors and relished the wind that blew inside, the unusual moon with its bluish tint making everything colder. Shadier. The moon made the entire night feel off. As if she were looking out at an old, forgotten film rather than reality.

Anabel spun around. She felt something glide across her shoulder, heart lodging in her throat. Until she noticed the drapes. The billowing drapes. She gripped her chest and went inside toward the bathroom.

It was a mistake coming here. Maybe Chrys *was* cruel. Maybe she invited Anabel to show her what she'd lost. Remind her that she was too late. Or maybe Chrys was pushing her. Testing her, and she was failing.

In the bathroom, Anabel stared at her reflection. Her wild mane of dark hair, her elfish face, and her huge dark eyes that always made her look lost or helpless. *Stupid.* Stupid zombie makeup and stupid hope that led her to this place. She ran the tap, because of course the water ran just fine. Maybe everyone in town had lied about this place being too dangerous. About it being shut down and uninhabitable. About it being cursed. Maybe the entire sinking forest was a cover-up, a money pit the town founders used to embezzle fortunes. Maybe Anabel's dad broke his back for no reason.

She scrubbed at her face furiously, washing off the powder that made her brown skin pale. She was engulfed in the dark when Chrys's whispered voice called, "*Anabel. I'm sorry, Anabel.*"

She quickly rubbed the water from her eyes, looked behind her, and glanced into the room, but there was nothing there. No one was standing in the bathroom except her. She was losing it. This place. Something was wrong with this place.

When she turned back to the mirror, a scream ripped from her throat. Santa Tierra stared back with her skull face and tattered brown dress.

Everything inside Anabel erupted. Falling back, she cracked an elbow against the wall, pain shooting up her bones. She bolted from the bathroom, nearly tripping on a broken piece of floorboard she was sure wasn't there before.

There was a horrible buzzing in her ears. The room was dim, but it didn't prevent her from seeing the tangle of stringy blond hair splayed over the bed. Elisa stared back at her, hollow cheeks and empty eyes. Flies buzzing from her open mouth. Dead.

Dead. Dead. Dead. Dead. Dead.

A strangled scream burst from Anabel. She ran for the door and rushed outside into the dim hallway with crooked pictures and peeling paint. A figure's fluttering black veil turned the corner, a scrape of nails against the decaying walls. Everything was different. Everything looked old and withering. She wanted to scream, but she couldn't make a sound and the music was so loud she was afraid no one would ever hear her. She went the opposite way, toward the main stairs.

She grabbed hold of the first couple she could find and shook them apart. "She's dead," she yelled into their faces, but they swayed in her grip, eyes cloudy. They were dreaming. Was she dreaming?

She grabbed the more lucid of the two—a girl in a ragged flapper dress and a dark stamp of circles under her eyes. "She's dead," Anabel repeated. "Elisa is dead in there!"

"Hey." Chrys showed up, her cold fingers gripping Anabel's feverish arm, pulling her away before she could shake loose the girl's teeth. "What's going on?"

"Chrys!" Anabel threw her arms over her. "Oh my god, you're okay." Chrys held her close, inhaling her hair, warm and alive, but then Anabel felt nails sharpen against her back.

She pulled away, watching Chrys's face flicker between panic and something colder before reverting to normal. "It's okay," Chrys soothed. "Elisa is fine. Look—" She pointed to the bottom of the steps, where Anabel could see the tail end of Elisa's pink dress before it disappeared toward the dark. "She was probably just scaring you. Why don't I get you a drink?"

A prank? Anabel shook her head. "No. I don't want another drink. Can you just—look in the room—" She pulled Chrys toward the hall, marveling at its now-meticulous state, before peering into the bedroom she'd ran out of. The door was still open. "See!" But when they looked inside, the bed was empty. The crisp white sheets untouched. The room whole and welcoming.

Anabel felt her heart contract, twist in on itself.

Chrys wore a pitying look. "I'm sorry, Anabel. Let me go get you something to drink. Stay here and try to breathe. It'll all be over soon."

"The party?"

"Yes."

Anabel swayed on her feet. None of this was right. She knew what she saw. Chrys grabbed hold of her hand, smiling softly. Her finger traced Anabel's palm. It was a game they used to play. Writing invisible words on their skin and guessing what it said. GO.

Anabel's throat went dry. Go? Chrys wanted her to leave? She let go of Anabel's hand, still smiling like she hadn't even registered the word. Like she wasn't even fully there. Anabel didn't recognize this Chrys at all.

Chrys's hand touched Anabel's cheek as if checking for a temperature, but she lingered before letting her hand fall to her side. "It'll all be over soon."

Chrys left her in the hall again, the bedroom still empty save for the distant sound of buzzing insects. Maybe the person dressed as Santa Tierra took Elisa's body. Maybe they were hiding her in another room. Or maybe it was just a prank and Elisa was downstairs in the kitchen with Chrys, laughing at Anabel's horrified scream. *Go.*

Anabel checked the closest rooms, but they were all empty, dark like cavities that lead to nothing. A rotten scent filled her nose, growing worse by the second.

The hall seemed to constrict until she could barely squeeze herself out. Or maybe her panic was just too big. When she stepped out onto the mezzanine overlooking the lobby, it was empty. No one was there, though the music was still blaring downstairs—a disjointed ballad that turned her stomach. The people were all gone like they'd never existed at all. No dreamers. No servers. Everyone left.

Anabel swayed in place. "No, no."

This couldn't be happening. This wasn't real. She made her way down the stairs, shaky hands gripping the railing that was flaked with rust. The chandelier was missing crystals and overwhelmed with cobwebs. The steps had holes. It had all gone rotten. It had all aged in a matter of minutes.

"Hello?" she cried. Nothing.

The kitchen. Chrys said she was going to get her a drink. She wouldn't have left her here alone. Anabel went to the unmanned radio first and turned off the music. The silence was worse. An echo of wind and creaking wood. She passed the mirrored alcove they were all in earlier. The cushions were gutted, the coffee table collapsed. The infinite, cloudy mirrors reflected her pale, frightened face.

"Chrys?" she called, gulping hard, making her way to the swinging doors off to the side that led into the kitchen. She tried pushing a door open, but it was stuck on something, only budging when she put all her shoulder's weight behind it. The door moved, and she slipped on something wet, plummeting into the dark room and onto the sticky floor. The ground was uneven beneath her. She was tangled around someone else's legs. When her eyes adjusted to the dark, horror wrapped itself around her throat.

The twins. The twins were tangled in a heap on the floor, mouths gaping. Limbs—oh god. They looked like broken dolls. A *prank.* Anabel's body vibrated.

She scrambled off them. "This isn't funny. You can stop now!"

The twins didn't move. Their chests didn't rise and fall like something alive would. *It's a prank. Just a prank.*

"Please stop." It was impossible. They were practically husks. Anabel touched Blair's skin with the tips of her fingers, and her body was paper-thin. Disintegrating. As if she'd been decomposing for years.

Anabel covered her mouth, backed into the door, backed into the hall, and let the door swing shut on the gruesome scene, stifling the stench of corroded metal and old forgotten things.

She didn't think she was breathing right. Maybe she'd forgotten how to breathe entirely.

She shouldn't have come here. Anabel ran for the front door, needing to leave. Needing to find anyone else.

And she found her. Chrys stood at the entrance, her lace gown dirty and tattered. Her face sunken in and ashen. Anabel felt everything inside her collapse. "Chrys? Chrys, what's happening? What's wrong with you?"

Chrys came closer, her voice a cracked, wispy thing. "Did I tell you my mom was supposed to work here? She was here on opening day, before she started using."

Anabel shook her head. "What does that have to do with anything? What's going on?"

"It's bad soil, Anabel. We were already tainted from the start." Chrys reached out a pleading hand, but Anabel was backing away. She was afraid of this Chrys. This Chrys wasn't right. None of this was right.

A wail vibrated around the lobby, shaking the chandelier, causing Anabel to lose her footing. She clutched the end of the banister, the old wood cracking in her grip. Like a flicker in film, Chrys's expression changed. Morphed into something bitter as she came closer. "You can't build on bones. We should've never built on her land."

Anabel couldn't take it. She ran past her friend. She'd come back with help. She'd always come back for her. The front door was solid wood. A fortress door. There was no handle, no lock. She tried pushing it open, but it wouldn't give.

"I never wanted you to come here. I'm sorry, Anabel. She knew my weakness."

"Then help me get us out!" She turned to plead with Chrys, but it wasn't Chrys standing there.

It was Santa Tierra. There was no mistaking her face for a mask. Where her eyes should have been, there were two dark pits. Her bone mouth was stripped of muscle and flesh.

Anabel cried like something wounded. She backed away and ran up the stairs. There had to be a way out of here. The stairs were withering with each step, collapsing under her weight. The entire lobby seemed to be disintegrating in front of her.

Michael stood at the top step, his tuxedo in strips. His muscular shape was gone, leaving nothing but gray skin over a skeleton. "How long have I been here?" he asked. "Is anyone even looking for me anymore? You'll help me, right?"

Anabel was sobbing. She was slipping back, the stairs too

precarious. Michael reached out as if to rest on her, but she could barely support herself anymore. She pushed him away and, like a sack of bones, he tumbled down the stairs. She only had time to see his neck at an odd angle before the ground swallowed him up.

The land will take back.

"I'm sorry. I'm sorry." It had turned into a chant as Anabel climbed what remained of the stairs, jumped onto the mezzanine with holes that revealed the hotel's desolate bones, stumbled down the hall, and pushed her way into the collapsing room where she'd found Elisa dead.

The hotel must've swallowed Elisa up too because she was no longer there, but Anabel couldn't stick around to wonder about it. The second-story balcony looked out over the forest, still glowing blue from the moonlight.

Anabel peered down. The roundabout road was still there, jagged stones in a sea of gravel. The fall could kill her, but so could staying here. There was no other choice. She looked once behind her.

"I promise to come back for you, Chrys. I promise."

She jumped, closed her eyes, and braced for the blow.

Anabel cracked open her eyes. She wasn't hurt. She wasn't in pain. But she was distraught.

She sat in the alcove, the mirrors reflecting the party in full swing. Elisa, Michael, and the twins were dancing beneath the glowing chandelier. No.

No.

She was too stiff to move. Too petrified to scream. From the reflection, she saw Chrys sit down beside her. Beautiful, beautiful Chrys. She perched her head on Anabel's shoulder, grabbed her hand warmly in hers.

Chrys's fingertip traced a pattern on the inside of Anabel's wrist.

NEVER LEAVE

She could never leave. She would rot here, sink into the ground where nothing flowered. Except she wouldn't be alone again.

From this angle, Anabel could see the front door, open and waiting for the next guests to arrive. She saw a tattered brown dress and a black veil. Santa Tierra was leaving. But in place of the skull was Anabel's own face reflected back. Dark wide eyes no longer innocent.

"What a lovely, lovely face."

The land will eventually take back when she's hungry, when she's had enough. Sometimes places are never meant to be disturbed.

THE VISITOR

Kalynn Bayron

All day I counted down in hours. Big chunks of time seemed to go by quickly when I kept track that way. But in the afternoon I switched to increments of thirty minutes, then fifteen. The anticipation grew as the moments passed. All the excitement, anxiety, and fear gathered into a ball in my chest. I kept finding my jaw clenched, my shoulders tight, my thoughts racing. By the time the sun tucked itself behind the horizon and the clock lurched past the 8:30 P.M. mark on Halloween night, time felt like it wasn't moving at all. I looked at my phone for the hundredth time that day.

"Checking your phone every ten seconds isn't going to make the time go by any faster, Toya," said Ari.

"No, I know. I just—" I sighed. She knew how much I loved being home with my dad on Halloween. At least she thought she did. Nobody—not even my girlfriend—knew exactly how much I wanted—no, *needed*—to be home on the spookiest night of the year.

"You don't have to explain it to me, babe," Ari said, kissing me gently on the cheek. "I know it's your thing. And your pop's. You know something?"

"What?" I asked.

"Your dad is the only grown man I know who gets this hyped about Halloween. He's almost as excited as my little brother." She laughed. "October first rolls around, and it's like a switch flips in his brain. He's ready to go. Especially these last few years."

I looked at my lap. She was telling the truth, but when she said it like that it sounded ridiculous. My dad was in his mid-forties, and even though Ari didn't understand everything that was behind his love of Halloween, I thought he should still be allowed to have a little fun if he wanted. Ari reached across and closed her hand over mine.

"I hope I didn't upset you," she said. "I love you and your dad. I think it's sweet that he takes it so seriously."

"It was my mom's favorite holiday," I said.

Ari's mouth stretched into one of those tight, fake smiles—the ones you show to grieving people when you don't really know what else to say. "I know," she said gently. "And that's why I'm gonna get you home so you and your pops can celebrate. Is he doing a costume this year?"

"I don't think so," I said.

"Good," Ari said. "I don't want to see him dressed up like an elf ever again. I've seen some things that can't be unseen."

I laughed. "His candy cane stockings were way too tight. He was mortified when I told him."

Ari grinned. "You know what else? There's a blue moon tonight."

"For real?" I asked. "Is that a big deal?"

"Kind of," Ari said. "Some people think it's like a symbol of new beginnings, big changes, stuff like that."

I side-eyed her. "Who is *people*?"

"I dunno," Ari said. "Witches and shit."

"Witches?" I narrowed my eyes at Ari. "You fell down a Reddit rabbit hole or something?"

"Maybe," Ari teased. She had a love of all things scary, all things strange. She'd probably understand if I told her the real reason Halloween night was so special to me, but I wasn't quite ready to do that. Not yet.

Ari and I laughed together as she drove me home. A wave of relief washed over me as we drew closer to my house. I'd be there in time to hand out candy to the trick-or-treaters and watch scary movies the way I used to when my mom was still alive. It was a tradition me and my dad had carried on, and it was more important to me than Christmas, more important than her birthday or even the date that marked her passing. A numbing ache gripped my chest, but I shoved it away. I didn't want to feel that terrible, heavy sadness. People told me the grief would ebb and that I would find some kind of normalcy on the other side of all this sadness, but as time passed, the pain worsened. I loved my time with Ari and with my dad. I loved them both, but the happy moments with them were like putting a bandage over a broken bone. It felt like it would never be enough to drown out the ache of my mom's death.

Ari patted my leg and then returned her hand to the wheel. We'd spent the day shopping for candy and discount decorations to save for the next year. I did her makeup, and the shimmery orange swipes of eyeshadow against her deep brown skin made her look even more gorgeous than she already was. She caught me staring and glanced over at me.

"See something you like?"

"Only every single time I see you." That was true. This was one of those happy moments, and I tried desperately to hold on to it.

She grinned.

Just then, a beam of brilliant bright light lit up the inside of the car as someone on the road behind us flipped on their high beams. Ari's hand flew up to block the reflection in the rearview mirror.

"Damn!" she yelled. "High beams are illegal when you're behind another car, asshole!"

I turned around to flip the driver off but couldn't see anything in the glare of the headlights, which meant whoever it was wouldn't be able to see my gesture. I did it anyway, just to make myself feel better.

Ari brake-checked the driver, and I almost flew into the dashboard.

"Sorry!" Ari said as I readjusted myself in the front seat.

I was fine, but the driver was now tailgating the hell out of us. Ari made a quick right onto my street, and the car followed behind us.

Ari huffed. "This jerk lives on your street, Toya."

I couldn't see enough of the car in the glare of the lights to know if it was one of my neighbors or not. Ari pulled into my driveway, and a navy-blue Honda Civic with tinted windows revved its engine and sped past us.

Ari shot whoever it was the bird, then turned to me and shrugged. "I guess he had somewhere important to be."

"I guess," I said.

So did I. I leaned over and kissed Ari before hopping out and heading inside. My hands were already starting to sweat, and my thoughts were racing again. Did I have everything I needed? Did I have the right outfit? Would everything go the way it had gone last time? A part of me hoped it would, but there was another part that longed for something different, something more.

"Pick you up for breakfast tomorrow?" Ari yelled as she leaned out the window.

"Waffle House?"

Ari grinned. That meant yes. "See you at nine?"

"Make it ten," I said. It was going to be a late night regardless of which way things went.

She backed out of the driveway. "Happy Halloween, babe!" she called.

"Happy Halloween," I said quietly.

I glanced down the street, and as her car disappeared, I noticed that the blue Civic had pulled over and parked in front of a house at the end of my street. I couldn't tell if someone was still inside, but the lights were off and the street was quiet.

I quickly climbed the front steps and readjusted the scarecrow I'd made from some of my dad's old clothes and a hay bale I'd snagged from the craft store. The scarecrow's face was hideous. Under the deep purple sky and twinkling orange lights I'd strung through the porch railing, he was absolutely terrifying. I'd attempted to paint an insidious little smirk on the repurposed

Michael Myers mask, but it had turned into a horrifying scowl. I wondered if he was too scary for the trick-or-treaters.

As a scattering of clouds pushed in, I avoided looking directly into Mr. Scarecrow's face and went inside to find my dad on the couch, remote in hand.

"Where you been, baby?" he asked. "It's getting late. I was starting to get worried."

"I know. I'm sorry. I was with Ari."

I fell into the couch next to him and glanced at the time on the face of the big grandfather clock sitting in the hallway. The thing was a relic from another time, but my mom loved it. She said it looked like something that belonged in a haunted mansion. The gold-plated pendulum swung back and forth in its glass housing and kept time in a series of soft clicks, like a metronome. 8:45.

"I was watching the time," I continued. "You know I wouldn't miss this for anything in the world."

"I'm always a little nervous," he said. "Not really sure how . . . well, I'm just glad you're home. We can get our movies going and—"

The doorbell rang, and a jolt of excitement coursed through me. I exchanged glances with my dad, and he nodded toward a bucket brimming with candy, little plastic spider rings, and pencils with black bats on them.

I greeted the first group of trick-or-treaters just as the streetlights flickered on down the street, casting a gauzy haze across the pavement. A stiff wind swept a pile of amber- and russet-colored leaves into a little cyclone, and the kids squealed as they ran through it on their way to the house next door.

"How long do you think the kids will be out?" I asked, closing the front door.

My dad shrugged. "No later than nine or ten probably. It's already getting dark. I know me and your mama used to have you in by eight thirty." A pinched expression distorted his features, like it physically hurt to talk about her. Missing her was like that sometimes.

"I'm gonna go freshen up," my dad said.

"Okay," I said as he disappeared upstairs.

I answered the door as another group of trick-or-treaters came bounding up the front steps. As I shoveled candy and pencils into their plastic pumpkins and pillowcases, I peered down the street and noticed that the blue Civic had changed position. It had pulled in front of a house just three doors down from mine. Gray smoke from the exhaust pipe billowed into the chilly evening air. Someone was sitting in the driver seat, but I still couldn't make them out.

I shut the door again, and this time I slid the dead bolt into place.

My dad came back down wearing freshly pressed dress pants and a cabled evergreen sweater. He had a fresh lineup from earlier in the day and was wearing the glasses that my mom always said made him look like a librarian. Seeing as she'd been a writer, that was a compliment.

"You look really nice," I said.

His big brown eyes were glassy in the flickering light of the TV. "Thanks, baby. Are you going to change?"

I nodded. "You wanna take over candy duty while I go do that?"

I handed him the bowl of candy and hurried up to my room. I shrugged out of my T-shirt and sweats and into a pair of black jeans and a chunky red sweater. I was halfway through twisting my braids into a high bun when my attention was pulled to my bedroom window. The heavy curtains were drawn, but from behind them came a noise—scratching, like fingernails dragging across the glass.

My heart thudded and my palms were slick with sweat as I turned toward the sound. My gut twisted into a knot, but I pushed away the feeling and marched up to the window. Gripping the curtains with both hands, I yanked them open as a loud crack split the air. A flash of lightning illuminated the willow tree just outside my bedroom window. The wind pushed the branches around, and they scraped against the glass.

Relief coursed through me. I didn't know what I'd expected to find—some hideous monster waiting to attack me? A dude in a mask armed with a butcher knife? It was Halloween, after all. Rain began to pelt the roof, building to a steady drum.

I grabbed my shoes and met my dad in the living room.

"Ready to start the movie?" I asked.

My dad looked me over. "You look just like your mama. Absolutely beautiful."

"Aw, thanks, Dad," I said.

In the stretching shadows and the dappled glow from the Halloween lights, his face looked drawn, like his skin was stretched too thin over the bones beneath. He pointed to the TV. "I've already got the movie queued up. *Nightmare on Elm Street*. The original."

I sat next to him, and we watched Freddy Krueger slice and

dice his way through a bunch of high schoolers' nightmares as the rain continued to fall outside.

"The trick-or-treaters are probably done," my dad said. "Nobody is going to want to be out in this rain."

The TV flickered, and then the picture froze on Freddy's hideous face before it went out and the lights snapped off. The hum of electricity stopped, leaving only the sound of the pelting rain. My dad tilted his head and stared up at the recessed lighting. The light from the kitchen flickered on, but everything in the living room remained silent and dark.

"You think the whole block's out?" my dad asked.

I quickly got up and went to the window. Our neighbors' porch lights were on to the right and left of us. "Everybody else still has power."

"It's probably just the fuse."

"I'll go check," I said.

Dad nodded. "I'll get the flashlights just in case." He disappeared up the stairs.

Ding-dong.

I rolled my eyes. "Kids need to take their bad behinds home," I grumbled to myself.

The sound of the rain was like a blanket of white noise. The trick-or-treaters were probably soaked to the bone. I grabbed the bucket of candy and pulled open the front door only to find . . . nothing. There were no trick-or-treaters with bags at the ready, but my makeshift scarecrow was doubled over, his hands made of gloves stuffed with hay touching the ground in front of him. I reached out to readjust him when a bolt of lightning split the air and lit everything up in one brilliant flash. My heart jumped into my throat, and I stumbled back inside, slamming the door shut. I pressed my forehead to the wood and tried to catch my breath.

"Get it together," I said quietly. This was not the night to be losing my cool.

The living room was still cast in shadow, and my dad hadn't returned, though I could hear him rummaging around upstairs. I gathered myself and went down the hall to the basement door. I pulled it open, and the stairs descended into the dark. I hit the switch. There was a soft click but the light didn't come on. I flipped it off and on again and still nothing.

"Dad?" I called over my shoulder. My voice echoed through the quiet.

He didn't answer and probably couldn't hear me if he was fishing around in the upstairs closet looking for a flashlight.

I grabbed my phone, flipped on its flashlight, which did almost nothing to help illuminate the dark space below, and descended the steps. *I'm not afraid of the dark,* I told myself a hundred times before I reached the bottom step.

The basement was unfinished, perpetually damp, and smelled like dirt and dust. The fuse box was on the back wall. The outlets in the living room were funny. They popped whenever more than four things were plugged in at the same time, and we were constantly having to reset the switch. I swept my light around as I crossed to the rear wall and reminded myself that I was absolutely not afraid of the dark. I narrowly avoided the booby traps of old furniture and broken gardening equipment. My mom's stuff was down there too—her old desk, her clothes neatly folded and stored in big airtight plastic bags. I avoided that corner of the basement and went straight to the fuse box.

The light on my phone dimmed and then went out completely, plunging me into an all-encompassing darkness.

"You gotta be kidding me." I tapped the side of my phone, and the light flickered back on. I swept it around the room, fearing that in the three seconds I was in the complete dark, something had come into the basement and was waiting for me in the shadows. When I was sure nothing had crept up on me, I turned my attention to the fuse box.

The rows of switches behind the gray metal panel were numbered, and each one corresponded to a certain section of the house—kitchen, bathroom, Mom's office, bedrooms one and two. The switch labeled LIVING ROOM was tripped, so I pushed it back into place.

I waited in the dark for the familiar sounds of the TV to trickle down, but instead I heard heavy footsteps—shuffling . . . dragging. I swept my phone's flashlight up to the ceiling as the steps cut a path from the hallway into the kitchen where they stopped at the top of the basement steps. The door groaned on its hinges, then gently clicked shut.

"Dad?" I called as I moved to the bottom of the steps. "You find the flashlights?"

I expected him to be standing at the top of the stairs but found only the closed basement door. An overwhelming urge to sprint up the steps consumed me, and I didn't hesitate. I took them two at a time and almost fell into the kitchen. It was dark and empty—my dad was nowhere to be found. A chill ran up my back and forced the air right out of my lungs. I gripped the edge of the counter to steady myself.

Making my way to the living room, I saw that the lights

had come back on and the TV was in the process of resetting itself.

"Dad?"

"Be right down," he called—from upstairs.

I glanced back down the hall toward the kitchen as my dad came down the stairs carrying several flashlights and a box of AA batteries.

He stopped in front of me. "What's wrong? You look shook."

"I—were you just down here? In the kitchen?"

He glanced down the hall. "No. Why?"

I shook my head. "It's nothing. I'm a little on edge."

"It's Halloween," he said. "It's understandable."

I helped him switch out the batteries in the flashlights, and we settled back down in the living room. The time on the clock in the hallway read 10:30, and my eyelids grew heavier with each passing moment. My dad was already asleep by the time Mrs. Voorhees took her revenge on the first set of kids at Camp Crystal Lake. I checked my phone: a text from Ari confirming our breakfast date and one from an unknown number. I opened the message and found it empty. I deleted it and made sure my alarm was set for 11:45 P.M.

My attention was drawn to the hallway. I couldn't say for sure why—a noise or a feeling like I was being watched. Something moved in the shadows. Or maybe it was just a trick of the light. Could've been my imagination or maybe . . . something else entirely.

"Dad," I whispered as fear stole my breath, rendering my voice weightless and hollow.

He didn't stir.

I couldn't bring myself to look at anything other than the floor as I perched on the edge of the couch, my heart drumming in my chest.

Suddenly, I was aware of a familiar sound—the lock on the back door turning and the door yawning open.

I was on my feet and shaking my dad awake. "Dad! Wake up!"

He awoke with a start and jumped up like something was chasing him. He moved to the front door, but I grabbed his arm and yanked him back.

"It was the back door. I—I think it's open." My breath hitched in my throat. "I—I think somebody's in the house."

His eyes grew wide, and he straightened up. He crept to the hall closet and took out the steel bat he played baseball with on the weekends, gripping its taped handle until the skin over his knuckles was stretched thin. He slowly moved toward the back of the house with me following along behind him. I didn't have a weapon, but I had my phone unlocked and ready to dial 911 if needed. We rounded the corner at the end of the hall and found the rear door sitting wide open. The rain puddled on the hardwood floor, and the wind whipped through the hall. My dad quickly shut the door and locked it.

"I think it was just the wind, baby. Must've pushed the door open."

"That's exactly what people say right before a serial killer jumps out and stabs you seventy-six times."

He shook his head and chuckled. "Grab me some towels, would you, baby?"

I nodded, and as I rushed to the closet in his room to grab them, a familiar scent wafted past me—vanilla and cocoa butter.

My heart ticked up. I ran to get the towels, and when I came back, my dad was standing in the hallway, phone in hand, staring down at the screen.

I approached him, a stack of neatly folded towels in my hands. "You okay?" I tried to look at the screen.

"Someone just called me."

I set the towels down and stepped toward him. "Okay? Who was it?"

"The caller ID said unknown, but when I picked it up, I swear it was . . ." He lifted his head, and his gaze met mine, and I knew.

"That's not supposed to happen," I said, realizing that something had changed—in me and in the makeup of this very important night. That feeling inside me that hoped the night would go according to plan grew smaller with each passing moment, replaced with the growing urge to put a stop to this terrible pain. I knew there was a way to do it—but could I actually go through with it?

Dad checked his watch. "Never mind. It's almost time."

We quickly laid the towels across the soaked floor and went back to the living room. We sat next to each other in silence as the credits rolled on the horror flick.

My alarm cut through the quiet at exactly 11:45.

My dad let out a long sigh, then slowly turned to me. Stretched across his face was the giddiest smile I'd seen in almost a year. He took his hand in mine and squeezed.

The wait was almost over.

I turned off the TV and went to the floor-length mirror in the hallway to straighten my shirt and make sure I still looked put together.

My dad adjusted his tie and gently touched his neatly trimmed beard. "Your mom always liked the beard. Didn't like it too long, though. 'Keep it short and sweet,' that's what she always said."

The grandfather clock ticked toward midnight, and then, just as the hands overlapped at the top and the low chime erupted from behind the beveled glass in the lower door, another sound drew my attention to the front of the house.

My dad's head snapped up, and we both listened as a set of footsteps ascended the stairs outside. Above the soft patter of the rain and over the chiming of the midnight hour, I heard it.

A soft thud. A short dragging rustle. And then—a voice.

"Toya."

I gripped my dad's arm. Every year we waited for this specific, impossible moment. We went through our rituals: scary movies, candy for the trick-or-treaters, the decorations and the lights. They were like beacons in an endless abyss of grief. We didn't know how, but we knew why—Mom loved this time of year. Every Halloween with her was a celebration, and the time in between was always a slow crawl to the next year. Now it was here, and there was only one thing left to do.

I went to the door, my dad trailing behind, and put my hand on the knob. The footsteps came to a stop on the other side of the door. I didn't lift my gaze to peer through the window, I simply turned the knob and pulled the door open.

My dad gasped, and then there was silence. I held my breath and lifted my head.

She stood on the front porch, still as a statue, the moonlight breaking through the thick cloud cover just enough to reveal the details of her. She wore a flowing cream-colored gown, her feet bare on the dampened porch, a sprig of baby's breath tucked behind her left ear—and a mask that covered the upper part of her face. Her deep brown eyes searched my face, and as she gazed at me, the familiar glint of recognition lit a fire in her. The corners of her mouth drew up into a smile as she extended her cupped hands toward me.

She'd never done that before.

Her expression was almost always far away, like she was concentrating very hard on something, like she couldn't quite see me. But this time, her eyes were clear.

She leaned toward me again, and I cupped my hands under hers. Our fingers were so close, I could feel the cold radiating from her. She dropped several small objects into my upturned palms, then stepped back and tilted her head toward my dad.

He smoothed the front of his shirt and pressed his shoulders back, lifting his chin to show her he was okay—as if either of us really believed we could be okay without her.

She looked upon him, nodded, and turned her attention back to me as I studied the objects she'd given me—a locket, a gold ring, and a small brooch—all things that had been in the casket we buried three years ago.

She took another step back.

"Please don't go," I said. Tears filled my eyes, and I wanted nothing more than to reach out and fold myself against her the way I had when she was alive.

She gazed down at the threshold, a barrier she'd never crossed. She'd explained it to us only once, and we didn't question her. She could cross it if we invited her in, but under no circumstances were we to do that. The danger, she said, was too great, and she didn't trust herself not to hurt me or my dad. She'd asked for time, for patience, as she adjusted to her new way of existing. It had been three years since a stranger had made her into this undead thing. We buried her in the cold earth, thinking we had come to the end of our time with her.

When she appeared on our doorstep the Halloween after her death, we'd realized how wrong we were. But her stay was brief, her explanations impossible. The evidence of the bite on her neck had already faded.

My dad threw himself into research and study of the undead, of the creatures myth and lore called vampires. But when the change was complete, she had to go away. She did it for us. To keep us safe. But I hated it. I didn't want her to go. I didn't want this once-a-year visit to be so brief and so filled with things unsaid.

"I don't want you to go," I said, my heart breaking open. I didn't want to go another year waiting for her and missing her so much it hurt.

She sighed and closed her eyes. "There is no other choice."

There was. She knew it and I knew it but could she do it? *Would* she?

I realized in that moment that this night would be different. The signs had been there all day, and I didn't care about the promises I'd made before. I made a choice right then and there—I didn't want to be without her. I couldn't do it anymore. I held my breath, shut my eyes, and spoke the words I'd promised never to say.

"Mom. You can come in."

My dad gasped so hard, he began to cough. He grabbed me and pulled me away from the door.

"Toya!" he hollered, his tone a mix of absolute terror and despair. "No! You're not supposed to say that! You swore!"

My mother stalked into the room, over the threshold, and pulled the mask away from her face. The whites of her eyes were now bloodshot, the unnatural length of her teeth made them visible just outside her top lip. The look of pain and pity that creased her brow and turned her gentle smile to a frown scared me in a way I'd never been before in my entire life. She was my mother and not my mother at the same time. That pitiable expression shifted, and in its place was the look of hunger, of starvation.

In the blink of an eye, the front door was closed and locked. She stood in the shadows just inside the door, her body melding perfectly with the dark.

"Toya, baby," she said in a voice I didn't recognize. "What have you done?"

A BRIEF INTERMISSION

Sara Farizan

"Um, hello? There's hardly any cheese on here!"

I know there are worse jobs out there than working at the snack shack at the Stars under the Stars Drive-In theater. There are, however, times when I want to jump up on the counter, raise my hands in the air, and scream, *I quit! And yes, I promise you that your battery is going to die if you don't turn your car engine to accessory mode!*

Before I can tell the sunburnt gentleman with an unfortunate beard that he has received the standard amount of cheese on our nachos, Rusty ladles a large helping of hot yellow goo all over the chips, some of it landing on the customer's fingers and on the counter too.

"There you are. Enjoy!" Rusty says with a bright smile, the kind he gives to kill with kindness, emphasis on the kill.

"Hey, watch it," the customer says, cheese oozing down his elbow as Rusty continues to pour. "That's enough!"

"Glad to hear it," Rusty says. "The movie's about to start. Wouldn't want you to miss it." His smile now slightly maniacal. The customer backs away, swearing at us under his breath before he exits the shack. Rusty's smile immediately morphs into his usual frown.

"So accommodating," I say, shaking my head. Rusty grabs a box of Junior Mints he definitely didn't pay for and pops one in his mouth.

"Please tell Harry about it. Then maybe he'll fire me."

I let out a snort. There was no way Harry was going to let either of us go, especially since the place was busier than it ever had been in years. And the fact that nobody wanted to work here because . . . well, I didn't believe all those rumors anyway.

"Garbage is looking pretty full," I say as I wipe up the cheese Rusty left behind.

"It sure is, Afsaneh," Rusty says, leaning against the candy counter. "It was full earlier too when I took out the first batch." We stare at each other for a moment like Toshiro Mifune and Tatsuya Nakadai in *Yojimbo* during the final showdown. Rusty's the first to draw his weapon. "We could just let it overflow. Let the trash build and build until we're all buried in ketchup packets and chewed-up mac-and-cheese nuggets, and *then* Harry will fire us, but only if he can find us underneath the deluge of waste!"

I roll my eyes and grab the plastic bags out of their bins. Rusty at least helps me tie one of them up before I head out back. It's not like I'm some princess who can't stand to get dirty. It's just all the rats by the Dumpster make my skin crawl. It always seems like they only show up when I'm on trash duty—or maybe Rusty sees them too and doesn't care. I trudge from the snack shack past the screen on Field 1 that's showing the latest superhero movie. Field 2 is playing *Jaws*, which surprisingly always gets a crowd even when most people have already seen it year after year. I know exactly which part of the movie it is from the sound coming out of the speakers. The woman is about to go skinny-dipping, unaware she's going to meet her demise as a shark's chew toy when the ominous John Williams score begins.

I throw one of the trash bags up into the dumpster, giving myself enough space in case something wants to scurry out of there. Thankfully, there are no little friends trying to say hello. I get ready to heave the next bag over, when I hear a scream that doesn't belong to the victim in *Jaws*. It's a guttural, low voice in pain, and there's a smell of iron in the air that makes me queasy.

"Not again!" the voice bellows. I drop the bag and rush over to the poor guy. I step in some mush, look down, and see that the rats I'm usually so worried about have been put out of commission, their entrails leading the way to my boss, Harry, who is screaming as he bats away something by his ankle. It's dark, making it hard to see, but it doesn't look like he's swatting at anything but air.

"Harry!" I scream. The bottom of his right pantleg is drenched in blood and looks torn up, like something's been chewing on him. "Get away," I say to whatever is chomping on my boss, but I still can't see anything. Harry slaps at the air by his leg one more time, and I can hear an animal wail. Harry's leg stops jerking around. The cries of the animal grow faint. Dust kicks up in the air as though something is running across the dirt road that leads to the driveway exit. I take Harry's hand and try to help him up, but his eyes roll back into his head, and he lies limp on the ground.

"Somebody help!" I scream before I grab my phone to call

911. I look down at my boss's leg that continues to gush blood, a puddle of it now by his foot. There's a little bit of his shin bone poking out and teeth marks from *something* surrounding the wound.

⁂

"Hey kiddos," Harry says from his hospital bed. I think he always calls us kiddos because he's unsure of Rusty's pronouns or how to pronounce my name. There's more color in Harry's face than when the ambulance took him two days ago, which makes me feel a whole lot better, but he looks worried and has dark circles under his eyes. He looks a lot older than his sixty-two years. Right now, he looks about eighty.

"Hey, Harry," Rusty says, placing a popcorn bucket full of flowers on his bedside table. Rusty's made an effort in dressing up for Harry by wearing a black leather jacket and a T-shirt without nacho cheese stains. I usually only see Rusty in our work uniforms: blue polo shirts with stars on the front and back and our workplace logo in fifties-style type on the front. Rusty's work shirt is always too tight for him, and mine is too baggy for my short and slight frame, which is fine by me. I always have my black hair in a high ponytail, even when I'm not at work. Today I'm wearing a yellow collared shirt I'd wear to a debate team meet and a blue blazer. My corduroy pants sometimes make a swishing sound when I walk.

As much as Rusty complains about work, Harry's always been good to us. He lets us eat whatever snacks we want. He doesn't care about Rusty's black nail polish or neon yellow hair when other employers in our town have, and when I called in "sick" after Lily broke up with me, Harry didn't push and told me to take all the time I needed.

"How are you feeling?" I ask looking at his bandaged leg. I shudder, thinking about the chunks of flesh I found missing when I called 911. The paramedics told me whatever bit him had managed to break Harry's tibia and asked me if he'd been bitten by a bear. I didn't have an answer for them.

"I feel right as rain," Harry says, trying to loosen the needle in his hand connected to his IV. "Doc says I've got to stay here a few days, but you two have got to help me out of here."

"Um, what?" Rusty asks.

"I don't think that's a good idea," I say, gently resting my hand on Harry's, hoping he'll stop fiddling with his drip.

"You don't understand," Harry says. "I've got to be at the drive-in tomorrow."

"Why? We're closed," Rusty says. I never understood why Harry closed every year on Halloween, but it had something to do with the rumors surrounding the drive-in. Some people said the place went downhill after a car crash on the grounds in the late fifties. In the seventies, the drive-in was a seedy place showing gory B movies and X-rated films. There were rumors of customers being strung out on drugs and booze, swearing they saw a lot of unexplained and strange stuff that had become town lore over the years.

"I've got to be there. Take care of some old family business," Harry said, trying to push himself out of bed.

"Come on, there's no way," I say. "You're in no shape to work." He looks at me then, his eyes wide with fear, but his body slowly relaxes back into bed.

"Then I . . . I need you two to do something for me. But you have to do exactly as I say."

"Will we get paid overtime?" Rusty asks.

"Exactly as I say," Harry says, ignoring Rusty and staring right at me, gripping my hand in his until I feel my bones might break.

"You sure we can't turn on the lights?" Rusty asks, our flashlights shining the way for us as we make our way to the projection booth.

"Harry said not to," I say.

"Yeah, but—"

"We promised," I say, thinking it's silly too, but I'd never seen Harry that serious before. Sure, there were times when he'd lose his cool when a customer was drunk on the premises, or I'd see him panic when that kid needed the Heimlich from shoving too much popcorn in his face. But seeing Harry in that hospital bed, so much smaller than he usually was, I wanted to do this for him even if it was ridiculous.

"*You* promised," Rusty clarifies from behind me as I walk up the stairs.

"You don't have to stay." But I really want him to. I haven't been here alone at night without any of the lights on. Even with the light from the blue moon and the stars above, it was too dark for my liking. Lily once told me that the moon had great control over our emotions—she was always into astrology—and I never really paid it much attention. But something feels different tonight. I feel like I might break down and cry at any minute.

"And miss a free movie? Not on your life."

Rusty and I go to different high schools, but if we went to the same one, I don't know if we'd hang out. He's tall, really into geocaching, metal music, and reality shows about ghost-hunting; he has a neck tattoo of Clifford the Big Red Dog taking a piss; he loves horror movies and books; has a long-term girlfriend named Ruby who doesn't seem to like people all that much; and I think he's repeating his senior year for a second time. I'm short, a junior, on student government and the debate team; I'm Persian with incredible thick and well-shaped eyebrows—they're my best feature; and I keep breaking up and getting back together with Lily. Sometimes I think maybe we should just stay broken up because college-application time will be stressful enough.

Rusty and I butt heads about who should do what at work, but the one thing we have in common is our love of movies. Criterion Collection titles, foreign films most people in town haven't heard of, B movies starring Dick Miller and some kind of monster, cult classics, mainstream blockbusters—we love to talk about *all* of them. We disagree a lot, especially when it comes to director Ingmar Bergman, who Rusty adores and I find way too existential to be enjoyable.

The thing is Rusty appreciates that I'm familiar with Bergman's work the same way I am thrilled that I can bring up Kiarostami's *Taste of Cherry*, and we can discuss it without my having to explain anything. I tried showing it to Lily when I recorded it off the Turner Classic Movie channel, but she fell asleep twenty minutes into it. Maybe we really aren't meant to be together.

The film reel cannisters I'm supposed to look for are labeled 1959 ANNIVERSARY, but I don't know what movie is on it. Harry told us to start playing the movie at 9:00 P.M., make sure it was running okay, change the reel when there was two minutes of the movie left on reel 1, and then get the hell home. Under no circumstances were we to talk, interact, or touch any guests that might arrive.

Rusty crouched down and pulled at a loose part of the wall Harry told us about.

"Found it," Rusty said, shining his light on a safe hidden in the wall. "What's the combination?"

⁂

"You ever seen the 1988 remake?" Rusty asks as 1958's *The Blob* plays on the big screen. "It's a Frank Darabont film, so it looks great, but Kevin Dillon is no Steve McQueen."

"I'll be sure to look into it," I say, watching the reel on the projector about to come to where we need to change it. I wish Rusty was paying as much attention as I was. He's just sitting back, eating candy he pilfered from downstairs. I hold the other film cannister from the safe close to my chest, ready to switch over as fast as I can, just as Harry instructed. The back of my neck is sweaty. "Okay, let's do it."

Rusty takes his time getting up and starts to feed the second cannister of film while I make sure it keeps playing without a hitch.

"Are you sure you're doing it right?" I ask him.

"Harry really freaked you out, huh?"

"*He* didn't." That thing that chewed on his leg did. I didn't tell Rusty about what got Harry because Harry didn't tell his doctor or nurses. All he said was he couldn't see what it was that bit him. That was half true, he couldn't *see* the animal, but I had a feeling Harry was holding back. The first reel's film pools at my feet while the second film reel plays. The intermission ads of that era light up on the screen. An animated hot dog, popcorn bucket, soda, and candy box all march in a line and sing. Rusty joins in a deadpan voice, nowhere near as cheerful as the dancing food: "Let's all go to the lobby, and have ourselves a snack."

I lead the way, and Rusty follows as we walk downstairs and outside. I begin to book it to my mom's car. I can't hear Rusty's footsteps behind me. I turn around and see he's sitting on a picnic table near the snack shack, his feet on the bench, watching the intermission ads playing on the screen of Field 1, telling the audience the show was going to start in five minutes, but there was plenty of time to grab a tasty treat while bandstand music played in the background.

"Harry told us to leave," I whisper-scream to Rusty. I worry he can't hear me, until he turns his flashlight back on, but this time it's under his chin, casting shadows across his face as he turns toward me. "Should we tell scary stories? MUAHAHAHA!"

"Cut it out," I hiss. "We have to go."

"Why? We might as well watch the movie," Rusty yells.

I rush toward him, grab his arm, and try to drag him off the table, but he won't budge.

"We're not supposed to be here," I plead.

"You're freaking out over nothing," he says. He was about to argue with me some more when a car engine began to roar behind us. "They're here . . ." Rusty said in a little-girl voice, mimicking Carol Anne from *Poltergeist*, a movie Rusty loved and made me watch with him. I felt bad for the kids getting scared in the movie and didn't enjoy it so much.

"Please, let's go," I whimper.

"I don't see a car," Rusty says, looking over his shoulder. "Don't you want to see who shows up? I mean, who is Harry playing these movies for?"

"It's none of our business. Besides, maybe it's just some tradition of his or a superstition or something. Let's get out of here!" I'm worried about that *thing* still being out here and wanting some new flesh to take a bite out of.

A car engine hums behind us. Then the faint sound of a song drifts in the air. I don't know the band or the name of the song, but it sounds familiar and like it's from the 1950s. It's a slow tune, and the guitars sound like they're being played underwater. I turn around, only able to see headlights shooting out a bluish-green hue slowly heading toward the screen. As the lights pass us by, I can't see a car attached to them.

"Holy shit, look," Rusty says pointing at the grass. Tire impressions on the ground begin to appear as the unattached headlights "drive" on. My body stiffens. I want to run. My brain is telling me to get away from here as fast as possible, but my body has checked out.

The closer the headlights get to the screen, the more a car begins to present itself. A whale of a teal-green Chevrolet with giant winged taillights surrounded by a blurry fog parks right in the front row. When the fog that only appeared around the car fades I see the back of the heads of two passengers inside through the car's rear window.

"A ghost car!" Rusty exclaims, clapping me on my back. I shudder when he touches me, because I realize this is actually happening. "Harry's been holding out on us!" I keep staring at the car and watch the driver put their arm around the shoulders of the rider in the passenger seat. "Whoa! Afsi, check this out!" Rusty shoves his phone in front of my face. It's on video mode and pointed right at the Chevy, but nothing shows up on his phone. "Maybe I'd better get closer."

"No," I finally manage to get out in a whisper. I grab his arm and pull him back. "Harry said we're not supposed to." I must sound so pathetic because Rusty turns to look at me.

"You don't look too hot," he says. "Come on, let's get you a drink." He holds on to me and sits me down on the picnic table bench. "I'll be right back." I clutch his hand. Instead of leaving to get me a soda, he sits down beside me. "Okay. We'll wait here awhile."

I can hear the speakers announce it's time for the feature presentation, but I can't tear my eyes away from the car. The motor is turned off, and the song is replaced with the sound from the movie as it begins to play.

"What the hell is a *Gidget?*" Rusty says, looking up at the screen.

"It's a Sandra Dee movie," I whisper, relieved that I'm not so shocked that I'd give up a chance to one-up Rusty in movie trivia. "She learns to surf. Has a crush on a guy named Moondoggie."

"Huh. I guess you would have to be dead to enjoy a movie like that."

"It started a whole genre of surfer teen movies. It can't be that bad. Also, um, what are we supposed to do?!"

"Not sure. Maybe we should call somebody?" I don't answer him. "Come on, I set that one up for you! Who you gonna—"

"I got it," I hiss, turning to him. He gives me a grin that I'd love to wipe off his face with my fist. "I think we should quietly hide out in the snack shack, wait out the movie, and hopefully the, um . . . vehicle will go away?"

"Yoo-hoo!"

A shiver pulses through my entire body when I hear a high-pitched voice. Rusty and I both look at the teenager who stands beside the passenger side door of the Chevy. She's wearing saddle shoes, a long pink skirt, a white sweater, and a high ponytail without a blond hair out of place. "I'm sorry to be a bother, but would you mind bringing us popcorn and some Cokes? Harry usually brings them out to us when we arrive."

Rusty finally shuts up. The one time I'd like him to do the talking.

"Oh, I'm sorry, where are my manners? I'm Penny Ridgeheart. Bert, don't be rude, introduce yourself," the ghost says. She looks solid, not transparent like in the movies. Her car buddy slides through the driver's-side door without opening it. He stands up, beaming at us, wearing loafers, slacks that are up way too high, and a tucked-in linen shirt, and his dark hair is so slicked back, it almost looks plastic.

"Hi there. Bert Clemons. Sorry to give you a scare. I suppose Harry didn't tell you about us. Where is the old sport, anyway?"

"The ghosts are talking to us," Rusty murmurs. I think I make some kind of noise in agreement while my mouth is dry and open.

"Everything jim-dandy?" the dead guy named Bert shouts at us. His smile is still tacked on. "We sure could use those Cokes."

"You promise you're not going to possess us?" Rusty yells. Both Penny and Burt laugh.

"Gosh, that's a good one," Bert says, wiping at his eye with his index finger. "Afraid that's not in our repertoire."

"I tried it once," Penny admits. "It gave me the heebie-jeebies!"

Rusty nods and slides off the table. He starts walking toward the snack shack.

"We're still on the clock, Afsi. And the customer's always right," Rusty says.

He's so full of crap! He never cares about what the customer wants! But he's left me alone as the sole focus of our only guests. They're still smiling at me. I find their overly chipper demeanor more unnerving than the fact that they're spirits from another realm. I run after Rusty, only to hear Penny call out, "If it's not too much trouble, some candy would be swell!"

Bert shoves his nose in his bucket of popcorn as he leans against the hood. Penny sits in the passenger seat with the door open. She takes another whiff of her candy box like she's huffing a can of paint for a high. Rusty and I stand a few paces away from them, observing as they go through every snack we have, not eating any of them but smelling them over and over again.

"Ugh, that's good," Bert says.

"Forgive us, we only have so much time," Penny says as she comes up for air. "We can't eat, but the smell, it, well . . . it gives us a satisfying sense memory."

"Hey, we all have our things," Rusty says with a chuckle. I can't believe how cool he is with all of this! "I'm Rusty. This is Afsaneh."

"What a beautiful and unusual name," Penny says, looking at me. "Is it . . . Spanish?"

"Yeah, I like Rusty too," Rusty says, fielding the microaggression and pretending she was talking to him. I appreciate it. "And I'm not sure of its origin, actually." We don't have to do the whole "where are you from" game. Though I guess I could turn the tables, ask where they're from. Heaven? Hell? Somewhere in between?

"It's nice to meet new folks," Bert says. "Though we're sorry to miss Harry. He's a good man. Most of the time."

"Oh, Bert, don't be a fuddy-duddy. That was so long ago," Penny says. "And you can't blame him for his grandfather's mistakes."

"What about last fall?" Bert asks her. "He didn't even come say hello. He just left a measly bucket of popcorn and two sodas for us on the field. I almost ran them over."

"We should let you finish the movie," I say, taking a step back.

"We've seen this movie dozens of times," Bert says. "If I have to hear about how dreamy Moondoggie is one more time—"

"It's the movie that was playing the night we checked out," Penny explains casually. "I think Harry thinks it's sweet or a part of how we're able to come back, so we haven't had the heart to tell him we wouldn't mind a little variety."

The same movie for decades. If it was *The Lego Batman Movie,* maybe I could do it, but I'd never say that out loud.

"Why isn't Harry here? He's had it with us?" Bert asks.

"He's in the hospital," I say. Penny looks distraught. Bert raises an eyebrow. "He's going to be okay. He just couldn't make it tonight."

"Is he sick?" Penny asks.

"No," I say, the words coming out more naturally even if every so often I keep backing away inch by inch. "He got attacked by something."

Penny and Bert share a look with one another that is a little too knowing for my liking.

"Did Harry tell you about our arrangement?" Bert asks. I shake my head. "I was a senior in high school when I brought Penny here. Asked to borrow my father's car. Isn't she a beauty?" I nod. There's a lot about the fifties that doesn't appeal to me, but boy, could they make beautiful-looking cars. "It was a big night because I asked Penny if she wanted to go steady."

"I said yes, of course! I mean, look at that dreamboat!" Penny says to me while touching the pin on her sweater.

"The dreamiest," I say out of fear. Men all kind of look the same to me. I know some of them are handsome, but, like, they're not terribly exciting.

"And it was the luckiest night of my life," Bert continues. "Until it wasn't. Story goes we got hit by a truck when we exited the drive-in. The drive-in didn't have the proper lighting on the road back then. At least, that's what our families were trying to convey to Harry's grandfather when they were looking for some compensation. Harry's grandfather said the crash didn't happen on the property, so it wasn't his fault. I guess that never felt right to us because something keeps us coming here every year on the night of the accident."

"Not the most romantic of anniversaries," Penny says, rolling her eyes.

"At first, we kept to ourselves, but as the years went on and car models changed, we sort of stood out," Bert says. "Then, when the place started becoming filthy, well, we just couldn't abide."

"All those nudie films and movies with men killing women with knives," Penny says, making a face of disgust, "and all the guests doing drugs and drinking. Some of the men had long hair, and the women had tattoos. It was awful! I have a feeling they were communists."

"Say it ain't so!" Rusty says in mock shock, his eyes bugging out of his face.

"I know, it was unbearable," Penny says, not picking up on Rusty's sarcasm.

"This place used to be wholesome. A place for families," Bert says. "Sure, us kids used to come here to neck, but it was respectable. Men and women indulging in some heavy petting, but nothing more. It was decent and pure. An all-American place where people knew how to fit in with one another. The way society ought to be."

The hairs on the back of my neck begin to prickle the more Bert gets worked up about how things *used to be.* Whenever someone talks about the "good old days," they forget to mention who it was "good" for.

"That's when we started putting on a show," Penny says, wiggling her eyebrows. "Flattening tires, scaring junkies in the bathroom, coming up with new ways to keep people away from here."

"When Harry took over, we made sure to pay him a special visit," Bert says. "But Harry understood why we were upset. He cleaned the place up, played better films, put money into better lighting and safety measures. And he closes every year for one night only so we can have a nice, quiet, pleasant evening for the three of us."

"The three of you?" I ask.

Bert grins before he puts two fingers into his mouth and lets out a loud whistle.

"Nanette!" Penny coos out into the night sky. "Nanette, come on, girl!"

A small whimper gets louder and louder as dirt and grass kick up into the air. The *thing* that had attacked Harry makes its way into the light shining down from the movie screen and reveals itself to be a cocker spaniel, tongue wagging as she bounds into Penny's arms. Penny fawns over the dog, petting her shiny fur coat and talking to her in a baby voice.

"Penny's just wild about Nanette," Bert says. "She brought her with us on the night of the accident. When your girl wants something, you make it happen for her, right?"

"Yeah," Rusty and I both say. Bert looks at me in confusion, and I think it may be best for my safety not to explain further. "For whatever reason, Nanette is able to stick around places when we can't. So, when Harry didn't treat us right last year, and the theater was, um . . . getting a little overcrowded with unusual characters"—Bert looks pointedly at Rusty when he says that—"we thought it'd be for the best to leave Nanette behind for a bit. Make sure Harry and the customers got with the program."

"That's right," Penny says to Nanette in a baby voice as she holds the barking dog up in the air. "We want this place to be just like we remembered it! Don't we, honey? Now that we know the theater is in good hands with these fine young folks, we can all leave here together."

"You will be here next year, won't you?" Bert asks, his smile now more threatening than nice. "Keep the place in tip-top shape?" He extends his hand out to us. I don't move. I remember what Harry said, not to get too close. Rusty doesn't seem to care about Harry's warning.

"Yeah, no sweat," Rusty says, shaking Bert's hand. It's a surprisingly solid handshake—I had thought Rusty's hand would go through Bert's.

"Good," Bert says. "We wouldn't want to have to leave Nanette behind again. She can be a real terror." He looks Rusty up and down. "And maybe you'll want to wear some more professional attire." He lets go of Rusty, who stays standing stick-straight in front of him.

The music from the movie swells, and I look up briefly to see THE END pop up.

"Looks like we better be going," Penny says in her regular tone of voice, cradling Nanette to her chest. "Give Harry our regards, won't you? Hope he feels better soon."

"Good to meet you, kids!" Bert says. "Don't do anything we wouldn't do!" The perkiness in his voice is now dripping with passive-aggressive menace. They both enter the car as the credits roll. When Bert puts the car in reverse and does a three-point turn, the fog surrounding the car fades away. The farther the car gets away from the light of the movie screen, the more the car changes.

The headlights are smashed, the doors are caved in, the windshield is shattered, and the car is rusty, worn down. My stomach drops, and I dry heave when Bert, Penny, and Nanette stop to wish me farewell. Bert's body is severely burned, portions of his skull poking through the skin of his forehead, and the eyeball in his right socket dangles like a yo-yo below his chin. Penny's ponytail is gone, as are her ears, her nose, and her lips, which makes her smile all the wider. Nanette doesn't look like a dog at all. Her gnashing teeth look like they belong to a tiger, and she's triple the size of a wolf. Her eyes are fiery red, and her snout is that of a pig's. Her ears have been replaced with scaly horns. The only cocker spaniel thing about her are the patches of charred fur in random places on her reptilian body.

"See you at the movies!" Penny says with a gleeful laugh. The car slowly rattles down the field until it disappears before it makes it to the exit.

I put my hands on my knees and continue to heave, this time throwing up a little, tears forming at the corner of my eyes. When I stand back up, Rusty hasn't moved at all.

"You okay?" I call to him. The blue moon suddenly begins to glow brighter as he turns to face me. His hair is combed back, slick, blond, without a hint of neon. He's wearing a sweater vest, khakis, and a pair of loafers. His neck tattoo and nail polish are gone. There's a smile on his face that I've never seen on him before. It's devoid of humor or passion. It's just plastered on the way Bert's was. The scream lodged in my throat comes out as a gurgle.

"It's a humdinger of an evening, isn't it?" Rusty asks with a sincerity in his voice that almost makes me cry. "Gee whillikers, it's a school night! I'd better get home and finish my homework!"

GUESTED

Rebecca Kim Wells

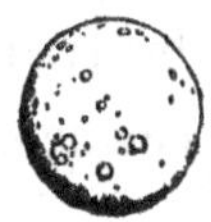

You are cordially invited to
a Halloween Extravaganza
372 Highland Avenue
Saturday
7:00 P.M.
~ *Guests Provided* ~

The envelope was inside your locker on Friday morning, a heavy cream-colored affair embossed with a lacy black pattern that reminded you of masquerades. Your hands trembled as you ripped open the seal and pulled out the invitation. The paper smelled like dusk and roses. Your eyes flitted over the mundane details of address and time before coming to rest on the words printed at the bottom: *Guests Provided.*

The locker next to you slammed, and you jumped. Fingers with brightly painted nails plucked the invitation out of your hands. You turned to see Kayla brandishing the paper in your face. "Tell me you're not going," she said. "*Please.*"

You looked away. "You know I have to go."

The thing about Kayla was that she was the only one who had kept you grounded over the last two years, the only one anchoring you when what you wanted more than anything was to step off the ground and float away. And now she thought what you were doing was wrong.

You agreed. It was risky. Dangerous, even. And not because the party was being hosted by Tyler Hemming, a high school sportsballer cliché who, two years ago, you wouldn't have touched with a ten-foot pole. But—

Excited cries erupted down the hall as other locker doors opened and other invitations fell out. When you looked back at Kayla, she was frowning at you, her eyes narrowed.

"Come with me," you said impulsively, as though that would change anything.

You wished it would. You broke up a few months ago—your fault—and even though you were still friends, even though it was for the best, even though, even though—even though *everything*—sometimes you still missed her so much, it hurt to breathe.

Especially when she was standing right in front of you smelling like her favorite honey and milk lotion and there were ribbons threaded through both of her braids, and her nails were painstakingly painted orange and black with a tiny perfect jack-o'-lantern grinning on each pinkie.

"You know my mom would kill me if I went to a Guested party," she said. You knew this was true. Mrs. Choi thought Guested parties were white-people nonsense or the work of the devil. Sometimes both.

Kayla handed back the invitation, then touched your arm hesitantly. "But seriously, Nina. Be careful."

"I will," you replied, though it felt like you were crossing your fingers behind your back while you said it.

Win costume of the century.
~ Guested ~

Two years ago, Penny went to a Guested party and came back wrong.

Nobody believed you. That was the worst part.

It was subtle at first. She used to crochet while the two of you watched TV together. After the party, she stopped crocheting. Then she stopped watching TV, right when *The Untamed* was getting really good. She quit the soccer team. She stopped fighting you for the last mandu and started ignoring Mr. Zuba, the crochety family cat who only liked her. And then, when it was time to go to college—early-decision acceptance to Amherst, she had been so nervous and so excited when she applied—she just . . . didn't.

Instead she skipped graduation and got a receptionist job at a dentist's office and moved into her own apartment and basically stopped talking to you.

Your mom called it growing pains, an assertion of independence, and after that she didn't really call it anything. She said you just had to give Penny space.

You knew better. Because your older sister might be growing up, might have left most of her bedroom behind when she moved out, but the real Penny would *never* have forgotten Cappy the stuffed capybara. Or her underlined and annotated set of Jenny Han novels. Or the too-big flannel shirt that used to be your dad's.

That person, whoever she was, wasn't your sister. Something bad had happened at that party. And you were going to prove it.

⁂

When you got home after school there was a note on the fridge with a smiley face and money for pizza—Mom was working late again. Picking up extra shifts at the hospital was kind of her mode these days. She used to say it was to save money for your big Korea trip, but after Penny moved out, she stopped talking about it.

You pulled out your phone and texted a smiley face and a pizza emoji to Mom. Then you scrolled down to the text you had sent Penny this morning.

Will you be around later?

You could see that she'd read the text but hadn't responded.

You sighed and pocketed the pizza cash. It wasn't even 4:00 yet. She was probably still at work.

This, you had to admit, was really just you telling yourself a story to cover up the fact that she was definitely ignoring you. Though that didn't mean it wasn't true. And if she was at work, then she wasn't at her apartment.

⁂

After Penny moved out, you threw yourself into research, starting on social media. Guested parties were notorious. Anyone lucky enough to score an invitation would want to show off.

Hours of scouring Penny's friends' profiles yielded a rough timeline of that night—artfully arranged and filtered pictures of party invitations giving way to dashed-off captions posted from the steps of mansions giving way to blurry, too-loud videos. You studied each one carefully, noting the way delighted shock rippled through the crowd every time a new Guest made an appearance. A cowboy, a T-rex, Benjamin Franklin himself . . . Bethy Clinton *was* the leather-trench-coat-clad badass from that old virtual reality movie—you had to work hard to see underneath the Guest to the girl who had led your high school soccer team to a district championship last year. Each Guest was so eerily perfect, it was as though they had swallowed their hosts whole, as though the person who had walked into the party had never existed in the first place.

Your chest tightened as you watched. After a while you had to hide your phone under a pillow and squeeze your eyes shut, counting up by sevens until you felt like you could breathe again. You wanted to tell yourself it wasn't real, that it was just a trick of shadows and light. But deep down, you knew that wasn't true.

To your frustration, you could only find Penny on the peripheries. On the edge of a group picture taken before the party. Laughing in a video as an astronaut argued with the cowboy, and then started making out with them. You couldn't find any posts of her Guest, but when you spotted her in the background of a selfie walking upstairs with a Guested technician, your stomach clenched. You knew then. You knew even if you couldn't yet bring yourself to voice the words.

The possibilities are endless.

~ Guested ~

Penny lived in one of those complexes where every apartment looked identical from the outside. You'd gotten lost the first time you'd come here, and even now you had to consult the signs splitting complex North from South and apartments 1–35 from 36–70 to find your way. To combat the sameness, most people decorated their entryways, putting out SPEAK, FRIEND, AND ENTER! or WIPE YOUR PAWS! mats and seasonal wreaths on their doors. Not Penny. Apartment #38 was a mud-brown door and a plain black mat.

Your mom had gotten a key only after she had promised never to use it without Penny's permission. Now you slipped the key into the lock and waited, holding your breath. There was only silence from inside, so after another long moment, you opened the door and stepped in.

It was a depressingly spartan space. Penny's room at home was lush and cozy, all soft colors and fluffy pillows. This studio looked like a hotel. Impersonal. Anonymous. Just being there made you want to cry. Instead you gritted your teeth and forced the tears down. There wasn't much time.

You rifled through the apartment as carefully as possible. This was your last chance before the party tonight. Your last chance to find something—anything—that would tie Penny to Guested, Inc.

Twenty minutes later you were almost ready to give up when you saw the glint of metal in the back of the closet. You shoved clothes aside, your heart pounding. Penny's treasure chest.

She'd had it as long as you could remember, a large wooden chest with metal rivets that always reminded you of pirates. When you were little she hid candy inside. Later it became storage for her stuffed animals, journals, sports trophies, A+ school assignments . . . You hadn't realized she had taken it with her.

You slowly lifted the lid . . . and stared down at a neatly folded set of sheets. You sat back in disappointment. "Shit," you whispered. And then, because it made you feel about half a percent better, again: "Shit!" You slammed a fist down on the sheets in frustration—and felt something solid underneath.

You snatched up the sheet, rummaging through the chest. "Please, please please . . ." Halfway down the chest you found it—egg-shaped, gray and smooth like a river stone, small enough to fit in your palm. You stared down at it, puzzled. And then you heard a key turn in the door.

You startled upright and hit your head on the clothing rod. "Shit!" Head smarting, you grabbed the stone and dropped it into your pocket, then banged the lid of the chest down and piled clothes over it. The door opened as you lunged away from the closet, leaving you standing awkwardly in the middle of the apartment as Penny came in.

She stopped. "What are you doing here?"

"You're early!" you blurted.

"The office closed early today. And you didn't answer the question."

"I, um—" You stuffed your hands in your pockets, and your fingers found the crumpled twenty. "Mom's working late and she left me money and I thought maybe you'd want to get pizza and watch a movie and pass out candy?"

You used to do that all the time. Once you grew out of trick-or-treating, it was your favorite part of Halloween—candy and a movie, not necessarily scary, with Penny.

Her eyes just narrowed slightly. "And you couldn't text or call?"

"I texted you! Besides, when's the last time you returned a text or call?" you shot back.

Penny opened her mouth, and you willed her to snap back the way she used to. Instead she shrugged and shook her head. "No thanks."

She seemed to have bought your excuse. Letting it lie would have been the smart thing to do. But a wave of missing your sister broke over you so strongly your chest ached. Even now, you wanted to believe that you were mistaken, that this *wrongness* about her could be mended if only you tried hard enough. "What about *The Nightmare Before Christmas*?" you pleaded. *Nightmare* was one of Penny's favorite movies—you used to watch it at least once a month, singing along to the songs and arguing about whether it belonged in Christmas or Halloween.

"A Christmas movie in October?" Penny scoffed, and your skin crawled. The real Penny had *always* been Team Halloween. "I don't have time tonight. You should get going." She looked pointedly at the open door. "And give me that key, please."

You didn't want to give her the key. It felt too much like letting go of the last of your sister. But what else could you do? You dropped it into her open palm and stopped yourself from screaming as you did. You walked by Penny—Penny's body, anyway—and you didn't stop shivering until you were on your bike and pedaling furiously away.

After you had exhausted social media posts from that night, you moved on to Guested, Inc. You were puzzled to discover that when the company first launched, they were aimed at corporate retreats. *The perfect partner to enhance your team-building*—that was on their website archived in 2015. It seemed like a weird fit to you. You weren't surprised to see that they had quickly pivoted—in 2016 their website boasted *the world's most exclusive costume party* and *be someone else for one night only.* They would provide Guests for anyone who paid an exorbitant fee, of course, but they did most of their business in October. What better costume than to invite someone—some*thing*—into you, to play the part that you assigned it?

You remembered when you started hearing about the company, the *Guests*—from whispers and video reels of Penny's richest friends' richest friends—the laughter, the strange, almost unnatural scenes, things that frightened you enough that your mom told Penny to stop showing you her phone.

When you were old enough for your own phone, you hunted them down again. Guested parties still scared you—but there was something alluring about them too. You—thirteen, gawky, anxious—allowed yourself to imagine being someone else. To be freed from yourself, from the burden of making decisions, of feeling the awkwardness of not knowing how to act, how to *be*—just for one night. You yearned to attend a Guested party for years. Until the night of Penny's party, you yearned.

Guested, Inc., claimed their service was perfectly safe. That what happened once the doors were closed was foolproof, a process presided over by highly trained technicians—they had a patent on some hydrotherapy equipment that you didn't fully understand, and you were frustrated that you hadn't found any references to exactly *how* the process supposedly worked. That once the Guest had arrived, company hosts would watch over you, keeping you safe from real harm until the experience was over. *100% Satisfaction!* the website boasted. *A night you'll remember forever.*

But if that were true, why were there lawsuits and settlements and NDAs? The company had tried their best to scrub the internet, but the evidence was there, scattered through years-old Reddit threads and archived pages, a few oblique mentions on now-deleted videos. It took three months for you to piece it all together, for you to be sure. Even then, the relief of *knowing* was far outweighed by the dread that settled into your bones as the truth became clear.

Per the website, the Guested process was simple. *Tell us who—or what—you want to become. Relax as our certified technicians work with a Guest to make your dream a reality. Wake up with memories to last a lifetime.* But the whispers you found said that not everyone who attended a Guested party woke up.

Penny had gone to a Guested party and asked to become someone else. But whatever Guest Penny had hosted that night . . . they hadn't left. The Penny who returned from that party wasn't your sister. She was the Guest.

⁂

Why would a Guest take over a body?

A lot of people—well, only Kayla and your mom—asked you that when you brought up your suspicions. They indulged you at first, but it was obvious they didn't believe you. After a while you learned to keep it quiet, this creeping suspicion, this nagging certainty that all was not well.

The truth was, you didn't know for sure why Guests would stay. You came across a lot of conspiracy theories on the internet—everything from Guested, Inc., planting Guests in strategic locations to mount a campaign for world domination to aliens to butterfly effect sagas about mass assassinations to ghosts. But none of that explained why anyone would care about planting a Guest in an average Korean American suburban teenager. And as far as you knew, Penny hadn't suddenly turned into a superspy. She just . . . wasn't there anymore. And if you couldn't get her back, the only thing you could think of to do was prove that Guested, Inc. had done this—to her and all the others.

Who will you be tonight?

~ Guested ~

Tyler's house was already loud by the time you arrived at 7:07. Fashionably late wasn't really a thing when it came to Guested parties. No one wanted to miss the spectacle.

Tyler lived up in the hills, in a neighborhood populated by gated driveways half a mile long. It was the sort of place where some kids had literal castle-type towers for bedrooms. Being around this much money creeped you out, and you felt both out of place and out of breath by the time you puffed up the sloped driveway and parked your bike by the front door.

"Nice ride!" called Dylan Angeles. He snickered as you flipped him off. You took a moment to mess with your hair—safety first, but wearing a helmet did some supremely unflattering things to your haphazard braids, which were Korean dark but (sadly) white frizzy.

Your phone chimed.

Are you at the party?

It was Kayla. You didn't want to lie to her. Yes.

Be safe. Please. <3

You stared at the heart for a few beats longer than you should have. Maybe she meant it. Or maybe it was just her last-ditch effort to get you not to go.

A chorus of howls broke out in the backyard, raising the hair on the back of your neck. You shook it off, rolling your eyes. It was a full moon—a blue moon, according to Kayla—tonight, at a Halloween party. Of course people would start howling.

You pocketed the phone without responding. Then you headed inside.

There was an attendant—a real-life doorman—checking invitations as you stepped inside. He gave you a pointed look as you handed yours over, and you fought the urge to smooth your hair again.

"Nina, you made it!" someone squealed. You turned to see Charlotte Baker at the top of the staircase.

She was wearing a diaphanous pink gown with a tiara. It wasn't hard to guess what sort of Guest she would request. She ran gracefully down the stairs and engulfed you in an enthusiastic hug. She was enthusiastic about everything and everyone. It would have been easy to hate her for being so rich if she weren't so damn sweet and generous about it.

"Princess?" you asked, pointing at the tiara.

She grinned ruefully. "I know, I know. I just love the pretty dresses, okay?" She looked you up and down. "I want to say . . . Sherlock Holmes?"

"More of a generic detective type," you said, pulling a magnifying glass and a notebook out of your trench coat pocket.

She laughed. "I'm so glad you're here. I mean, how often do we get two full moons in a month? It just feels like tonight's going to be extra special."

You smiled awkwardly. Now that you were here, you kind of wished you had made more of an effort with your costume. Not that it was important—it so *wasn't* the most important aspect of tonight. Still, you already felt like a short, stubby, round-faced duckling surrounded by deeply confident swans on a daily basis. Wearing a too-big trench coat and Converse sneakers next to Charlotte's princess gown just felt like overkill.

Magnanimous, Charlotte continued. "The Guesting starts at seven thirty, but there are drinks and hors d'oeuvres out now. And you *have* to go check out that moon if you haven't yet. Get comfy!" She was taking the role of hostess seriously, as Tyler's girlfriend.

Behind her you could see the second-floor staircase was roped off with a sign saying AUTHORIZED PERSONNEL ONLY. Your heartbeat quickened. That was it. All the Guested equipment was behind that sign. All the answers you were after. All you had to do was get to it.

It had taken a while for you to figure out a course of action. You'd reached out to a few papers, but none of them took you seriously.

The Guested, Inc., headquarters were across the country—there was no way you could get there, and even if you did, there was no way you'd be able to sneak in without getting detected. You couldn't just start posting on the internet—you'd seen enough of their legal team in action. You needed proof. And the only way you could think of to get it was to get yourself an invitation to a Guested party. That, of course, was a different sort of problem.

There were only a few kids at school whose families were rich enough to bankroll a Guested party. After careful consideration, you narrowed the list down to one top contender: Tyler Hemming. The biggest thing he had going for him was that he wasn't *as* insufferable as the rest of the list, which included a girl who found a way to wrangle a mention of her family's private jet into pretty much every conversation. You also knew that his big brother Zack, with whom he was extremely competitive, had been at the same Guested party as Penny.

First you volunteered to work a group project in physics with Cat Gutierrez and Charlotte Baker. Charlotte was so nice it was easy to invite her to a classic movie night at the local theater after the project was finished. From there it was simple enough to bump into her at lunch and sit with her and Tyler and the rest of them, to make your way from outside the group to the fringe, then the inner fold.

Tyler himself wasn't that bad, especially when he was on his own. Sometimes you talked about real things—your parents' divorce, his mom dying. Once you even talked about Guested—really talked.

"Isn't it dangerous? I can't believe your dad is cool with it."

Tyler rolled his eyes. "My dad couldn't give less of a shit what I do. He'd be a hypocrite if he did, though—he's Guested tons of times with his buddies. It's totally safe. They have all sorts of monitors, and you have to sign off on your Guest. It's all on the up and up."

"Don't you think it's weird, though?" you said. "No one even knows what the Guests really are."

"Oh, lighten up. Haven't you ever wanted to be someone else? Zack said you haven't lived until you know what it's like to be a T-rex. Night of his life and all that. Besides, the videos are killer."

"Whatever," you replied, and he laughed and tossed you a soda, and you went back to *Mario Kart*. You didn't tell him that you'd wanted to be someone else, somewhere else, for years. That you felt completely empty sometimes, like there wasn't anything in you at all but the determination to see this through.

It was easy to drop enough hints, easy to wait for the announcement that Tyler and Charlotte were hosting a Guested party for Halloween. Everything went according to plan. Everything except for one thing: you lost Kayla.

⁂

Charlotte hugged you once more before floating toward the next arrival. You melted back against the wall and surveyed the party. A gaggle of soccer girls waved at you, and you waved back. There were a few boys sitting awkwardly in the living room, and you could tell this is the sort of situation where there would usually be alcohol. Without that particular lubricant—thanks to Guested, Inc., safety policies—everyone was nervous and no one knew what to do with their hands.

Then Tyler himself arrived, and the party perked up. An older woman stood next to him, impeccably dressed in a custom suit, her hair shaved on one side and layered with blue highlights on the other. She looked *cool,* but also like she'd tried too hard to get there, and you distrusted her instantly.

"Welcome!" she said brightly. Her tone made it clear she was accustomed to being listened to, and the conversation about how many cookies Todd Campbell could stuff into his mouth at once cut off. "I'm Fiona Kessler, and I'm so excited to share Guested with you tonight. As I'm sure you're aware, Guested is a one-of-a-kind immersive experience perfect for Halloween celebrations. Past participants have described the experience as freeing, mesmerizing, even simply indescribable. And we are incredibly proud of our return rate—over ninety-five percent of participants come back a second time."

You zoned out as she continued to extol the virtues of the Guested experience, coming to only as the room broke into raucous applause.

Fiona smiled. "Ready, everyone?"

A few people clamored to be at the front of the line, and Fiona beckoned Tyler and Charlotte forward. A Guested technician checked their names against a list on their tablet, and then escorted them upstairs. You watched them go, remembering Penny walking up the stairs. You were going to have to follow them. You didn't feel ready. Now that you were here, you remembered that you were afraid, and suddenly that was all you could feel.

You turned around and grabbed another soda. There was time, you told yourself. You had all night.

⁂

The first footsteps came sooner than you expected. Tyler first, and then Charlotte, but . . . different. Your stomach twisted as you saw their faces.

Charlotte—not Charlotte, the Guest inside of Charlotte—peered imperiously around the room. "This place is a sty," she said, and the way her voice had shifted, just slightly, made you queasy.

Tyler—no, the Guest inside of Tyler—was a knight. He immediately jumped to rearrange furniture and set a chair atop the coffee table, creating a throne for Charlotte to sit on. A cowboy came down the stairs, followed by a tiger. You couldn't stop looking at the tiger. They were human still, but also *not*. Your eyes wanted to see a tiger no matter how you told them otherwise, and there was something in your brain that shrank and curled in primitive fear as the tiger moved through the room. How were you the only one seeing this? Everyone else seemed awestruck and eager.

You had to get away. You turned around and bumped into Amelia Earhart holding hands with Eleanor Roosevelt.

"Sorry," you muttered, pushing past them. Suddenly you were certain you'd made a massive mistake. You thought you could sneak upstairs undetected, but there were more of the Guests with each passing minute. Soon they would all be Guests, and you would be the last one left. What would happen then?

There wasn't enough air in the room. You broke through a group of Olivia Rodrigos, desperate for an exit—and saw that the second-floor staircase was, for the moment, unguarded. It was now or never. Heart pounding, you ran up the stairs.

As massive as the first floor of Tyler's house was, the second and third floors impressed you more. The hallways went on and on, with far more rooms than inhabitants, especially since Zack had left for college. Now the doors were closed.

You crept down the hall, toward the guest bedrooms. Light shone underneath the doors, and you paused, listening for any indication of what was happening inside. Hosts had to tell the technician who or what they wanted their Guest to be, you knew that much. And the waiver you had to sign to come to the party mentioned hydrotherapy tanks and asked whether you had a fear of tight spaces. But beyond that, the procedure remained opaque.

The door at the end of the hall sighed open, and you froze. Seconds ticked by as you waited to see who would come out—but there was no one. You tiptoed toward the room and peeked inside, holding your breath.

Boxes emblazoned with the Guested, Inc., logo were stacked in neat piles, and there was a laptop open on the desk. You pulled the egg you'd taken from Penny's apartment out of your pocket. You'd been so certain that it was tied up with Guested, Inc., but it didn't seem to fit with anything you saw now.

You went to the laptop and tapped the trackpad. Password-protected. You turned back to the boxes. The first few were filled with equipment you didn't recognize, but the top box on the second stack yielded a set of heavy manuals. You pulled them out and flipped through the pages—entire chapters on the hydrotherapy tank setup and takedown procedures, the questions to ask participants, all the things you'd read hints of on the internet. And then—*Anomalous Outcomes.*

In the event a Guest refuses to leave
the host at the appropriate time,
see Procedure #F5.

You folded the corner of the page over and flipped forward.

Procedure #F5

1. *Note the host's details, including personal identification and health information.*
2. *Prepare Report #J4, including Appendix #2: Host Pre-Interview.*
3. *Submit Report #J4 to manager on-site; cc: home office manager and legal manager.*
4. *Submit Confidentiality Agreement #8 under manager supervision.*

This is what you were looking for. Proof that they knew that Guests could hijack their hosts' bodies. Not only that, it happened often enough that they had an entire *procedure* for it. Hands shaking, you ripped out the relevant pages and stuffed them into your pocket. You could do something with this. You could *change* things.

"What are you doing?" said a sharp voice.

You shot to your feet, looking up to see Fiona Kessler standing in the doorway. Fear spiked through you—and then rage. "Nothing! Got lost. I was looking for a bathroom."

Fiona nodded. "And those manuals?"

You shrugged. "I got curious. I've—I've always thought it would be cool to work at Guested."

"And you thought corporate espionage would endear you to us?" You swallowed. There was a strange smile on her face, and it suddenly occurred to you that whatever she was—Guest or human enabler—you had to get out of there. Now.

"You're right," you said. "You're absolutely right, that was a complete lapse, and it won't happen again. I'm sorry, I'll just get out of your hair now—"

But there was movement in the doorway—Todd Campbell was blocking the way. Not Todd—the Captain America Guest inhabiting his body.

Your breath left your body in a rush. "Look, I think there's been a mistake—"

"Yes, I do think you've made a mistake," Fiona agreed. She pointed something at you—a Taser?—and the world went hot and spiky and dark.

⁂

This is what happens in those rooms:

They strap you into a hydrotherapy pod. They attach monitoring cables to your temples, your wrists, your ankles. They close the pod, leaving you in water and darkness. You are alone—until you are not.

They skipped the part where you would talk to the technician about who you want to be, what Guest you want to invite in, but I know now. I know everything about you. You'll see.

⁂

The truth about the Guests is so simple, Nina.

Once upon a time a man went out into the wilderness. Having summited mountains, he now went down into the dark unknown places of the earth. There, three days deep in the darkness, he stumbled upon something he should never have seen. Rather than leave us be, he asked himself—so predictable! So human!—how he might exploit us. And we agreed.

Guests have no need to share profits or fight over contracts. We play our part willingly, feed off of our hosts' emotions, their brightness, their life. And if one of us occasionally overstays our welcome . . . Well, the humans at the top agree it's a fair price to pay for the immense success that Guested, Inc., has become.

Soon you will wake up and go downstairs, dizzy, disoriented, ready to escape Guested, Inc., forever. Tomorrow when Kayla asks, you'll be disappointed and maybe a little heartbroken. You'll say that she was right, that your mom was right, and you didn't find anything. That you want to mend fences with Penny, who is actually worried about you. Then you'll apologize—profusely!—for how obsessed you've become with the whole "Guested thing."

Kayla might look at you, puzzled, for a moment, but she'll be so relieved that Guested is in the rearview that she'll be happy to loop her arm around yours and never speak of it again. Three months from now you'll be back together.

Penny will start talking to you. She'll apologize for being so distant. She'll tell you about going to therapy and you'll cry together and laugh together and start having movie nights again. At Christmas, your mom will surprise you both with plane tickets to Korea. Isn't that the life you so desperately wanted to return to?

They will all be happy with the person who leaves Highland Avenue tonight, who takes off her helmet without worrying about how her hair looks. The girl who puts Guested, Inc., behind her for good. Isn't that the person you truly wanted to be, in the dark places of your heart?

I can see the things that hurt you. I can feel your fears and wants and secret dreams. I will be you better than you can be.

You were right, Nina, in the end.

Sometimes the Guests do come to stay.

You were also wrong.

Your sister isn't one of them.

But now you are.

ROCKY ROAD WITH CARAMEL DRIZZLE

Kosoko Jackson

I.

"What's wrong with you?"

There are many ways that sentence could have been said, depending on the inflection. Put the emphasis on the right word, and it might have sounded like concern. But the way my best friend, Amber, chooses to say it makes her voice sound like a white-hot needle sizzling as it pushes through my skin, searing my flesh.

She knows, that's the kicker; she just doesn't *want* to know. All she wants to do is enjoy her evening, celebrate Halloween, and be a normal teen. She doesn't want to be the best friend of the boy who ruined last year's Halloween in Wyndy Hallows. She wants to shrink away from the spotlight that makes every imperfection, every flaw, every blemish look larger than life.

Doesn't she know I want to do the same thing? After all, I'm the one the beating happened to, not her.

"I'm fine," I whisper back to her, tugging on the sleeve of my flannel shirt with my left hand, pulling it over the wrist of my right. Amber narrows her, well, amber-colored eyes—the reason she has her name—her lips curving downward into an ugly scowl.

"You're lying, Julian. At least try to be better at it if you're going to do it."

Another knife that perfectly finds its way through my presumably well-crafted armor. That was always Amber's skill. A reason why she's debate captain at our high school and most definitely going to go to some Ivy on a debate scholarship, even if she doesn't want to jinx it by saying it out loud.

"Sorry."

Why am I saying sorry? I'll kick myself for that later. We both know why I'm wincing. Ever since the beating 365 days ago, my right wrist hasn't been the same. It throbs when it's too cold, burns when it's going to rain, and feels cold when it's going to get hot outside. My own personal barometer.

But that's not the only thing that hasn't been the same. The past 365 days have felt like a blur. Like the world has been played around me at five times the normal speed. I barely remember it all. The attack. The hospital. The days in between. Almost like they didn't happen or are some hazy dream falling more and more out of reach the more I try to grab on to it. I guess that's how the mind deals with trauma.

Besides, thinking about it hurts too much. So instead, I focus on what I can: Amber's burning gaze. One of frustration and annoyance.

I hear her let out an angry sigh, the kind that makes her

nostrils flare. She shifts her weight from her left to her right foot, scanning the party.

"Where is he . . ."

He being her ex-boyfriend, Todd. Well, *boyfriend* is a strong word. I guess *situationship* is better.

"You think he'll actually show?"

Amber shrugs. "He said he would."

"Todd says a lot of things," I mutter around the rim of my red cup filled with Sprite. I keep looking forward, avoiding the burning death glare she's giving me.

"You want to explain that further?"

I don't because Amber doesn't actually want to hear it. Todd was one of the people who I saw when, well . . . when my face was being bashed in by my attackers. He never confessed to the police what he knew, even after he came to my bedside, like he wanted my forgiveness, with that signature British accent of his.

But if I tell Amber that, she's going to think, once again, that I'm making this all about me. How she can't have something for herself and everything in her life has to be connected to my trauma. She'll call me . . . what was it . . . a *heat vampire.* Sure, she apologized for it, but words like that? Wounds like that? They don't go away so easily. Not like the broken bones, pulled muscles, and bruised skin of 365 days ago.

But what me is there without Amber? It's been the both of us for as long as I can remember. She's accepted every part of me, even when my parents didn't. Even when they pushed me aside or told me to keep my gayness to myself, she was there for me. And I like to think that, eventually, she'll be there for me again. Because, if the opposite is true, then who do I have in my corner?

Being alone, truly alone, is worse than being relegated to the side. At least, that's what I keep telling myself.

"I meant, I'm sure he'll show. He just might not come when he says he's going to come."

Smooth save, Julian. It seems to be good enough. Amber's tight shoulders relax, and she lets out an audible sigh of relief.

"Yeah, maybe so."

The only reason I'm here is because of Mom. According to her, one year is long enough to hide in the house.

"You can't let your life be defined by that night, J," she'd said this morning, leaning against the door. "You can't let him win."

Him. As if saying his name is some curse. I wish she'd just say it. You can't let Ian Wilson and his privileged impenetrable shell of power, money, and connections keep me from living my own life. Sure, he attacked me. Yeah, he and his friends cornered me, taunted me, called me names you told me to stop saying when I was explaining to you and the sheriff what happened, but that doesn't mean I shouldn't show my face and hold my head high. And, of course, how can I forget, when we were told—by his parents' lawyer, our lawyer, and everyone who thought they had a right to comment on the situation—that it would be *better* for everyone if we just let it fade away because did I really think the mayor's son, whose family goes back four hundred years, would admit guilt?

I push those thoughts back when the chorus of students currently crammed into the home cheer when the front door opens. I don't even need to look up to know who it is. In fact, I do the opposite; I fold in on myself, shrink into the shadow my body pools around me, hoping I can disappear. It's not a reaction I'm proud of, but it's damn near automatic.

Most people in Wyndy Hallows open themselves up, peacock their bodies, if you will, when Ian Wilson shows up. They think, *Maybe if he notices me, he'll smile my way. Maybe he'll say something, a compliment. He's so handsome with that perfect jaw and perfect hair and perfect everything.*

I know people think that because they're the same thoughts I used to have. The same thoughts that made me feel that maybe, just maybe, I deserved a happy ending. I should try to fight for some morsel of happiness. Everyone else in our high school gets it. Why can't I?

And where did that lead me? Being called a faggot. Cornered. Beaten. Broken.

Amber perks up just like everyone else, scanning his posse of friends, looking for Todd. I don't need to look at her or Ian's friends to know what the little squeal she lets out means—it tells me everything I need to know.

"Go," I say, gesturing.

Amber may have the silver tongue of a serpent, but I also know she listens to her parents. I know Maria told her to take care of me. She was my nurse during my recovery, and I've spent more days than I can count over at their house. To Maria, I'm the son she never had. Amber won't go against her mother's wishes, no matter how much she wants her own happy ending.

Unless I let her.

"I'm just going to go and look at the library we saw when we came in," I tell her. "I'll be fine, promise."

Amber's deep soulful eyes flicker from me to Todd back to me. "Are you sure?"

"I'm sure."

"You're not going—"

"Just go," I interject, cutting her off before she can say what I know she's going to say.

You're not going to get yourself beat up again, are you? Like what happened was my fault.

I don't know why I care about Amber's happily ever after. Maybe it's because she's been my best friend for as long as I can remember. Or maybe it's because I still want *someone* to be happy. Or maybe, deep down, her and Todd doing whatever her and Todd will do means she'll be as far away from my orbit as possible, and I don't have to put up with her constant grazing jabs.

That's most likely it.

II.

Whoever's house this is has good taste in books.

Ten minutes in, and I've already clocked nine first editions, more than a dozen translated versions of classics, and books by authors I've never heard of, most of them hidden behind a glass wall with a lock on it. So close but so far away at the same time.

Some of the books are out, clearly placed for us commoners to touch. Normal bestsellers, generic run-of-the-mill books everyone's heard of if they care anything about literature. It's almost as if those books are a bait-and-switch to detract the eye from the books hidden behind the invisible glass barrier.

I know what it's like, to be one of those books. Something fragile hidden behind glass so that no one can touch you, but everyone can look at you. I wonder if they feel anything. Wonder if the age they are, and the emotions the author put them into, and the emotions the reader poured into them, brought them to life. Do they know that we watch? Do they know they can't be touched? Do they yearn to fulfill their pur—

"Did you hear me?"

The answer is no. Turning to the voice, a girl not that much older than me with dark, raven-colored hair pulled into a ponytail leans against the wall, chewing gum. She eyes me with a bored expression, blowing a bubble and popping it.

"Come again?"

She pushes off the wall and at the same time, points her thumb to the adjoining room with the sliding wooden door half open. "I asked if you're down for something freaky."

Usually when someone asks a question like that, my first instinct is to avoid them as quickly as possible. Questions that feel like dark, cold black holes, where a specific answer will send you tumbling down an endless spiral that you can't pull yourself out of—those are the types of things I like to avoid. Recently, shrinking myself has been my MO: Don't be noticed. Don't be seen. Don't put a target on your back, period. Something like this breaks all those tenets.

But there's something about the girl that makes me think that at the bottom of the black hole, there may be a glimmer of hope.

Or a glimmer of something, maybe just something to make this party go by faster, before Amber goes searching for me, finds me, and tells me rather than asks that we're leaving.

"Yeah, sure, why not?" I reply.

A grin like wildfire spreads over her face. She pushes off the wall. "Monica."

"Julian."

She gives me a curt nod before leading me to the adjoining room. Sitting around a Ouija board on the floor are two others I don't know but who quickly make introductions.

"Samantha."

"Carson."

"You ever used one of these before?" Monica asks as I close the door. The muffled sounds of the party barely make it through the thick wooden sliding door.

I shake my head, moving forward to the only space still available after Monica sits: the spot closest to the door. I sit on my knees.

"Where did you find it?"

"Over there." Samantha points to an open trunk.

"So you were snooping," I say.

"*Snooping* is such a charged word." Carson grins. "I would say . . . *investigating*, you know?" He winks. It's a charming smile and almost . . . almost makes my cheeks burn.

"Well, anyway, we have it out now. Between being out there or in here, where would you rather be?" Monica asks, leveling her vision with mine. "Especially now that Ian Wilson's arrived."

The name cuts sharply through the center of my body. Of course, Monica knew. Everyone in town knew. Carson clears his throat, trying to break up the heavy silence in the room while Samantha shifts her weight.

"Are we going to get started?" Samantha asks, pushing her blond hair over her shoulder.

"Before my twin chickens out, please," Carson adds.

"Hey!" Samantha glares, leaning forward, and presses her hand on the board. Carson follows suit, then Monica, leaving only me.

"You know this thing is supposed to summon the dead, right?" I ask.

"Call on the dead," Monica corrects. "And come on, it's All Hallows' Eve. We should have a little fun, right?"

Playing with the dead seems like a pretty loose interpretation of fun, but what else do I have planned?

"All right," Monica says as she clears her throat. "Do you all know what to do?"

Carson and Samantha nod, but I purse my lips into a frown.

"Don't worry," Carson whispers, leaning into me. "You'll catch on. Not like there's anything on the other side anyway, right?"

He's right. When I was being beaten to death, I thought it was going to be the end of me. That I was going to drift away into someplace nice and warm and pretty and beautiful. I thought I'd find some perfect afterlife or go through some sort of judgment. But I remember only feeling the cold concrete under me. The feeling of warm blood pooling around me.

What they've sold us about the afterlife is a lie. Just like friendship. Like love. Like justice. Nothing is real except for what I can see, feel, and touch.

"Right," I say, turning to look at Monica. "Ready."

"Close your eyes, all of you. Each person will say the chant three times, then take a ten-second break. Then I'll say it three times at the end. We'll go counterclockwise. So, Carson, Samantha, then Julian. Say it three times by yourself with a ten-second break between each person's set. Understood?"

"Got it," we all respond.

She nods, shifting her weight before beginning the chant, one Samantha and Carson know like the back of their hand. "Go."

Spirits gone and still here bound
Ones in the shadows and worlds around
Hear our prayers and heed our call
Awaken, victims from your undue fall
Complete our quest, then take your leave
On darkest of nights, this Hallows' Eve

We repeat the chant together, following the pattern and instructions to a T. It's nice to not have to focus on the world outside, to only focus on the words. It makes everything melt away, like time almost stops. Samantha's voice feels distant as she speaks, finishing her incantations. I can hear her, but just barely, enough to know when it's my turn.

After everyone goes through their chant, I contribute, but what follows isn't what I expect. There's no bang. No fire. No noise. Just . . . silence. I wait ten seconds, then fifteen, then twenty, and I finally sigh and lean back, opening my eyes.

"Guys, I don't think—"

I don't get to finish my sentence because the words are sucked right out of me. Standing in the center of where the Ouija board should be is a man shrouded in darkness like a cloak haphazardly wrapped around himself with a pair of black, raven-like wings, not made of flesh or bone, but smoke. His head is covered in too much darkness to see any features, only an endless space where a face should be. I sense only darkness, pain, fear, and anguish.

"Hello there, Julian," he says, his voice not fully spoken but felt, like I know what he's saying even if I hear nothing. "You called upon me, and I answered. What is your wish?"

III.

The first thing I notice is that I'm the only one who can move, like everyone else in the room is frozen in space and time. Can they breathe? Or are they locked inside of their bodies? Can they sense everything happening around them?

I turn slowly to the being shrouded in darkness. "Are they okay?"

They're the first words I've said in what feels like hours. Before, no words would form. Not because I didn't want to say anything, but because everything was so cold. Like some chilled lasso was wrapped around me, keeping me from speaking.

The creature turns its head slowly, examining everyone else in the room.

"They are fine," it says back to me. "Time isn't moving the same for them. When this is over, less than a second will have passed. In fact, for them, you are the one who is out of sync."

I have no question where this thing came from or that it is some demon we summoned from the other side of the veil. What makes a shiver go down my spine is the memory of every fantasy or horror story I've ever read. Creatures like this care little about humans, and if you summon them, they always want something in return.

Slowly, the demon steps out of the makeshift ring. It walks around the circle, surveying Samantha, Monica, and Carson. It sniffs them, dragging a tongue that shoots out from the darkness along their necks.

"I should ask the same question of you," the thing asks.

"In what world would I be okay?" I reply slowly, carefully. "I just—"

"Not that," he replies, so curtly and coldly that it's impossible for me to even question him. My vocal cords feel frozen. Is this magic or just fear?

"You carry so much pain inside of you, Julian," he says walking slowly toward me. Once he's standing in front of me, a single finger, bony and long, slips out from under the cloak of shadows and tips my chin upward to look at him.

My heart is racing so fast I should be unconscious and dizzy from the rush of blood. But instead I feel . . . still, locked in this moment, unable to move.

"I know what they did to you," it whispers. "I know how they broke your spirit. . . ."

The bony fingers move up from my chin and then to the side of my face, right above my right eye, where the scar will be forever—the scar from Ian's family ring that cut into my flesh when he punched me, the final punch I remember. A constant reminder of the hate crime that went without punishment and led me to the moment where I am now.

"That's such an ugly word, isn't it?" the being asks. "*Hate* crime. Aren't all crimes fueled by hate?"

"Not all of them."

"But many. So many moments in human history can be linked to those. You are such . . . vengeful creatures. No better than animals."

"We're not all bad," I remind him. "There are some good ones."

Ignoring today as evidence, when I say that, the first person who comes to mind is Amber. She might not show it in the moment, but I know there's a part of her that still cares. Yes, she acts like she has a monopoly on how the event marred her. Which, I get it. She found my bloody, bruised, beaten body with torn flesh and an exposed bit of skull, skin flap pulled back from the constant beating. She's the one who was torn between saying something or saying nothing. Putting her friend or the man she "loves" first. To me, that wasn't a choice, but I like to think that if I were in her shoes and in love with someone who could change my life, someone as powerful and well connected as Todd, someone who, if I played my cards right, could yank me out of poverty and whose family could change the course of my future . . . I could understand how she made the choice to be silent.

That doesn't mean I don't hate her for it.

The whole time I'm remembering Amber and my history, the being is staring at me. At least, I think it is. There is no face under that black hood, just pure, never-ending, cold darkness, but I feel like there's a person there, a heartbeat and a soul buried deep in that darkness. Trapped in . . . whatever dark magic we let free.

"What do you want?" I finally muster, though my voice cracks.

"You should answer that question, should you not? After all, you summoned me."

"We all did," I clarify. "It was just a prank."

"Perhaps."

I shake my head. "Not perhaps. It was a stupid joke. And sure, even if I do agree we summoned you, there's a key word you're missing there: *we*. Not just *I*. They should be here too."

"They are not you."

With a casual flick of its right hand, each of our bodies are thrown backward, each of us slamming against the respective wall behind us. Carson's stonelike form hits the wall, and I see a trickle of blood drip down from the back of his head. Monica lands against the bookshelf, a dozen or so books toppling on top of her. And Samantha lands safely, as safe as she can be, on the couch. Even my body lurches from the magic; my back slams against the wooden wall, white-hot pain spiraling outward. Before I can stand or even process how much pain I'm in, a cold hand wraps around my throat, lifting me off the ground. My vision, blurred for only a moment, focuses on the dark maw in front of me.

"Do you know what is needed to cast dark magic?" the being asks. "It's not a spell, or a gift. It's not even blood, or a dead animal or sacrifice. It's pain. Pure unfiltered pain. That's what binds us all, every speck of magic across the universe. From European lore to Japanese mythology, to cast a spell dripped in darkness, you need pain. That's why their spell didn't work before.

"I am only here because of you, Julian. Because of the pain that has gone unquenched. The lust for vengeance that pulses within your heart. That spoke to me. It called to me. I hunger for a taste of it. And in exchange, I can grant you your deepest desire. You may have all summoned me, but only one of you has a soul that screams, for I can see what is in your heart, Julian—your deepest desire, and I can grant it for you."

Its grip hurts, and it feels like the cold is digging into my flesh, burning it, but not so much so that I can't let out a raspy reply while my legs dangle inches from the ground.

"I want to go home."

"Try again," it says. "You can lie to your family and to your friends, but not to me," it says, leaning in close. As it moves forward, I expect it to do what it did before, to have a slithering dark tongue slide against my skin. But instead, the maw where its face should be consumes me. For a moment, there's only darkness; not just the sight of it, but the feeling of it. Endlessness, weightlessness. All of it. There's just vast nothingness.

And inside the all-consuming darkness, I see my past self. I'm looking at my body from above, witnessing Ian and his friends kicking me and breaking me, both body and soul, like it was theirs, and they could do with it what they wished.

My past self, bloody and bruised, is looking up at me.

"I remember this," I whisper to no one. I remember looking up into the sky and thinking I saw myself in the clouds. I thought I was dreaming, my brain fracturing and trying to make sense of everything that was happening. I remember reaching up into the skies, trying to grab at the hand that was reaching down. I thought it was an angel, that Mom and Dad were right about going to church and what the afterlife was. I assumed the angel just looked like me.

But was it actually me? Because I'm looking down at myself right now.

From above, I reach out desperately, completing the cycle, trying to pull my own self from the darkness like I wish someone had done for me that day. I remember reading somewhere that it only takes one person to change the course of history. I wish someone had been brave enough when it mattered to be that someone for me.

But the moment I try to reach forward, I'm pulled back. The darkness rushes around me like a vacuum, yanking me back upward by a hook in my navel into the sky. I take a deep breath, as if I hadn't been able to breathe for the past minute. I stumble backward, and my back slides against the wall.

"You want them dead," the creature says matter-of-factly. "A very human emotion. No one would fault you for what they did to you."

"I don't want revenge," I breathe out, voice broken. I clutch my throat, feeling the remnant of the cold touch of the thing hovering lazily before me. "I'm not that . . ."

"Not that type of person? Everyone is, Julian. Deep down. Everyone wants revenge on those who wronged them. Do you think it makes you a better person if you hold back? It doesn't. They will never learn. None of them. Your desire to take the high ground will not bring you peace."

"I know how this works," I interject. "Making a deal with a

demon. I've seen these stories before. They never end the way you think they will. The human is always given the short end of the stick."

"And what makes you think I want anything in return?"

"Demons always want something in return."

The creature stares directly at me, and though it doesn't have a face, it almost feels like it's smiling.

"Julian, what is the cost of your sanity?" it asks. "What's the cost for you to feel in control of your own destiny for once? I saw the same scene you did, witnessed those men taking from you the one thing every human should feel."

"And what's that?"

"Safety in their own skin," it says without hesitation. "They robbed you of that, took it for themselves, as if they had a claim to it. All because of who you are."

"You're asking me to murder someone. For any reason."

"No," it says, holding up one bony finger. "I'm not asking you to do anything. I'm giving you an option to shape your future. *How* you shape it is up to you. What you do is up to you. I am simply the tool with which you do it."

"No one should play God," I counter.

"You're not. You're simply . . . how should I put it . . . playing conductor. Deciding how fast the train goes.

"Julian, they decided their own fate. Be it you, another person, or another god, they decided where their path would end. I am simply helping you expedite it."

I look at Carson, Samantha, and Monica's bodies. Those wounds from the impact against the wall don't look good. My gaze shifts to look toward where I'm assuming Amber is, frozen in time, in the middle of a conversation with Ian. She's looking at him with those doe-like eyes. Like she can look past what he did to me because it didn't happen to her.

I wonder how easy it is to do that. To compartmentalize situations and put them in neat little boxes. Pack them up here and there. Sort them and organize them to suit however you see fit. I wish I could do that. I wish I could forget things, put them aside and open them only when I was ready for them.

But I can't. What happened to me is as much a part of me as my Black skin or my coils of hair or my dark eyes. No, this scar runs deeper than that; it's burned into my soul.

"I have a question," I mutter, not turning my body to face the demon.

"Anything."

"You're a being of magic, right?"

"In the simplest of terms, yes."

"Will they do it again? Ian and his friends. Will they hurt another person?"

The demon is quiet for a moment. "The future isn't set in stone, Julian. There are many different outcomes, and I see them all. Each choice, making another. But I can say, in the majority of them, someone else suffers the same fate as you. And in most of those, justice isn't served."

That's all I need to know.

I turn on my heels to face the demon. "Everyone in my life talks about how they want to help me heal. How they want me to get through this or be how I was before. But that's what they don't understand. I can't be like that. That version of me is gone. Ian and his friends killed that part of me. And I'm just trying to find a way to live with such a large part of me dying right before my eyes. Understand how I wasn't able to save myself, my innocence, but also understanding there was nothing I could do. That this wasn't my fault."

I swallow thickly, my voice cracking. "I won't let them do what they did to me to anyone else. I won't let a system that is meant to protect people like me let down another person. It's too late for me, not because there isn't a path of recovery that I can walk down, but because I don't want to. I want to see them suffer. I want to make them feel ten thousand times the amount of pain they made me feel. Can you make that happen? Can you help me?"

At first, the demon doesn't move. It simply stares at me like it's deciding what fate to pass. But then, slowly, it raises its right sleeve, a hand extending out from under, and it moves its hand over its face from left to right, the smoke disappearing, revealing the face of a boy no older than me, his right eye foggy and a gash like an animal slashed him over the same side of his face. There are flecks of glass stuck in his skin, pebbles and pieces of stone, a chunk of skull where his forehead is exposed to the air.

But under all that, there's a handsome face. A sharp jawline. And in his left eye—untouched, somehow—there's a vibrant crackle of mirth and life behind it. Like he was a trickster or a bad boy before . . . whatever happened to him happened.

"I would be honored to help you, Julian," he says, a small smile painting his lips. The demon extends his hand, no longer bone, but that of a human. The robe is gone, replaced with a black hoodie torn and tattered, covered with blood, a pair of dirty sneakers drenched in mud, and ripped pants that give me a glimpse at his right leg, twisted backward, but somehow still able to carry the weight of his body.

"What happened to you?"

"I'll tell you once you're done," the demon whispers. "Once you've crossed over, I'll answer any questions you have. And maybe, I'll show you that not everyone, in this world or the next, will let you down."

He wiggles his fingers gently at me, beckoning me to take it. I have so many questions. So many unanswered thoughts and feelings, but his hand is like a gravitational pull, reeling me in. The longer I stare at his hand, at the lines and how soft his skin looks, the more I can make out . . . everything else around me becomes foggy. The smell of asphalt. The taste of blood. The sound of sneers, Ian's sneers. The vision, in the corner of my eyes, of his friends standing above me, sneering, waiting their turn to get a punch or two in on me.

"Take my hand, Julian," the demon says. "And let's tear them limb from limb."

And though his words make no sense, and though they are filled with so much vitriol and hate, I can't help but place my hand in his.

IV.

When I open my eyes, the first thing I feel is my bones; they aren't where they are supposed to be. Some are broken, barely hanging on to the tendons that connect them to my muscles. There is so much pain, rippled pulses that move through my body with each labored breath. It's easy to want to give up, but as my fingertips feel the cool and wet asphalt under me, I understand where I am. I'm back in this alleyway, one year ago, moments after Ian and his goonies killed me.

Or at least, that's how it ended before.

I've been given another chance; an opportunity to change my destiny and to rewrite the past, but unlike before, I'm not helpless. I'm not caught off guard. I'm not hoping for someone to save me, crying out silently to the heavens for an angel or God to spare me. I will be my own savior.

Standing up doesn't hurt as much as I thought it would, or as it should. In the reflection of the puddle that I was lying in, where my blood has mixed with the oil and dirt from runoff, I see myself. Much like the boy who I saw in the house, I look like death has claimed me just moments before. I look like I should have crossed over to the other side.

There will be time for that later.

Ian and his friends walk away from me, with their backs turned to me. I can hear them laughing and joking, praising each other for a punch or two they landed on me, as if defeating someone helpless who wasn't fighting back, someone who was begging while choking on their own blood was some sort of badge of honor.

"Did you hear how he screamed?" Todd muttered. "Didn't know he was a squealer."

"Not like he stood a chance against The Squad," Ian said, the other boys echoing back the title.

In another life, I might try to reason with them. I might try to understand why they hate me, to spend my last few moments on this earth trying to make amends to find some common ground. But right now? All I want to do is hear them scream.

My body, and whatever is inside of me that's keeping me alive that burns in the center of my chest like a battery running on overdrive, knows what to do. I raise my hand, twisted and broken bones mangled and barely attached to one another, pointing my palm at them. I make the motion of squeezing my right hand halfway, and as I do, their shadows stop, causing them to stop as well.

Ian is the first to notice. He curses under his breath, muttering how he must have tripped over something or his shoelace got caught in some groove. But as he turns around, his eyes land on me, and confusion in that moment turns to horror.

I don't give the others the same moment of grace.

"Die," I whisper.

I complete the squeezing action, my fingernails digging into my bruised and cut palm. As I do, the shadows expand and combine, molding into one black circle like a pit of tar. Slowly the boys begin to sink down. They scream—of course they scream—but nothing stops the slow descent into the darkness.

Not their begs.

Not their pleas for their mothers.

Not them apologizing to me, or to whatever God will listen.

There is no God here tonight. Only me, and I am vengeful.

The last thing I see, as one by one they slip into the silent darkness, is Todd's confused look. He was never like Ian and the others, and maybe in another life, if there was more time, perhaps he could be spared. But he drank from the same poisoned lake as the others. He is not innocent. None of them are. And as quickly as the ring of darkness came, it disappears, the boys with them, nowhere to be found. Not even a moment passes before the pain returns; every wound of mine reminding me it exists.

I collapse to my knees, coughing up blood and bile, so much blood and bile. As I sway and fall backward, I don't have the energy to brace myself for the fall. But, as death returns from turning its gaze away from me for those few moments, I see him. I feel him, his lap cushioning my head to protect me from the fall.

"You," I say. Well, not really say. I can't speak; my esophagus is shattered. I think it, and he hears.

"Me." He smiles, stroking my forehead with his hand. He looks like before, bruised and beaten, broken and scarred; like me.

He's beautiful just how he is.

"In your last moments, you called out for God to help you, for anyone to help you," he says. "Most people do. God and the angels didn't answer. But the same demon who saved me when my father killed my mother and threw me in a ravine because I saw him, leaving me for the bears to feast on, heard you. And he sent me to give you the same option he gave me. A chance to find peace before you pass on."

The pain hurts so freaking much, but I don't mind. It's . . . nice to feel, to be grounded to something. To know this won't be forever but to also know I'm feeling this because I'm back, writing my own ending and not letting them write mine.

"Tell me, Julian," the boy says. "What's your favorite ice cream flavor?"

"Rocky road," I say without hesitation. "With caramel drizzle."

"Hmm." He smiles. "That sounds good. Tell you what, when you pass over, when you open your eyes, find the nearest ice cream parlor, and I'll be there waiting for you, with a double scoop of rocky road with caramel drizzle to share. My treat. My way of welcoming you to the other side."

The boy looks upward to the sky, and my gaze follows. It's going to rain soon. It always rains in Wyndy Hallows around this time of year.

"I've been alone for so long," he whispers. "And something tells me you have too. Perhaps we can be alone together?"

I want to tell him how nice that sounds. How just hearing someone want me, bruised and beaten, broken and vengeful, unforgiving and unashamed, sounds so freaking nice. But the sound of a familiar voice, a panicked and scared voice coming toward me, breaks my thought.

Gently, the boy leans down, brushing his bruised lips against my own busted ones.

"Find me," he whispers, fading out of vision in the span of one blink. But I'm not alone. My head doesn't hit the ground. Instead, his lap is replaced with Amber's hand . . . the last thing I see is her tearful, scared face.

The last thing I hear is her saying, "Hold on, help is coming."

Sorry, Amber, I think, though I know she can't hear. *I've been holding on long enough. It's time for me to go. But don't be scared.*

I'll be seeing you on the other side.

I'll see you on the other side.

I'll be seeing you. On the other side.

THE THREE PHASES OF GHOST-HUNTING

Alex Brown

PHASE ONE: KNOW YOUR HISTORY

OCTOBER 31: 9:02 P.M.

The ghost of a pirate haunts the Golden City Mall food court.

Well, okay, the pirate doesn't haunt the food court *because* it's a food court. I think. According to local legend, Terrifying Bob *allegedly* buried his forbidden treasure one thousand paces inland from Angler Rock. And yes, Angler Rock *was* responsible for his ship wrecking. Or that's how the story goes, anyway. Nowadays, that would put Terrifying Bob's treasure right under the middle of the food court.

Even death wasn't enough to stop Terrifying Bob—rumor has it that when the mall closes napkins will float around as if a heavy wind were inside. Of course, no such wind exists.

The worst part of Terrifying Bob's reign of terror, though, is that occasionally people's food will disappear. They'll sit down to a nice Sbarro pizza, get up to retrieve their wayward napkins, and when they get back to their table, their slice of greasy, commercialized New York pizza will be gone. Weirdly enough, it's only pizza that gets stolen. Everything else—the O'Charley's sandwiches, hibachi-style teriyaki chicken, and Ben and Jerry's ice cream are all left alone. Terrifying Bob won't even mess with the Jollibee, which makes me sad on his behalf.

Anyone with a pulse would think that the strange occurrences in the Golden City Mall would be worth investigating. Sadly, no ghost-hunting shows have decided to drop in.

So that's why I'm spending Halloween in the Golden City Mall food court—dressed as a fashionable witch—with my best friend, a microphone, a few tea light candles, and a to-go box of Sbarro pizza. Sure, we could be going to a cool party, or getting jump-scared in our town's haunted corn maze, but instead we're doing a public service. We're going to accomplish the impossible: contact Terrifying Bob and ask him to leave the napkins and the Sbarro in peace.

"You really think we're gonna talk to Terrifying Bob?" Iris asks as a smile tugs at the corners of her mouth.

I shrug. "Maya said we would. That's good enough for me."

"Daisy," Iris replies, her small smile twisting into a frown. "Madame Maya is a con artist who scams tourists at the boardwalk. Last year she told me my grandfather sent his best wishes from *beyond the veil*. He's still alive!"

"Everyone makes mistakes," I say, waving her point away. "Besides, it's Halloween *and* a blue moon. The boundary between our world and the spirit world is weakest tonight. There's no better time to contact Terrifying Bob the Pizza-Stealing Pirate."

She sighs, tapping the top of the Sbarro box. "If you say so."

"I know so," I reply as confidently as I can. I love so many things about Iris Chen, like the way her warm brown eyes always have a hint of mischief in them, or how her laugh sounds more like a weird sound effect in a movie than actual laughter. And I love that she decided to spend her Halloween with me, ghost-hunting instead of going to Sara's party. But sometimes her skepticism about the supernatural can be a little bit of a buzzkill.

Even though Iris doesn't believe in ghosts, I want to make sure that our last year together is something she'll remember forever. I don't know where either of us will end up after we graduate, but I know everything we do this year has to make me hard to forget.

I wink. "On the small, teensy tiny, absolutely minuscule chance that nothing happens, we'll still have fun, right?"

"You know these things are only fun because of you," she says with a smirk.

A blush creeps into my cheeks. I wish it away, but the more she looks at me, the hotter my face gets. "I knew my awful dad jokes were good for something."

"Ah yes, it's the dad jokes, and not how scared you get while talking to absolutely nothing, that keeps me entertained."

"But you *are* entertained?" I wiggle my eyebrows at her.

She playfully nudges me with her elbow as she asks, "Okay, so what's the first part of your dastardly plan?"

"I was hoping you'd ask! First, we need to conduct an interview. All good ghost-hunting investigations have them."

"Who're we interviewing? The ghost?"

"Marcus."

"Your brother? Seriously?"

"He's here almost every night watching the security cameras. He's seen some things. And it was a condition of my deal with your mom, so . . ."

The only reason we were able to be in the mall after hours was because my brother's the night security guard, and Iris's mom *happens* to be our town's mayor. We promised to stay confined to the food courts, with Marcus supervising us at all times. In exchange, we'd record everything and release it as a podcast. Iris's mom figured it could be a fun way to encourage even more tourism. Ghost-hunting evidence goes viral all the time—there was no harm in trying to chase a little bit of that fame too.

Iris starts to open the pizza box, but I pull it out from under her. "*And* we shouldn't eat the pizza. It's our offering for Terrifying Bob."

"I'm sure he wouldn't mind if I had a slice—"

"*Iris,* we don't want to be rude and steal Sbarro from Terrifying Bob."

"Unlike Terrifying Bob, I'm *actually* hungry and could *actually use* a pizza."

"I thought of that," I reply, pulling two to-go pizza slice boxes out of my tote bag. "We should have enough time to eat these before—"

"Excuse me, youths, are you loitering in my mall?"

I roll my eyes as Marcus strolls up to the table. "Why're you like this?"

"Because I can be," he replies with a smirk. "By the way, your ghost-hunting hobby is lucrative for me, Tiny Satan. I'm getting overtime pay for this."

I punch him in the shoulder as he slides into the chair next to me. "Do you have to use the nickname?"

"It's not really a nickname. It's a way of life."

Iris snorts. "He's got a point."

Marcus tips his hat at me. "So, are we gonna do this interview thing? Scott said I couldn't be out for long."

"Your boss has no appreciation for anything weird or wonderful," I reply while Iris turns the mics on. I gesture to the table next to us, where everything's ready to go.

Marcus chuckles as he moves one seat over. "I tell him that every day." He puts his headphones on, and I do the same. Thankfully, I set up the microphones as soon as we got there. The food court isn't the best place for podcasting acoustics, but Golden City Mall management didn't want us going anywhere else, so we made it work.

"Okay," I say as Iris gives me a thumbs-up over Marcus's shoulder. "We're going to check levels real quick—"

"Levels?" Marcus says, his voice quirking up in surprise. "Look at you go. You're sounding like a little pro."

"And you're sounding extremely punchable."

"Ouch. Violence is never the answer, Daisy."

"Anyway," I say, rolling my eyes as I speak into the mic. "I'm Daisy de la Cruz, and I'm here with the worst older brother to ever exist, Marcus."

Marcus leans in closer to the mic. "That's a little harsh, considering you couldn't do this without me."

"Technically we couldn't do this without Iris's mom. Shoutout to Mayor Chen for being a badass."

Iris grins at me. "Levels are good," she says as I shift in my seat.

"Ready, Marcus?" I ask. He nods. "Great. So, Marcus, what do you do?"

"I'm a part-time security guard for the Golden City Mall, part-time student at Greenbrier Hills College, and a full-time lover of long walks on the beach and scary movies."

I mime throwing up. He flips me off as I say, "Sir, this is a podcast, not a dating app."

"Why not both?"

"You're the worst," I reply, completely monotone. "Let's cut to the chase. Have you seen anything weird on the night shift? Napkins moving around, pizza disappearing, things of that nature?"

"Not really. It's pretty boring at night. I *wish* something cool would happen, though. Might make this job interesting for once."

Iris stifles a laugh as I ask, "What was the point of putting you on the podcast?"

"Because my sparkling personality elevates your art."

"If you don't have anything useful to say—"

"Wait, wait, wait. Okay, I do have *one* story."

"A real one?" He nods. I cross my arms, skeptical. "Fine. Go."

"So, there was a blue moon a couple of years ago, and we had a power surge around three A.M.—"

"Three A.M., also known as *the witching hour*—aka when spirits are more active," I add.

"Allegedly!" Iris shouts.

"Allegedly," I reply. "Keep going, Marcus."

"Right. The power goes off, and the whole mall sounds—I

don't know how to describe it. Kind of like it was crying? It was like a cross between a wail and a sob, but if it was amplified and slowed down. Like, really, really slowed down. It creeped me out. Shivers down my spine, goose bumps, the whole nine yards. But I wrote it off because shit happens, you know?"

He shrugs but shrinks a little in his chair. He swallows before continuing. "And then . . . maybe I fell asleep, and it was all a dream, but I . . . I saw something. On the cameras." He pauses, voice trembling as he says, "Eyes."

"What?"

"Eyes."

"In the food court? Were they by the Sbarro?" I ask.

"No. I mean, yeah, the eyes were by the Sbarro. But they weren't the only ones."

"You mean—"

"Everywhere," Marcus says, eyes wide and alert as he stares at me. "Didn't matter which camera I was looking at. The escalators. The merry-go-round. Kiosks. Bath & Body Works. There were at least fifty eyes in each frame. And they all looked the same. Glowing. White. No pupils or irises. Just . . . devoid of color. Of anything."

I blink, mouth hanging open as I take it all in. "Why . . ." My voice trails away as I slowly remember how to talk. "Why didn't you tell me?"

Marcus exhales deeply, leaning back in his seat. "I know you're into this stuff, Daisy, and I wanted to, but—I don't know. I still don't understand what I saw. And I'm not sure I want to."

"Well, I do," I reply.

Marcus nods. "I figured. That's why I'm here. I'm not excited about seeing the eyes again, but I'm also not about to leave you alone with them."

"Wow, thanks!" Iris's voice drifts into the microphones, sounding like an annoyed whisper. "She wouldn't be alone!"

Marcus shakes his head, pulling his headphones off. "Sorry, Iris. I didn't mean it like that."

"How *did* you mean it?" she asks as I start packing up the mics.

Marcus shrugs. "It's just hard if you don't believe in this stuff. That's all."

Iris's dark brown eyes became dangerously bright. "If anything out there wants to *prove* it exists, I'll gladly acknowledge it," she drawls. "I'd love to see a bunch of disembodied eyes creeping out of the darkness. Sounds like a fun night to me."

"You and I have very different ideas of fun," Marcus replies, standing. He grabs the pizza box and takes out a slice before I can stop him. "Nice of y'all to supply your interviewee with food," he says, biting off nearly half the slice in one go.

"That was for the ghost," I protest, but it's too late. He swallows the other half in another giant bite.

Marcus lightly hits my shoulder. "I think Terrifying Bob owes me one after that whole creepy eye show." He checks his phone. "Looks like my twenty minutes is up. Gotta get back to the security room. Capitalism calls."

"Bye, loser," I say to him as he leaves.

"No funny business, Tiny Satan," he replies, pointing up to a camera. "Remember—I'll be watching."

Iris snorts as she moves next to me. "That wasn't reassuring at all."

"Nope. But at least we have a good place to start."

She nods. "Phase two?"

"Phase two," I say, with a smile.

PHASE TWO: COMMUNICATION IS KEY

OCTOBER 31: 10:30 P.M.

"Do we have to use the spirit box?" Iris groans.

"You want proof, don't you?" I ask as I turn it on. Static roars out of the small handheld radio before it choppily starts searching for frequencies.

Iris sighs. "All that thing ever does is catch snippets of sounds that you *think* are words."

"Not true," I counter, turning it up. "We got the word *help* that one time, remember?"

"We got something that sounded like the beginning of a cough that you interpreted as 'help,' yeah."

"It was totally *help*."

"No, it was—"

"*Iris*," the spirit box chirps, cutting her off.

"Oh shit," I say, scrambling toward the camera we set up. "Are we recording?"

"There's nothing to record."

"It just said your name! You didn't hear that?"

"I think it said 'virus.'"

"Seriously?"

Iris shrugs. "Confirmation bias. Learned about it in AP Psych.

You heard my name because you wanted the spirit box to say something."

"*Or* because that's what it actually said."

"Look, when the spirit box can speak in a full sentence, maybe I'll listen."

"You know that's not how it works."

Iris walks over to our cache of ghost-hunting tools. She pulls out a voice recorder and sits down at a nearby table, patting the seat next to her. "Then let's try something a little more convincing."

I turn the spirit box off with a sigh and join her. The flecks of gold in her eyes shine brightly. People miss them all the time, but not me. That was one of the first things I noticed about her.

"You really want to do an EVP session?" I ask.

A mischievous smile pulls at the corners of her mouth as she shrugs. "You know what they say: when in Rome, use an electronic voice-phone thing to see what the ghosts have to say."

I squint at her. "You know full well it's electronic voice *phenomenon*, not electronic voice-phone thing. Besides, you hate EVPs more than the spirit box. Why would you want to do one?"

"*Hate* is such a strong word," Iris replies as I sit next to her. "I *want* to believe. I just haven't found anything to believe in yet."

Iris turns the recorder on. "This is Iris Chen. It's Halloween night, and I'm sitting here with Daisy de la Cruz. And we're trying to communicate with Terrifying Bob." She pauses for a few seconds and then continues. "Mr. Terrifying—"

"Can you take this seriously?" I interrupt.

"Terrifying Bob," Iris amends apologetically. "If you're here with us, can you please give us a sign? Bang on a table, flicker some lights, pick up a slice of pizza. Whatever you wanna do."

"We brought the pizza for you," I add. "It's probably a little cold now, and my brother took a piece already, but you can have the rest if you'd like." I open the pizza box as a sign of good faith. Hopefully Terrifying Bob is hungry enough to take the bait.

Anticipation ripples through the air as we wait. After a minute, I deflate, and Iris speaks again. "Terrifying Bob, are you trapped in the Golden City Mall?" Nothing happens. Iris shrugs. "Terrifying Bob," she continues, "is there anything you'd like us to know?"

Thirty seconds of silence pass before I ask, "Terrifying Bob, are you searching for your lost treasure?"

The lights flicker as soon as I finish my question. A chair next to Iris falls over, and I jump out of my seat. Iris stands too.

See? I mouth at Iris. My heart pounds frantically. An inanimate object just moved without any interference. There was no wind. No one bumped into it. It was the proof I finally needed to convince her.

She shakes her head, mouthing back, *Coincidence.*

I groan. Okay, a chair getting knocked down isn't enough. Time to change tactics. "Terrifying Bob," I say, with all the showmanship of a TV ghost hunter, "was that you? Can you give us another sign?"

The lights around us flicker. I point up to them, but Iris's expression remains impassive.

"Maybe they just haven't paid the electric bill," she replies.

I open my mouth to argue with her, but before I can, a loud *snap* crackles through the air as we're plunged into darkness.

"Great," Iris says, shining the flashlight on her cell phone. "The lights are out."

"Yeah, because it's a *sign*," I reply.

"Or we're having a power outage."

"Do you always have to—"

A strong wind gusts through the air around us, cutting me off. It whips our hair and rustles our clothes. I look at Iris pointedly, and she shrugs.

"AC," she says.

I shine my flashlight in her face. Iris holds her hands in front of her eyes, reeling back. Her eyes widen as I move the flashlight's beam up and over her head. A jagged shadow looms behind her. A bright white smile emerges from the darkness, flickering for a moment, before it vanishes.

Iris's eyes meet mine. *Is something there?* she mouths.

I nod.

A long arm with spiked barbs for fingers reaches for Iris as she takes a step forward. She turns around, facing the shadow figure as the lights burst back on.

I jump, my heart quickening at the sight in front of me.

Marcus stands where the silhouette was, hand stretched toward Iris.

"Umm . . . are you good?" I ask.

Iris walks with purpose, bridging the gap between us as she moves next to me. "Marcus?"

But he doesn't answer. He just stands there, holding out his hand, waiting for Iris to take it. He looks like he always does—tan skin, short black hair, heart-shaped face—with one exception.

His eyes. They're usually mischievous, but now they're blank, lifeless, and as white as freshly fallen snow.

Iris starts slow clapping. "Wow, good job, Daisy. How'd you get Marcus to agree to that?"

"What?" I ask. My brother watches us, unblinking.

Iris points to him. "You got him to turn off the power *and* wear those creepy contacts? Did you bribe him with endless coffee? Or finally take up his offer to start playing *D&D*?"

"I . . . I didn't do anything," I reply quietly. "This isn't me. That's not *him*." I know my brother, and the thing in front of us is a poor imitation. There's no life in his face. No sign of the person who tried to get our parents to name me Tiny Satan when I was born.

"Of course that's him," Iris says, laughing. She walks over to Marcus, waving her hand in his face. "Okay, this has been fun, but you can drop the act now."

"Iris," I hiss, "come back." Even though adrenaline rushes through my body, fear roots me to the ground. I want to warn her. Grab her and pull her away. Stand in front of her to block her from harm. But I can't. Something deep inside me screams, knowing that it wouldn't matter if I did anything anyway. Because that's always how it is with Iris. When her mind is set, there's no changing it, no matter how hard I try.

"Iris Chen," the voice inside my brother says.

"Marcus de la Cruz," Iris says, copying his strange cadence. "This isn't scary."

I clear my throat. "It *isn't* Marcus."

As if on cue, a tiny drop of red ripples across Marcus's milky white eyes like bloody ink. The lights flicker again. My brother's outstretched hand falls to his side. Two shadows spring out from behind him, coiling around his body.

Iris looks to her right, then to her left. She walks over to the Quiznos only a few steps away and checks behind the counter. She shakes her head and crosses the food court to O'Charley's. She examines it for a few seconds, then turns to me with a shrug. "Nothing here. How're you doing it?"

"I'm not. Why won't you believe—"

"Daisy de la Cruz," the thing controlling Marcus snaps, interrupting me. "Where is your sacrifice?"

I blink. "My what now?"

"You brought me an offering," the entity replies.

Iris nods. "Yeah. An offering of *pizza*." She strides over to the abandoned Sbarro box and opens it. "Half-cheese, half-pepperoni. Pick your poison."

"You poisoned it?" the thing that used to be my brother growls. "I thought you would be different, Daisy de la Cruz, but you're just like all the rest. A disappointment."

"Ouch," I say as Iris steps in front of me.

She glares at what's left of Marcus. "Daisy is a lot of things. She's late all the time, insists on dancing the Macarena at every party, and thinks ghosts are real, which they're not—"

"There's literally a ghost possessing my brother right in front of you," I chime in. But Iris waves my comment away.

"Like I said"—Iris reaches back to grab my hand as she continues—"Daisy is a lot of things, but she's not a disappointment."

I look at her, surprised. "You mean it?"

Iris squints. "Why would you even ask that?"

"I always thought . . . you know . . . that you wanted me to be more logical. Like you."

"Hell no," Iris replies. "In fact, you wanna know a little secret?"

"Sure."

She leans in close. When she whispers, her breath is hot on my ear. "I believe in ghosts too. I just thought it was cute to see you get all riled up."

My eyes widen. "Dude, what the fu—"

She lets go of my hand, covering my mouth. "Yell at me once this is over. Right now, we need to figure out what to do with Marcus."

I duck out of her grasp. "I keep telling you, that's *not* Marcus."

"She's right," the monster says. "But what *am* I? Isn't that an interesting question?"

We stand there, together, staring at . . . well, I have no idea *what* it is anymore. There's still the silhouette of a man, but it's taller than Marcus. Everything about it is sharp and jagged—and even though we're standing too far away to make out any actual details, they're there. Plain as day.

It's made of different shadows, all interlocking, all writhing and knocking into each other as if they're jockeying for the best position. Some of the shadows are long and wavy like tentacles. Others are more familiar: the spiky arms with clawed hands that reached for Iris, the two that initially wrapped around Marcus. They're gray and white and static and charcoal and changing, always changing.

Iris looks at me. "What do we do?"

I smile, grabbing a slice of pizza and a nearby voice recorder.

"We do what we've always done—get proof of the unknown." I take a few steps toward the shape formerly known as my brother. As I get closer, my hands shake uncontrollably. But I hold on to the recorder like my life depends on it. "Hello there. What's your name?" I offer the pizza as a greeting.

A tentacle slithers out from the silhouette, grabbing the slice and retreating into the monochromatic blur. There are a few seconds of silence before a voice booms around us. "Cheese is . . . acceptable. Though I would've preferred pepperoni."

"Um, okay. Sure. Sorry about that," I reply.

Iris runs up with a slice of pepperoni. "Here you go."

A spiky arm reaches out. Barbed fingers skewer the pizza and bring it back to the entity. Something that sounds like a burp fills the air shortly after.

I raise my hand. "Was that a . . . um, a proper sacrifice?"

"For now," it replies.

Iris and I exchange a glance as I continue. "Right. Can we get your name now?"

"Humanity has given me many names. And I have existed in more realms than I can recall. But here, I am known simply as Bob."

Iris's mouth hangs open. "Terrifying Bob?" she asks, looking down to make sure the recorder is working. "Are we *actually* speaking to Terrifying Bob, the pirate?"

"I was a pirate, yes," Bob replies, "though that was lifetimes ago."

I raise my hand and wait for him to nod at me before I say, "So . . . you buried something here and have been guarding it for hundreds of years."

Bob shrugs. "It hasn't felt that long to me. But yes, I suppose I've been here awhile. It hasn't been all bad. Mostly monotonous. Dull. Lifeless. As each day passed by, I wondered if there was more to this provincial life—"

"Was that a *Beauty and the Beast* reference?" Iris whispers to me.

I shrug as Bob keeps monologuing. "I'd resigned myself to a life of mundane woe. And then, one day, something extraordinary happened."

"You ran into a ghost at the mall?" I ask.

"No," Bob replies.

"You decided to get out there and see the world?"

Bob shakes his head. Well, he shakes what *used* to be *Marcus's* head. My brother has all but vanished, replaced by a tentacle-monster worthy of *The Thing*. "Not even close. But good try. The miracle that changed my life was this: one spectacular day, a human left an offering for me. It was a half-eaten slice of Sbarro's XL NY Supremo pizza. It sat on the table right there, calling out to me."

"I don't think that was for you," I reply.

"Of course it was," Bob's distorted voice booms around the food court. "Why wouldn't they pay homage to me?"

"Probably because they didn't know you were really here," Iris says, grimacing. "It was probably some inconsiderate shopper who thought they were too good to throw away their own trash."

Bob snarls. "You are WRONG." The shadows around Bob swirled violently. Thunder trembled through the air. The faint electric smell of lightning crackled around us.

Iris grabs my hand. Her eyes widen. She stands there, frozen, as I take a small step toward him.

"Hey, Bob," I say, as gently as I can. "If you want more pizza, we can help you with that."

The shadows stop. Everything stops. "You can?" Bob asks.

I nod. "I also have an idea on how to get you out of this mall."

"You do?" Iris's voice breaks.

I wink at her. "That's phase three."

PHASE THREE: ALWAYS HAVE A PLAN

OCTOBER 31: 11:50 P.M.

"So," I say, drumming on a table while Iris eats a slice of pizza. "Can I yell at you now?"

Iris squints at me. "For what?"

I ball up a napkin and throw it at her. "For pretending that you didn't believe in ghosts!"

"That's littering." She picks up the napkin, smirking. "And you left out the most important part of my confession. I think you're cute, Daisy de la Cruz."

A blush warms my cheeks. Awesome. The girl I like just said I was cute, and I'm on my way to turning into a tomato. "You were serious about that?"

Before she can reply, a black cat jumps onto the table. He meows, then rubs up against my arm, purring. I gesture to the pizza, and Iris hands me a fresh slice. I hold it out to him. His mouth unhinges like a snake, and he swallows it whole. His bright green eyes shine in the food court's fluorescent lights.

"Duh. You're the only person I know who could convince an Eldritch God to turn into a house cat."

He stretches and lies on the table. I scratch behind his ears as I meet Iris's gaze. "Ah, so it's just my sharp wit that you find attractive."

She smiles. "That's not everything. But it's a good start."

"If you liked me, why didn't you say anything?"

"I was waiting for you to figure it out." She pauses, her smile fading. "I'm not sure if I waited too long now."

"The college thing?" I ask.

She nods. "The college thing. I don't know if it's smart for us to start something when we don't know where we'll be next year."

I stop petting Bob, and he protests. "That's why I wanted to do this," I say, giving Bob chin scratches. He closes his eyes, purring louder. "I had to make sure you didn't forget me."

Iris reaches for my free hand. She laces her fingers through mine. "I could never forget you, Daisy de la Cruz."

Bob *meows* in what sounds like agreement.

"Sorry, I guess I fell asleep back there. I was more tired than I thought." Marcus says, walking up to us. "What's with the cat?"

Thankfully, my brother doesn't look any worse for the wear, considering he was possessed an hour ago. Once Bob agreed to become a cat, he left Marcus's body, and we put him back in the security office.

"We found him," Iris says. "Daisy and I are splitting custody."

"We are?" I ask.

Bob *meows* again. He sits up, staring at Marcus.

Marcus takes a weary step back. "Why do I feel like that cat can see into the depths of my soul?"

"Because he can," I reply.

"Riiiiiiiight," Marcus says, taking another slice of pizza. "Well, did you get the evidence you were looking for?"

Iris and I exchange a glance. "No," I say, as Bob *meows* again. "But that's okay. Some mysteries are best left unsolved."

Marcus sighs. "Bummer. I was hoping you'd figure out where Terrifying Bob's treasure is buried."

Iris and I both look down at the cat.

"Maybe that'll be our next adventure," Iris says. "What do you think, Daisy?"

"I'd love that," I reply. "On one condition."

"Name it."

"You have to officially go on record and say that you believe in ghosts."

Iris rolls her eyes playfully. "As long as you promise to still be cute for the rest of time."

"I think I can do that," I say as Bob jumps from my arms and sits on top of the pizza box.

"Then we have a deal, Daisy de la Cruz."

And it's there, right at midnight in the Golden City Mall food court, that Iris Chen kisses me for the first—but not the last—time.

NINE STOPS

Trang Thanh Tran

"*My name is Sabrina Pham, and I must tell you: if you stop watching this video, you will die.*"

The video is grainy, but I can see the girl's swollen eyes, how the delicate skin encasing them resembles seeded grapes in an otherwise normal face.

It's like looking into a mirror.

It means I'll think about her even if I close the app. It means I'm figuratively standing at one of the internet's dark orifices, lured by morbid curiosity over what it's offered as a Halloween prank.

My finger is hovering over the Start button when texts from Ramon slide in.

Are you on the platform?

im near the front be there soon in like 5.

"Oh shit," I mutter and roll out of bed, throwing on a floofy white button-up and a too-small vest. I've had all day to get ready for this hide-and-seek get-together, and even more days on top of that just to psych myself up. The girl on the screen judges me, though her stare hasn't changed. I pull the partition wall aside.

From the altar in the living room, Grandma watches me too, all flat eyes and stiff smile. She's been dead six weeks, but I still smell the Eagle Brand Medicated Oil she swore heals every ailment throughout the apartment. Already I want to sink back into my bedsheets. My phone buzzes with another text at the same time the video accidentally restarts.

"My name is Sabrina Pham, and I must tell you: if you stop watching this video, you will die."

"Very cool, Sabrina," I say. "Very cool." Then I step into the night.

90TH ST-ELMHURST AVE

Plumes of smoke streak from street vendors, making the air taste like charcoal and dripping fat. I've not eaten today, I'm barely dressed, but I am on my way: running toward the subway station. Ramon texts me that the train has paused at the stop before mine. Somewhere along the way, my friends are waiting.

The crosswalk light bleeds red as it counts down 7, 6, 5 . . . Torn between hurrying and bailing again, I glance down at my phone in case the group chat's blown up. Only the girl's wide and dark tunnel of a mouth waits. I don't remember pausing the video there, but I've long disabled autolock on the one machine connecting me to the rest of the world. I must have hit Play.

I'm out of breath by the time I've swiped through at the station. I take the next set of steps several at a time, brushing past a woman who's more bone than anything else—with limbs assembled in a green silk dress not warm enough for October. I don't see her face, and I feel ill as I run toward the subway doors Ramon's propped open waiting for me.

Dressed in his Miles Morales costume, he makes a *psssst* sound as he yanks me inside. Literally everyone gives us dirty looks. "On that Vietnamese time, huh?" Ramon teases. He's Dominican, but he knows me and he knew Grandma. If Grandma said she was fifteen minutes away, she was actually forty minutes away. If she said she'd be home soon, she was still taking her time at the corner store. But she always showed up eventually. I love that he loved her.

"I'm here," I say breathlessly as the train moves. He plucks my phone away while I'm distracted straining my neck looking for the woman in the green dress to show on the crosswalk below. Maybe in that half second my brain did register her face, she was really hot—because like Sabrina Pham, both have dug into the softest parts of my brain. A persistent earworm slurring, *Watch me.*

"Didn't I tell you not to open strange-ass links?" Ramon asks with a frown as Sabrina warns us both about impending death. "You're gonna get hacked." He probably expected this week's coping mechanism to finally be porn.

I shift on my feet for balance, then slap my hands together. "I literally have three dollars and seven cents in my Wells Fargo account, and I already forgot my PIN, so *please* hack me so I don't have to pay the monthly service fee."

He doesn't laugh, because he's worried, just like my parents are, about how much of a hermit I've become outside of school.

But on the internet, you're never really alone.

Browser cookies follow you site to site while the algorithm dredges up ads specifically tailored for your taste. Your search history joins the backlog at some data factory in the middle of nowhere. Siri, Google, whatever-the-hell is listening at all times for a request. Your camera light might not be blinking, but someone's probably watching, exploiting some download or malware, to blackmail you later. You could chat with a help bot for hours, and it'll stay polite.

And right now, I feel watched. Followed. Challenged, even, by the sad girl in the shitty video.

Ramon sighs and drops the phone onto my waiting palm. "You should try watching puppy videos instead." The internet's how I've kept up with friends. Little hearts, thumbs-ups, LOLs, and bad memes strengthen community. Just not for forever, apparently. My friends would do anything for me; I had to try harder too.

"I'll lock my phone after," I promise. "The girl . . . she just seems familiar." The earworm digs deeper into my brain. *"If you stop watching this video, you will die."* I swipe back to the video. "It's all over TikTok, so no way we're gonna avoid her."

"Okay, but this is in the spirit of Halloween," Ramon says, shaking his head. He points at the navigation pane near the subway doors. "We've got nine stops till we lose service. Let's *not* die, then."

82ND ST-JACKSON HEIGHTS

Sabrina must be in her room. She adjusts the lens, then settles in a squeaky office chair. A neatly made bed sits in the back, next to a small closet with closed panels. On the nightstand, a large brown rat scratches its glass cage. Ribbons and awards line the clamshell-white walls. At the center of the screen is her. "*You cannot go back. You cannot go forward. You can pause, but it'll catch up to you,*" she says. "*You have to finish the video.*" There's a dragging noise as she pulls thick candles directly in front of her. "*Here's a thing I learned in sociology class from some French guy: rituals, like a baptism, are actions that express a collective belief.*" She lights them one by one, the wicks releasing a swirl of smoke that momentarily obscures her face. "*It makes us feel . . . moral. Unearthly and part of something bigger. It creates meaning. It's why cheerleaders pep the crowd before games, choirs sing for their congregation. Some rituals are performed by a select few, hidden in code, because it's all about power.*"

The conviction underlying her voice hooks into me as her skin takes on a golden glow. Pretty and strange wrapped into one, not at all shy from attention. "She's definitely recruiting you into a cult," Ramon says as he tugs me aside so a zombie horde can board at the station. His brown eyes narrow at his own device. "Liam says he started it a few minutes ago. And that it gets creepy, for real." Ramon and his boyfriend always make it a point to each text me separately and in the group chat, but I didn't get that one. Maybe rituals are what hold friendships together too, and mine are being chipped away.

"*It's too abstract, right?*" Sabrina asks from the screen. "*I didn't believe it either until my sister died.*"

The entire world shifts under my feet. All my focus has siphoned to her eyes again. Red and puffy, like mine so much of the time, like a lot of people who have lost someone.

"We prayed for forty-nine days at the temple to make sure her spirit wouldn't lose its way in the afterlife. The monks would chant while I kneeled and bowed and offered incense. It gave me so much peace, until I realized it wasn't working fully." Sabrina flexes a green-veined hand. Its magnified silhouette dances in the backdrop, the fingertips in sharp points. *"She's still here because when the dead can't pass, they move with our shadows, waiting for us to notice. I feel her all the time following me."*

Invisible spiders climb my spine, and I shudder.

"Rituals are more powerful on special days. Tonight we have a blue moon, an extra one," the girl explains. I glance out the subway windows to catch this special moon that looks not special at all and yet ghostly all the same, like a rice paper wrapper soaked too long and hung up. *"Set her free with me. Help my sister move on."*

I turn back to my phone, but a different girl now fills the screen, too close and frozen inside a picture frame. "Oh shit," I say.

74TH ST-BROADWAY

Six months ago, a racist pushed Emily Pham from the A platform at the 59th St.–Columbus Circle station in front of an incoming train. She didn't survive.

Sabrina adjusts this candid photograph taken at a beach, never circulated on any news sites, so it can be seen: the two sisters sequestered under enormous sun hats, toasting their soft-serve ice cream. Sabrina's was chocolate; Emily's was vanilla with sprinkles.

"We should stop right now," Ramon says as he tries to cover the video. "It's getting to you. This is disgusting clickbait." He doesn't believe the photo, though Sabrina's talking about how talented of an illustrator Emily was, how her dream led her to a job in NYC but had an hour commute and four roommates. My heart hurts in so many different ways.

"No," I tell him. I have an internet addiction fueled by my complete inability to deal with real-life shit—see the Wikipedia article for Grandma—but maybe I can help Sabrina.

She strokes the edge of the frame, voice shaking. *"My parents should've known it takes more than just seven weeks to make my sister forget us. You see, people give rituals meaning. So I made my own for her, so she can stop watching me."* The girl plays a recording on her phone. It's the barest whisper: *Emily Pham.*

In the sound clip, the girl chants her sister's name over and over again. On the screen, her pupils slide to one side, revealing mostly white, as she talks to a shadow. *"There's so much I should've told you."*

I close my eyes and hear my grandma's voice warning me to not stand near the platform's yellow line. Whenever I fussed over her safety in return, she'd call me her con gái. I never found the words to convey that I'm not that, or a little boy.

I know all about the things you wish you could've said.

69TH ST

My shadow has curvy hips. Long enough hair. There's a protruding chest. To them, my shadow deserves to be killed, and so I should be too. I have monolid eyes and a wide nose that's beautiful and easily freckled. My face is an Emily Pham.

I watch my shadow and reflection inside the subway. It's gotten more crowded, not rush-hour level, but there're more monsters, comic book characters, and minions. Everyone pretends I'm not crying. You can love something so hard that you hate it at the same time. Each shortcoming hurts more because you care. The city and my body are like that.

A subway train car can hold two hundred people, and any of them can hurt you. More on a platform.

Mirror-you isn't always you-you.

The thing about living in New York City is that you'll feel like the main character even when no one's paying attention. We don't always get stars, but we have the moon, especially out here on the 7. The train runs on aboveground tracks, chasing the moon every night. I can never leave it or my body behind.

Even in a city of eight million, your grandmother can have an aneurysm in a place where she isn't found until hours too late. Even here, someone can die in slow motion.

Ramon draws so close to my phone that his head blocks half the view.

The chanting continues as Sabrina speaks. "*So many think pieces came out, but no one talked about how Emily loved painting her nails, even though she thought it flaked off when she made rice.*" She splays her hands out to the camera. "*This shade's called Back That Rose Up. It's the exact ridiculous thing that would have Em laughing out of nowhere for days.*"

"Why does she have a blender on her desk?" Ramon interrupts, pausing the video. At the far right side of the clip, a vertical stretch of machinery glints. When he sees my teary face, he relaxes his fist to a hand on my elbow.

"Does it matter?" I ask in too harsh of a tone. He cares for me; he's putting up with me. I try to joke instead. "Maybe she starts every day with a green smoothie. I don't know." But I'm not really taking in Ramon's reaction because I'm busy still watching Sabrina. Every word from her mouth strikes a tender part of me. For her, the news cycle must have been one long, unsatisfying obituary.

"*The papers forgot about her, but you won't, will you? You're good. Share this link now,*" the girl in the video says, "*on whatever platform—'scuse the pun—you have. I don't care if you only have two followers. You do it now. Please. Let me tell people about Emily.*"

My grandma didn't talk to strangers, but she always left money for the unhoused. My parents argued that we didn't know what they would do with that cash, but she said only her intention to help mattered.

I won't judge Sabrina for what she's asking from me, for what viruses this video might be spreading. My belief is what matters. Before Ramon can stop me, I click Share.

61ST ST-WOODSIDE

I'm bad at endings. Since my grandma died, I've left dozens of books unfinished, with so many dog-eared pages that the librarian will probably put a wanted poster out. But for once, I want to know what will happen. I want to see this spell—this ritual, this grief so real I can taste the bile in my mouth—finished.

Tweet. Post. Send. Blog. Leave a comment. The internet cookies do their thing. They reconfigure my algorithm like it's redone my brain. Or maybe that's the earworm: *If you stop watching this video, you will die.*

Ramon looks like he doesn't know what to say. My friends have been through multiple crises, celebrations, and coming-outs, but maybe this blue moon's the night they decide not to find me. No one has seen me this bad.

On the internet, I choose which versions of me to share. I am bodiless, a modern-day ghost connecting with cat GIFs, cartoon PFPs, and closed-off humans. My grandma didn't know the full me either. When I read about Emily's murder, I grieved. There is no version of me that is truly safe.

"*I saved a piece of her,*" says Sabrina as she holds up a vial containing sand. "*Repeat with me.*" The background chant gets louder.

"*EMILY PHAM EMILY PHAM EMILY PHAM EMILY PHAM.*"

"*Keep looking at me. Don't break eye contact.*"

"Emily Pham," I whisper, fully aware that I must be breaking down. I left the apartment too soon. I'm not ready to be in a world that moves on from tragedy so quickly. "Emily Pham."

She pours the sand into the blender.

I want a wall to feel secure leaning against; I want my grandma's arms around me, like when I was little. I'm so concentrated on the girl's eyes and chanting with the audio that I don't notice the rat in her hands until it's squirming and fighting and being tossed in with the sand. Paws scrape on the one sliver of glass that's visible on screen.

Sabrina switches the blender on, motor drowning out the

rat, and Ramon curses out loud. The sound clip has reached a maddening crescendo, the voice shouting so much that it's gone hoarse. The blender stops, then the girl removes the cup portion.

"She'll always be with me," she says. *"With you now, too."* Sabrina tips her head back and gulps down the sloppy mess, red dribbling from her mouth to the graceful curve of her neck.

52ND ST

She drinks and she drinks and she drinks and she drinks.

46TH ST BLIS—

"This train will now be making express stops," the conductor announces over the crackly intercom.

Sabrina is frozen in a frame, blood streaked all over her blue-tinted skin. Pure joy twists her features into something horrifying.

A series of grumbles in all different languages erupts around the train car as it barrels past a local stop. There are human faces among the masked and painted, but nothing makes sense.

"Those were ashes," I say, numb, betrayed, confused, about the piece of her sister that she threw in. I swallow down the bile collected in my throat. In my mind, the blades spin once more. You're not supposed to be hurt online.

"No, no, no, no. Come on, man." Ramon's call has gone to voicemail. His Spider-Man mask falls to the ground as he rakes hands through his hair, tugging at the thick strands in frustration. "He isn't picking up. Liam knows it's serious if I call."

Pings come from our phones at the same time. Our group chat is at the top of my messages.

Liam:

oh god im finishing that vid

it's so fucked up

call u after

"Why is he doing that?" Ramon asks, disbelieving.

My hands are clammy. Though the video is still, I can hear the sister's name. I can see her on the beach, lips kissed with sweet cream. "Because," I say slowly, "she said we would die if we don't finish." I'd been drawn to Sabrina, I'd felt kinship with her story, but Liam is plain old superstitious. He picks up gum-stained pennies, and he knocks on wood after every mildly salacious thing. There's no way he would stop, no matter how disturbing. "We have to keep going too."

"This is not the right kind of online therapy," Ramon snaps at me, as if Liam hadn't found it himself among trending topics and started minutes before us. "You need to talk to me, us, someone else about everything, instead of falling for this screwed-up hoax."

Loss is like swimming in an ocean, so I never found a way to begin. It just goes on and on in every direction. Do they want to know about her shoes still lined up on the rubber mat by our front door? Her mail—all in Vietnamese—that arrives, despite us writing *deceased* on the return envelope?

"There's only a minute left in this," I say shakily while the train continues on the express track. "Liam would say it's better to be careful, so I'm watching it either way."

Ramon lets out a long breath. "If she takes out another rat, I'm done."

No argument to that. The cup has been set aside as Sabrina grins right into the camera. *"It's like science, you know? You start with basic principles, and you work your way to new theories."* Her teeth are slushy red. *"You test those theories out. Again and again and again. A ritual."*

I wonder if she found conspiracists on the web. I wonder if she stayed up chatting with spirit medium bots. As easily as the world sees me as an Emily Pham, I could also be a Sabrina—desperate to see a loved one in their shadow.

"You can't ignore her now. My sister gets to live forever. Be remembered forever. She was never just a news story . . . she's everything to me."

The closer we get to the Queensboro station, the slower the video loads. Sabrina freezes frame by frame, sometimes no more than a bunch of pixels. It takes me a long time to notice, to be sure, that the dark slice of closet has grown behind Sabrina.

I pause the video so it can buffer. I swear I can hear Ramon's heart thumping. The closet has yawned open, and an abyss seems to stare back at us. My chest burns as if a woman's bony fingers are patiently ripping my esophagus apart.

QUEENSBORO PLAZA

The train stops at the next station. Some bros leave to hit up bars or transfer to more hipster-esque neighborhoods with better internet. It's the last stop before we go underground, so I continue the video, though a sicker dread has pooled in my stomach.

"No one pays attention until it happens to them."

Sabrina stops in the middle of her speech, head tilted as though she's trying to hear a train conductor over an intercom. The closet is wide now. It is a bottomless pit, and she turns to look, drawn away from her audience. We only see the back of Sabrina's unbrushed hair.

Ramon sucks in a breath.

"It's you. It's really you," she says, voice breaking. She gets up from her desk, the chair spinning. Her gait is a sleepwalker's. *"Emily."* Ramon turns the volume up. Another sound underscores the audio chanting, but the whispers escape us.

Sabrina stands in front of that rectangular cut of darkness, still, until long limbs emerge and pull her into an embrace. So pale, they almost blend in with the white pajamas she has on.

Sabrina melts into her sister's hug, sagging with relief, even as those monstrous arms tighten.

A split second, and blood spills down the bright satin, and Sabrina screams.

The video stops abruptly.

"What the fuck," I say finally. There are zero minutes left on the video. Ramon picks up his mask with a grumpy huff.

The closest passengers side-eye us wearily because of Sabrina's screaming from before. *It's nothing,* I tell myself. Curse, hoax, whatever, it is done. At a curve on the tracks, cell service zips in for a wild, erratic moment, disappearing as quickly as it came. Liam's text messages arrive all at once.

S TOP

Lng dont fin

Llxxxzzzzz

The tunnel swallows the subway train whole. Lights flicker on and off—the usual, illuminating everything in sepia tones. We're safe, right?

The emergency exit slides open at the end of the train car. No one perks their head up since it should've been another passenger passing between train cars. And yet, a chilling emptiness haunts that exit. It's strange in its familiarity, like a graveyard you walk past every day but only recently noticed.

I shove Ramon behind me.

Large rats emerge from the iron-toned darkness, their hairy forms agile over rushed feet. The roaches are worse—they dart along all the walls, some spreading their paperclip wings to fly right into the crowd. Panic starts slow, dignified with angry mutters of "only in New York City" and "what the fuck, MTA," until a costumed clown springs from their seat, waddling and screaming. Blue paint runs down their cheeks. Their two puffs of red clown hair are full of roaches.

"Oh, hell no," a middle-aged Black man says before he tries to peace out to the next train car, but the doors don't budge no matter how he or anyone pulls at them.

Several cell phones are out and recording immediately. *Don't*, I want to yell, but probably no one will be alive to post it online anyway.

The first leg hooks over the tiny platform connecting the two train cars.

"I'm sorry," I say to Ramon and grasp his hands tight, though now he pushes me away. So many hours and weeks lost to existing virtually, to not showing up. We could've had a beautiful blue moon. We could've survived had I been a better friend. "I'm sorry. I'm so sorry."

A slip of pale green dress flutters at the knee, haphazard rips that expose bones and slippery flesh. It's still a leg that would get catcalled on every street. In the thick air of an enclosed tunnel, she smells like expensive perfume—raspberries and vanilla and honey, all sweetened death.

Everyone else screams, but I only repeat her name.

LEYLA MENDOZA AND THE LAST HOUSE ON THE LANE

Maya Gittelman

There's an old man at the end of the lane, and you weren't always afraid of him, but you can't remember what it felt like not to be.

Everyone in your village calls his house The Vines because of the thick cables of them that smother the cottage like they're holding it hostage. Creeping and thickly twisting like great gnarled cobwebs, but thorny like the tangled claws of a beast. A starving briar-maw, waiting to cut into its next victims.

For most of the year it seems to be abandoned—that's the worst part, you think. The stone fence sunk into the lane, grave-like as it marks what was once, perhaps, a garden. But every so often, especially on the night of the thirteenth moon, someone catches sight of a light through the slats. A shadow slowly creeping past. Strange music coming through the creaking floorboards and shuttered windows. And when you get as close as you dare, just past the last well-looking oak lining the lane, the dry, sour smell of ancient things becomes sharp in your nose.

Tita Maria once told you that a long time ago, some men from the town went to see if the house was inhabited. They didn't expect to find anyone, loudly convinced the shadows were a product of the imaginations of bored housewives. They were going to take anything of value and knock the old place down.

As they approached, the story goes, the air became foggy and cloying with a tropical heat heavy with the smell of sampaguita, unimaginable in the cool Adirondack autumn. The first man swore he heard a howling, like a werewolf wild in fury at the thirteenth moon. The second said the scent turned sour, his stomach turning at the stink of rotting flesh. The last man laughed at his companions. He trod close, brandishing his fists. He didn't see the thorns reaching up from the earth to snatch at him until they enveloped him in a vicious embrace, tearing through his jacket to maul his flesh.

Now, no one gets close to The Vines.

Some say that the old man must've died alone there, and his lonely spirit lashes out at the villagers who never cared for him.

Others say he's simply an evil wizard who chooses to be cruel.

You and your cousins just know that he's ancient, an emblem of fear and death and terrible, violent loneliness, and that's enough to give you nightmares.

He is everything you are terrified of growing up to become.

Every Halloween, you and your cousins haunt your little Northeastern village tucked within the shadows of the Adirondacks. You're here because your mother's mother and her sister found jobs in the town's hospital, one of the only ways Filipinos could end up in Massachusetts for more than one generation. You actually have many cousins, but they're back in the Philippines. Here, you have four. Your father might have liked to move back home, but you'll never know. He died before you were born, leaving only the locked pocket watch you wear around your throat, so you have no siblings. You don't even have the key.

You could have been anywhere. Generations of Filipinos, ancestors braided into the rich, sweetbitter Batangueño soil, cut off close to the bud and shoved haphazardly into dry American dirt.

Your roots are transplants. No wonder you're not sure how to grow.

"Anak," your mother says, her voice snapping, brittle as the autumn twigs crackling in the forest at the end of the lane. "You're too old for this. This . . . *tomboy* thing, ha?" She says the word like it's foreign, because it is. It's not even the right word. You don't want to hear how she pronounces the right word. You can't even say it yourself yet. You don't even want to think it. You spend most of your time trying so hard not to think it that your heart might break from the effort. You're not even sure it *is* the right word. Or if a single word can contain it. That seems impossible. But whatever you are, you know *tomboy* is not it.

"Fifteen is almost grown. If you insist on going out on this terrible pagan night, you wear what I picked out for you. Won't it be nice to match your cousins?"

She says this last bit wheedlingly. Like she's trying to show something very obvious to someone very willfully ignoring it.

She doesn't see the irony. She never will.

"Come on, my lovely La-la," she croons, a sick musicality to her voice. "Look at it! Ganda naman, ha? It's going to be so beautiful on you!"

Your mother holds up the dress. It *is* pretty. It's an almost perfect replica of the dress you saw the Sugar Plum Fairy wear when your mom took you to watch the ballet. The beaded bodice is a bright, medicinal purple, the tutu real tulle, stiff lace that halos the waist. Lou and Lorna will be wearing the same.

She and your titas worked hard to make them, harder than they worked on the tin soldier costumes for Robbie and Diego.

But you worked hard on your costume too. You thought it was genius, a good compromise. You stayed up late after your homework for weeks, sewing and cutting and measuring, crafting the perfect Nutcracker costume. The design squared your shoulders, made straight lines out of the curves of your chest and waist. When you looked in the mirror through the brim of your hat, even—or perhaps especially—through the garishness of the costume, for once, you could almost see someone you recognized.

Your mother, her sister, and her brother's wife had thought their idea was the perfect group costume. Adorable. Appropriate. The girls in ballerina outfits, the boys as tin soldiers.

You don't want to be a soldier either.

"I'll still match them if I wear what I want." You don't say it insistently. You know better than that. You know how to modulate your voice, to bow your head so the thick curtain of your chin-cropped hair hides the heat in your eyes. To mask the rough rage that threatens to claw its way through your skin every time your mother or your titas or your teachers or anyone else in the world tries to tell you exactly how to be the perfect Filipina American daughter you are not and never have been.

You've studied the way Lourdes and Lorna talk to their mothers. Not to aspire. To *pretend*. To best mimic them. To crush your soul into the mold of someone your mother knows how to love.

"Yes," your mother allows, as if she's shoveling the acknowledgment out from under grave dirt. "But it won't be *pretty*. And it will stand out. You don't want to take focus from the kids, right? Aren't you a bit too old for that?"

You don't know what you're too old for. You straddle at this intersection of in between. Diego and Lou are both seventeen, Lorna and Robbie eleven and twelve, and you're the only child who's never really known how to fit between them. You're not Filipino enough for your family, not American enough for your town. Not young enough to wear what you want and pretend that it's all still in the name of playing pretend. Not old enough to wear what you want without your mother refusing you.

Not girl enough to feel at home in this body.

Halloween used to be your favorite day of the year. You could be a cowboy, a knight, a fashion icon, and everyone applauded.

Now it's just a sick reminder that anything close to who you might actually be will only ever be a costume.

"You're right, Inay," you tell your mother, your teeth gritted in a smile so broad, you're almost surprised she can't hear the blood rushing in your ears. "I'll wear the dress. I'll match."

"I knew you would," she says. She wraps her delicate arms around you. Your mother, with her friends and your titas and their anti-aging serums, the whitening creams, their magazine-ad plastic surgeries to change parts of themselves they never thought of changing before the ads.

All to affirm the way they feel in their bodies.

In their gender.

And yet yours and the way you want to express it is forbidden. A deformity.

A monstrosity.

You hug her back, because it feels good to belong. Even if the version of you who gets to belong is nothing like who you really could be, if you ever got the chance to find out.

So you take it even though it feels like you're suffocating, because this is all you have.

⁂

"What'll it be tonight?" Diego yawns, strutting in his soldier outfit. "Egg the school? Raw meat in the mailboxes? Carve Robbie's weird poetry into the oaks again?" He sounds as bored as the list.

"Maybe we could just take the kids trick-or-treating this year," Lou says nervously. She's always been anxious about getting into trouble, and now she's gotten old enough to worry about losing her scholarship. She has a life she's excited to grow into. Something she doesn't want to jeopardize.

The tulle itches.

It's tight, like your mother's embrace still hasn't let you go. It makes an itchy circle around your stomach, chafing your thighs.

It looks adorable on little Lorna, of course. And perfect on Lou.

You have to prove yourself tonight. To wrestle one element of control back into your life.

You couldn't stand up to your mother.

Maybe you never will.

But you can do this.

You open your mouth, draw in a deep breath.

"Let's go into The Vines."

⁂

"I still think this is a terrible idea," Lou says nervously.

"More interesting than anything else we could've done," Diego says.

"C'moooon, Ate," says Robbie. "I'm *bored* of being bored."

You're leading the group. Lou hurries to catch up, her eyes wide beneath perfectly applied sparkly purple eyeshadow. There's nothing wrong with the eyeshadow, you just wish your mother and her sister hadn't looked at you with mingled irritation and pity when you wouldn't let Lou apply it to you too.

"Leyla," she hisses, and your stomach gives a twist. You don't even hate the name, is the thing. You just hate the assumptions everyone makes about you because of it. "Don't you know what night it is?"

"Halloween," you say flatly. Lou makes a frustrated noise.

"Not just that!" She takes a shuddering breath. "*The thirteenth moon.*"

You hadn't remembered. The thirteenth moon, the night when the ancient wizard is meant to be at his most vengeful.

"Even better," you say through gritted teeth, and Lou groans, giving up. You nearly feel bad. This isn't her fault; none of it is. You glance at her. "You don't have to do this."

"I know," she says, her brow furrowing. "I just don't understand why you *do*."

Your resolve stiffens, and so does your spine.

"No," you say. "You don't."

You keep walking.

A wild, anxious humming fills your blood. The streets you know too well feel different tonight.

Or maybe they're starting to feel different anyway, because you are starting to let yourself recognize that you aren't the person you thought you could force yourself to grow up to become.

It takes a long time to reach the lane. It takes no time at all.

And then there it is.

The Vines.

"That's what I'm talking about." Lorna grins, sprinting toward it. Robbie and Diego hoot and follow her.

"This is so stupid," Lou whines, and the thing is, you know she's right.

Maybe there's nothing evil here at all.

Maybe this is just your pathetic, *childish* attempt at feeling in control of your life. Maybe you're taking tonight as permission to spiral into the very recklessness thrumming beneath your skin because you spend every *single* other day of your life constricting yourself into the shape of someone who gets to survive your mother's house, because that *is* the path of least resistance, the safest choice, and it's goddamn eating you alive.

Maybe that doesn't make you weak.

It just makes her cruel. Careless, at best. You understand why your mother is the way she is. That doesn't make it fair.

"Yeah," you say. "Fucking stupid." And you walk through the stone fence.

Lou groans and follows.

At first, there's nothing. Just the sounds of the other three laughing, kicking at rocks and leftover lumber, smelling the rotting flowers in what used to be a garden patch.

And then, with a sensation not unlike cold, manicured fingernails twisting in your gut, you realize it's not just rotting flowers.

"Sampaguita," you whisper, but it's already too late.

The fog curls in like a cloud settling on the lane. You can still see your cousins, but only barely.

"Did you hear that?" Diego says, his voice suddenly sharp with fear.

"Don't be a jerk," Lou snaps.

"I'm serious."

"I didn't hear anything," Robbie says, which makes it worse. Lorna gets into a fighting stance she must've learned from her tae kwon do class. The cousins huddle closer, their growing unease palpable.

Except for you.

You like it.

It makes you feel monstrous, cruel, but you *like* it.

They're fine. It's *fine*. This is a story, a myth. Your heartbeat roars in your ears, but even though there's fear there, it's tempered by something . . . else. Something reckless, and aglow.

Let someone else be uneasy for once. Let someone else be afraid. You don't know how, but you can tell that nothing here is going to hurt you.

Or maybe you just don't care, because the rest of the world already hurts.

The fog is thicker now, sitting heavily within the fence. Perhaps it spills over; you can't tell anymore. It reminds you, suddenly, of the way your mother talks about visiting her grandparents in

Tagaytay, the way the mountains in December would pierce through the clouds. She spoke of it like the sky was cutting off the land from itself. To you, it always sounded like something softer, almost magical. A blending of the earth and the heavens, a clear reminder that the lines between natural things almost always have the potential to be smudged, in the right circumstances.

Of course you'd see communion where your mother sees nothing but severance.

The fog thickens further. The strangest thing, perhaps, is that it's not cold, as the clouds on your mother's mountains were. It's warm, with slowly cloying humidity. And that scent, the sampaguita . . . with every breath you take, you realize. It's shifting.

"Ew, Lorna," Lou hisses, wrinkling her nose.

"It wasn't me!" Lorna says, stomping her little foot indignantly. "Robbie?"

"Not me either," he says. "Honest." They look around in worry as the smell gets worse. It doesn't smell like it comes from anything human.

At least, nothing human and *alive.*

"All right, happy now?" Lou asks. "Have you had your fun? Can we just go trick-or-treating, *please*?"

"You know what, this does kind of stink." Diego wipes a bead of sweat from his brow. "Like, literally."

Cowards, you think, but you don't say it aloud.

You don't like this version of yourself.

This you that revels in their discomfort because it almost aligns with your own. You *want* to be a caring thing. You want to be good to your cousins, to your mother.

You just also want to be good to yourself, and they're making it impossible.

The worst part is, they don't even realize they're doing it.

The humidity becomes heavier, and your father's locked pocket watch is warm against your chest. You don't want to grow up to be anything like your mother. You don't know if you want to grow up to be like your father. What would he have done in your place? Would he have been brave enough to venture ahead, kind enough to honor Lou's hesitation? Steady enough to not need this sort of risk in the first place? What would he want from you, for you? You'll never get to know.

The house looms large as you step closer. Your town's very own myth of what it means to be a ruin, a failure, a monster, made manifest in front of you.

Whoever you become, you are supposed to end up anywhere but here.

You're about to agree with your cousins. To give in, to give up. There's nothing here that can save you. There is no such thing as magic. There is just you, being an awful cousin.

And then, unmistakably, the earth begins to part.

Thick, thorny vines pierce through the cracks in the soil. At first, you can't believe what you're seeing. It can't be real. They thrash like the arms of a kraken: sharp, and volatile, and hungry.

Your cousins scream. They tug and tug at you to run.

You should.

You know you should.

You don't know what's happening. You don't know if this is the work of an evil wizard or if the earth simply decides to swallow people whole sometimes, but you know this is dangerous.

The blade-sharp bite of thorns whistle by your ears, the vines as thick as oak trunks now, strong enough to strangle even if the thorns don't cut you open.

Everything you've ever been taught is screaming at you to run. This is where defiance takes you. You think you're in control of your life? The very *ground* opens up to prove you otherwise.

Except—

Except you're already being suffocated.

You *know* what you'll find if you leave this place. You know who you are supposed to become, and you *can't* become her—you're just going to choke yourself pretending.

You know that.

Here is proof that there is something *else* happening, out here at the edge of the map.

Something unknown and full of potential.

You might never stand up to your mother. You will never get to see yourself in your father. You might never get to find out who you could be.

But you can do *this*.

You take a deep breath.

You keep going.

With each step, the fog grows thicker, mingling fragrance and rot. You hear howling now. It drowns out the fading calls of your cousins. Thick vines threaten your path, thorns growing long as limbs.

You step over them.

You're in front of it at last, this cursed place. Decrepit walls, peeling paint, cracked floorboards on the porch. Filth and cobwebs cake the windows. The snarl of vines, the same ones that still snag threateningly through the earth, coil almost protectively around the entirety of the house, as if snaring it in a lethal embrace.

At first you don't see past the shock of being this close, confronting in tangible reality the aged place that haunts your whole town.

But you do. You force yourself. And the longer you stand there, even through the chilling noises and the sickening smell . . . the less horrible it becomes. The peeling paint is actually a rather lovely blue beneath the cake of dust. The windows . . . when you peer close, they're stained glass, an intricate floral design. Your hand finds your father's pocket watch, as you're prone to doing when you need the reassurance that you are not entirely alone. It only kind of helps, but it only ever does.

This isn't a haunted house at all, is it? It's just what once was a home, made tragic by the same inevitability that makes everything tragic: time. It could be beautiful. It probably was.

You're just beginning to feel properly brave, almost brave enough to call this whole adventure a success and be done with it, when the door swings open.

"Hello," says the evil wizard. "I've been waiting for you."

A sharp thrill pierces your gut. The stories are true. Why did you think this would prove anything? You're a fool, pathetic and babyish in the face of such powerful unknowns.

This must be terror, you think. This must be the sort of terror you experience when you're about to die. This must be your life, flashing before your eyes.

And yet—

The evil wizard is old, certainly. Deep wrinkles crease his face, his sharply coiffed hair is the color of sword-silver. Yet he's smiling gently, as if he was expecting you. *That's what makes him more of a threat,* comes your oldest tita's voice in your head, but you push her away, take in the truth of who you're actually seeing. He doesn't look like an angry wizard, or even a conniving one. He looks comfortable in his body. Self-possessed. He leans on a carved ebony cane, peering at you with clever, earth-warm eyes. He's got a stocky frame, the sort where you can tell he used to run around a lot when he was younger, and when you step forward, you recognize with a jolt that his cloud-white shirt is a barong tagalog, the formal Filipino shirt Diego, Robbie, and your titos wear on special occasions. You've always coveted their barongs, while you were itching out of your skin in Lou's hand-me-down dresses. The loose fit, the intricate embroidery of the piña fibers. Barongs mean celebration, and it's jarring to see it on this man in the chill at the end of the lane, under the light of the thirteenth moon. The translucent hem sits over his forest-green trousers, where the embroidery continues, and you recognize the designs sprawling across his clothes as delicate, coiling vines. He tilts his head. Something occurs to you, and a fresh thrill spears through you.

This time, you know it isn't terror.

"My pronouns vary quite a bit," he says with a wink, as if reading your mind. "But you can go with 'he,' for now. Today."

Whatever you expected, it isn't this. Lack of monstrosity

aside, you've never heard someone speak so plainly about gender in this gentle, matter-of-fact way outside of the internet or the few books that make it through the library censors. You've never had anyone share their pronouns with you in person, especially not an adult.

"I—" you start, then stop. The wizard smiles at you. It's a peculiar, hollowing smile, as if he knows something you don't. Your mind is spinning so fast, it feels blank with it, a blur of questions and unease and . . . possibility.

You have no blueprint for this, no outline.

You get to fill yourself in.

"'He' for me too, please," you say, and with those five words, you feel in your chest something not unlike what it looked like when the vines split the earth. Something breaking through, wild and becoming.

Something with deep, deep roots, at last reaching the light.

The wizard's smile broadens.

"Certainly, young sir," he says easily. As if he sees past the scratchy tulle and the assumptions of your body and listens to the heart of you instead. The way you've always wanted.

A roaring fills your ears. This is who your town deemed monstrous? When they're the ones who trap you, as if their misconceptions of you are somehow truer than your own shifting understanding of yourself?

"Do you mind the name Leyla?" the wizard asks. His voice creaks with age, but there's something of a melody in it. "Just to check."

You think about it. You think about it properly for the first time in your life, because no one's ever asked.

"No," you say at last. "I've always liked it. I just don't like what people think it means about me."

A shadow crosses the wizard's face, as if he's remembering something painful. Only for a moment, though, and then that same strange smile is back.

"I understand," he says, and somehow you feel certain you can believe him.

"I like your shirt," you say, and his smile softens.

"Come inside," the wizard says. "I'll show you where I made it."

You follow him across the threshold. The door closes behind you and swallows the light. You shiver in the darkness, your fear rushing back.

"Sorry," he says. "This is the In-Between. I always mean to decorate it, you know, but why bother . . ."

What have you gotten yourself into? All you can see is a strange little mechanism next to the doorframe, silver and round, glowing as if from its own light.

"Just a moment . . ."

The wizard turns a key in the mechanism. The light flares bright, the wizard's hands sparking, and you're awash with a fresh wave of the scent of sampaguita.

When he opens the door again, your breath catches in your throat. You grip your father's pocket watch tightly.

The vines are gone. The lane is gone. Your town is gone.

The door opens to the most magnificent clothing workshop you've ever seen.

It's a room as vast as a greenhouse, and you can see morning light streaming through the enormous windows at the far end, no trace of Halloween night. It's also the coziest place you've ever been. There's what feels like an infinite number of textiles, bolt after soft, heavy bolt, fluttering their free edges as if eager to be shaped into a new garment. A well-loved array of scissors and sewing machines, measuring tapes and pins, some laid out neatly in massive shelves beside a wheeled ladder, others busily working away at garments of their own accord, fluttering through the air. There are designer's figures in half-made outfits, most of which combine suiting and dresses, cuts and textiles, in ways you've only ever imagined. In fact, this entire room feels like a version of your corner back home where you made the costume you didn't get to wear, only in its most ideal, enchanted form. At the center is the most beautiful desk you've ever seen, stacked with pages of designs.

"The desk is tanguile," the wizard says, for surely now you know he is a wizard. He steps to it. "Philippine mahogany, the very finest."

You follow him inside, trembling.

The magic of it, the cuts of his clothes, the kinetic energy of this workshop.

This place is an act of self-creation. Everything feels possible here.

You feel more alive than ever. This is terrifying. This is the best place you have ever known.

"This is . . . spectacular," you say softly. "It's like a dream." Like your own dearest dreams, you are too shy to say.

"Thank you." You look up at him, his wizened face, the small figure he cuts in the room.

"But," you say. "You're by yourself. Isn't . . . isn't that lonely?"

This time, the smile he gives you isn't frightening in the least. It brightens, sharp on his face like the flash of a needle.

"Oh, Leyla," he says. "I need you to know. I could not be further from alone."

He strides back to the door and guides you through to the In-Between. You realize with a jolt that you'd never told him your name, but you don't have time to dwell before he twists the key again and the door opens into a flourishing garden. The scent of fresh growing herbs thickens, and you can see tumbling hills beyond it, a sprawling series of cottages nestled within. There are people—other wizards, you feel suddenly sure—in all sorts of magnificent outfits, tending the gardens, bustling in their homes, laughing and living together. A community.

You barely have time to take it in before he whisks you back into the In-Between and turns the key again. This time it opens into a city, the air fragrant with street meats and calamansi. Someone wearing a flowing robe waves from atop the enormous flying lizard they're riding across the busy skies. Into the In-Between again, and you're in a towering library; again, and you smell the sharp salt of the seashore; again, and it's a humid jungle, the scent of sampaguita flaring with every twist of the key and flash of his magic.

"This is why The Vines seem abandoned most of the time," you realize aloud. The wizard smiles, pleased. He turns the key and brings you back to his magnificent workshop. You furrow your brow. "Then—why do you come back here at all? Why would you ever come back to this town?"

"You hate it now," he says, not unkindly. "And you have every right to, Leyla," he says, his eyes warm with understanding.

"Nothing feels like home when you are not at home with yourself. When you get as old as I am, it can feel good sometimes, to return to your roots. Imperfect as they may be, they're mine." He sets his jaw. "But I do it on my own terms."

"Why do you frighten them, then?" you ask. "I understand defending yourself—but why the thirteenth moon, why not just let them *see*—"

He draws himself to his full height, which is actually not very tall, but still impressive.

"Do you think they deserve to know the truth of me? The magic I am?" He shakes his head. "Not everyone deserves your full story, Leyla Mendoza. Sometimes you have to give up the idea that you can ever become someone they deign to respect. Sometimes you have to become the monster they think you are."

You think of your mother, and the way she'd look at you if you ever told her the truth about the daughter she thinks she has. You understand.

"The men I hurt," the wizard says, "they wouldn't have stopped, if I hadn't stopped them. I don't hurt anyone anymore. I haven't for many years. I just want to live."

Your eyes are brimming with tears, your heart bursting with hope and possibility and feverish envy. You want this more than anything. And if something like this, if a place like this, if a man like this can be real—you can do anything. Whatever comes next, you can face it. Because there is more to this world than a place that will choke you, and you finally have an example of who you might become. That's enough to make the future feel far less hopeless.

The Vines aren't ensnaring things at all.

It's ivy.

It's the roots you grow yourself, in the many places where you want to be planted.

"You're not a monster," you say softly. The wizard's smile is tender.

"I'm very glad you think so, my child. Come. Let's get you home."

That thrill in your gut flares again, and this time it *is* terror. You don't want to go. You're ready to beg to stay—and then you see it.

The little mechanism that controls the magic door. From this side of the threshold, you recognize—

"Where did you get that?" you demand, your hand flying to the watch around your throat. The very same watch embedded in the frame, except you don't have a key. "That's mine!"

The wizard's smile flashes with mischief.

"My father left it for me," he says. "He died before I was born."

"I . . ."

"Yes, exactly," the wizard says, with a wink. "Haven't been able to open it yet, right? Try this." He takes the key out of the watch and hands it to you. "Don't worry, I made a copy for myself a long time ago." He laughs, as if at a private joke, but that—he—you—this *can't* mean—

Of course. You should have known when you first saw the morning light.

Not only through space, then, but . . .

Time.

With shaking hands, you slot the key into your watch.

It pops open, revealing an intricate design of vines.

You take one last look at yourself, aged and laughing and so, so happy with the many lives you get to lead. Your future sprawls before you, because it is *your* future, and it is alive with multitudes of hope.

Your fingers spark.

The smell of sampaguita fills the air. It's coming from you, the magic that's always been in you, that you've finally given yourself the ability to unlock.

⁂

There is still an old man at the end of the lane, and you are still a little afraid of him, but you are not only afraid. That thrill that pulls at your gut is excitement. Possibilities.

You tell your cousins you found nothing in the house. You go trick-or-treating. You keep your tutu on all night, and it doesn't feel as suffocating anymore, because you know you're going home to the little corner of your room where you sew, and you're going to look up how to make your own barong tagalog. Your mother won't let you wear it yet, but you're going to get to one day.

There is a future ahead of you that you will get to grow yourself.

You can survive this.

You have so much to look forward to.

IN YOU TO BURN

Em X. Liu

Luce's first fire was a proper accident. Five years old, grandma's cigarettes, and a budding fascination with the way smoke curled into the crevices of their oil-spotted kitchen—all good for burning. She'd gotten her chubby little hands around the whole pack, managed to work a lighter somehow. The whole thing was over quickly, grandma running back into the room as soon as the flames had started to graze the top of their fume hood.

The next few were harder to deny, but not impossible. She's eight and there's a kid pissing her off on the playground, then the burning plastic slide. Static shock spark, they called that one. Freaky; thank god no one had gotten hurt. Luce only remembers the anger bright enough inside her chest to burn, her tight stance—all jaw gritted, nails digging into palms—and then the fire that licked up into the sky like it was hungry for more than just the playground.

She's twelve and trying to run away from home the third year in a row her mom said they couldn't afford to throw a party—Luce had nearly frozen to death on the beach, but the bonfire after that had gone on for weeks. The work of college kids, everyone said, drunk and messing with gasoline.

The old oak tree apparently struck by lightning, a scalded restaurant kitchen with the heat setting up too high. There were decent justifications every time, easy ways to make the world make sense. Magic wasn't real, after all. There were better, more mundane ways to explain things.

But Luce never saw the lightning. There were no college kids that night, just her. Maybe she's crazy, but all Luce remembers is the fire: inside her, and then out.

She's seventeen and angry again, always angry. Harley Tam is up in her face, a sneer spread over her mouth. It's always Harley—Harley who has always had everything, Harley who doesn't even have the poise to be humble about it, Harley who took one look at Luce in their first AP Biology class together and decided she was better. Luce hates her so much it hurts. They're talking about something that's supposed to be important, but all Luce can hear is the dripping condescension, the curl in her tone. All she can see is the way that she's looking down her nose at Luce, even though she's shorter.

She's seventeen and she's angry, and there's the fire, leaping eagerly through her veins.

There's the fire, and then—

⁂

The party's well on its way, a stinking, strobe-lit, teeming mass of people. Luce holds her plastic cup of orange juice—she pretended to pour in some soju earlier so Alice would stop insisting—and tries not to make eye contact with anyone as they shove past her and into the mix. Given the grim prospects of her usual clubs tightening security in the last few months, Alice had opted to shoo her parents and sister out of the household in time to repurpose the suburban monstrosity for her Halloween playground. Not that any of them had minded—Alice Sun is the apple of everyone's eye and is never to be denied, after all.

Luce included. Hence why she's sitting on the marbled counter of Alice's family kitchen, trying to shrink into her black hoodie as the bass pounds in the room next door.

"Where's your costume?" someone shouts at her as they go straight to the Jell-O shots lined up on the island counter. They've got a vibrant mask of makeup on, pink and blue eyes, a ghostly complexion, a classic Harley Quinn knocking back three toxic green blobs of vodka-infused gelatin before giving Luce another squinty-eyed look. "Who are you, anyway?"

Luce gestures weakly to the cat ears she'd reluctantly shoved over her unruly hair. She's in her usual getup of joggers and a black hoodie, her long—unstyled, admittedly—hair caught in as good a ponytail as she can make. Alice always says she can be hot if she puts in the effort, but Luce thinks that she's cute enough anyway, even without, so why bother?

"I'm Alice's friend."

"Oh," says not-Harley. "Where's Alice?"

Luce holds her arms up in the universal *beats me* gesture.

Eventually, when it's clear Luce doesn't actually know, the drunk girl frowns and wanders back out into the party. Luce slumps back. Not-Harley, indeed. Luce doesn't want to think about Harley—Tam, not Quinn—tonight, but she's always thinking about Harley in some form lately, so it's not exactly a surprise that this is where her mind has wandered yet again. She eyes the Jell-O shots like they might contain an answer for her. Or, you know, a path into not needing any answers. Maybe she needs to loosen up, the way Alice is always insisting. Alice, who is probably out there being the life of the party.

A sharp burst of feeling sorry for herself implants right underneath her sternum. Luce downs the rest of her orange juice. What the fuck is she doing? The thing is that Luce understands it's gauche to be like this. It's also that she can't really help herself. Alice was right that staying home instead of being here probably would've made her feel worse, but isn't that so much more pathetic? There's a pounding headache building behind her eyes. Luce knows that Alice has been worried since . . . But she hates being the cause of worry nevertheless. It's not like it's Alice's fault that—

She pushes herself off the counter, frustrated. Stupid that she can't even give name to it inside her own mind.

It's not Alice's fault that Luce still dreams of licking flames, wakes up with phantom smoke in her lungs. But that doesn't make it easier on either of them.

It's so bright inside the house, it barely looks like it's meant to be night outside. Maybe she'd feel better with the cool air on her face, the wide moon overhead. Blue moon, tonight, apparently. Luce doesn't usually believe in this kind of thing, but even through the window, it looms like something eerie, vast, and open, like it has a pull on them all.

She slips out of the kitchen and into the party. Here is a different kind of heat. Bodies pressed up against each other and Luce cramped in between, pushing. Lights overhead, flickering.

Everything is awash in beams of blue and pink and green, and maybe once upon a time Luce would've been able to lose herself in it. A lung-puncturing sadness joins the motley mix of malaise churning around inside her.

And then of course, of course—

Luce pushes herself out of the meat of the mishmash of bodies, and there she is.

Harley Tam is leaning on a billiards cue, long nails tapping on the lacquered wood. There's a little minicircle of admirers, lurking like they could leech even a hint of her essence, if they're close enough. She's slight—the cue nearly a height with her, but that doesn't stop her from eating all the light in the room. It's not a spotlight, but it might as well be; no matter the tint of the lurid glow, Harley shines.

Despite herself, Luce gravitates to the edge of the room. She tucks herself behind the doorway, out of view. Whoever Harley is playing with misses their shot, and Luce can see the curve of Harley's smirk from here. Her little court holds their collective breath as she pops a hip, leaning back to survey the scene.

She's barely dressed in costume. *Some Halloween party,* Luce thinks, though she supposes they're all a bit too old for it now. She can see the glimmer of makeup shining off Harley's forehead, a glittering mesh of blue scales, moving from thick, black eyeliner, a fierce mask that only makes her beauty sharper, hurt more. She looks otherworldly, something that doesn't belong in this badly lit high school. Harley finds what she's looking for, lines up her shot. She stretches her arm straight against the pool cue. The yawning beast tattooed on her skin shifts like it's alive, black and searing blues, curled all the way down her arm, and

Harley doesn't need makeup for her snarl to show what she is: dragon girl, barely contained, still feral.

Luce's chest is tight.

The last thing she remembers of the burning classroom are Harley's eyes, angry and as bright as the flames, and her clawing fingers. It's hard to shake that Harley's different now, but even Alice insisted it was all in her head. But that's the thing. Luce can't shake the image—Harley's furious mouth, shouting, the flames swallowing her whole. She doesn't remember anything after that.

Their classmates whisper, of course. About Harley reappearing weeks after, a ghost of herself. But still sharp, effervescent, beautiful. All her long black hair cut short and boyish, dyed a shimmering silver. Luce doesn't know how Harley's here, but that's a stupid, terrible thought. It's not like she can march up and ask in the hall either. What was she supposed to say? How come you didn't die like you should've in that fire?

Here now, Harley makes her shot. The shiny blue two ball sinks neatly into its pocket. Harley's grin is a slash over her face, a violent thing. She's surrounded by whoops, someone clapping her on the back, a friendly gesture, but when she looks up, she finds Luce through the throes of people, meets her gaze head-on.

In that moment, Luce could swear her eyes glowed electric, like from her memories. A streak of light, the only thing she could see before the darkness claimed her. Icy balm in the licking claustrophobic hot.

Harley straightens. She hands the cue off to someone else. Makes as if she's going to come near.

Luce fucking bolts.

She nearly breaks a vase, trips over some couple making out by the stairs and shouts apologies louder than she's spoken to anyone this entire night. Her breath comes hard and fast. She'd tried to confront Harley once, late one day, when school had let out and the sky was liminal-dark. Harley was loitering with her college friends, her glossy lips turned up in a pout while she cajoled cigarettes and booze out of the hapless frat boys already in love with her. It was easy to see where she'd be, come high school graduation—she probably already had a list of sororities trying to buy her favor. Luce wanted to—she didn't know what she wanted, only that seeing Harley limned in the early moonlight of summer, ethereal, like she was barely there, made something in her lurch, made her feel sick.

She wanted to know the truth, but there was the twitching thought in the back of her mind that the truth would be too much to bear.

She'd run away then too.

Luce basically trips her way up the stairs.

Alice's house is massive, winding, but there's still people everywhere. It's impressive how Alice herself has yet to be seen. Luce narrowly avoids getting a loud splash of Hennessy in her face when she tries to shove through a particularly rowdy game of Never Have I Ever, winces, shouts "Sorry!" behind her as she vaults over someone else's card game setup, then nearly gets tangled in someone's ill-advised mummy getup. Luce throws herself into the first closed-door room she finds and breathes a sigh of relief when it's blissfully empty.

She thunks her head back against the door, chest heaving.

"Fuck," she says aloud to the room. Bangs a fist against the door, too, for good measure. "Fuck!"

A spitting hiss answers her from the dark.

"Jesus, what!" Luce cries, nearly slamming her nose into the wall with how fast she skitters back.

She finds herself face-to-face with Winner's Mino in a cowboy hat. A quick scan of the rest of the room reveals, yep, three walls plastered with various old-school K-pop posters—Alice's sister's room is untouched from before she left for college. Which means the *hissing* . . . Luce slings her hands in her hoodie pocket and ambles over to the massive enclosure that houses Julia's bearded dragon. "Are you still hanging out in here, Jiyong?" she murmurs, pressing a finger to the glass. "Alice hasn't put you somewhere with more sun?"

In response, Jiyong flicks out his tongue.

Luce sighs. "Sorry for my potty mouth," she says. "I've been having a really bad day." The lizard's beady little eyes follow her around as she paces. Alice always used to be nerved out by the thing, so whenever Julia asked them to pet-sit, it'd been Luce who was tasked with making sure the little guy was nice and fed and happy. But that had been years ago. For some reason, the burst of familiarity makes Luce's eyes weirdly damp, but maybe it's the overstimulus of this entire night so far.

The last time Alice had made her come over to clean the lizard tank, they'd been sophomores and she hadn't known who Harley Tam was. It'd been a sunny day, and they brought all their supplies out on the deck, and Alice had sprayed her with the water, and Luce had gone home happy. That uncomplicated joy seems suddenly so out of reach from the version of her wringing her hands here, hiding from the world.

She lets her knees give out. Who the hell cares.

Harley looked beautiful. Harley always looks beautiful. That's part of the problem, isn't it? Luce doesn't know how to talk to Harley anymore; it'd been easier before, when they'd traded snarky insults in the halls, goaded each other about exam grades. When Harley would eye her up and down in the hall and raise an eyebrow at her outfit—her brother's old band tees and ripped jeans—and call her *brave* for daring to go out in that. When Luce would fire back with some bullshit about Harley's absentee father.

Luce hated her, which was an easy emotion.

Now it's hard to say what to name the molten mess of her chest when she thinks of Harley out there, changed like her, fundamentally different, but still the same. Especially when no one else but her seems to see it.

A loud bang, not lizard-induced this time, startles Luce out of her pity party.

"Holy shit," Alice Sun in the flesh declares, aiming a finger at her. "I've been looking for you *everywhere*. Bitch, seriously? What are you doing?"

"Hanging out with Jiyong," Luce says weakly.

Alice rolls her eyes. "I can't believe you left me alone out there!"

"Hey!" Luce cries. "I'm the one you disappeared on!"

"I told you I'd only be a few secs!"

"Yeah, well," Luce mutters. Her shoulders are sagging involuntarily. "I saw Harley."

Alice's mouth flattens into a line. "Did you say hi?"

"What? Why the hell would I do that?"

"I dunno," Alice says, and maybe Luce is oversensitive, but she thinks there's a hint of exasperation in Alice's voice. "You're right, you've been completely nonfunctional every time you even think about her, so I don't even know why I asked."

"That's not fair." Luce's voice comes out small.

All of Alice's sharpness melts away. She steps into the room, comes to crouch in front of Luce, who is still slumped in front of the lizard tank like a pathetic loser. Her best friend is gorgeous—not because she's pretty, even if she objectively is with her wide eyes and proud nose. Alice has always had a way of looking at the world with careful acceptance, taking all of Luce's moods in stride with an easy smile and toss of her curls. Had never said anything different to her since the fire, which is all Luce wanted.

"Lucy," she says now, and she hasn't used that childhood nickname since even longer. Luce's mouth trembles.

"I think this party was a bad idea," Luce mutters.

"Maybe," Alice concedes. "I'm sorry about being rude about Harley. I know it's . . . hard for you."

"Every time I see her, it's like I'm back there," Luce blurts.

Alice settles on the ground, legs crossed. She reaches out and takes Luce's hands in hers. "Yeah, and that fucking sucks. I know that's an understatement—"

"No, no," Luce cuts in, giggling a little. "It *does* fucking suck."

"Yeah," Alice says, shaking her head, "but instead of going on to me about how you think she's a witch or a ghost or whatever, maybe you should, like, try to talk to her?"

"I don't think she's a ghost," Luce mutters.

Alice gives her a look.

"Okay," Luce concedes, "but you have to admit, there's something weird! She looks so . . ."

"I'd be a little fucked-up, too," Alice says slowly, "if I'd gone through that, you know? Maybe she's just . . . dealing with it her own way."

A hiccup rises up in Luce's chest, embarrassingly emotional. She rubs her fingertips together. They still go numb at random times. She still remembers trying to pull at the classroom doorknob, the searing heat across her palms. Dull numbness afterward, but her hands had been slippery with blood.

"Lucy, it's not your fault, you know," Alice says suddenly, and Luce shudders, draws closer to herself. That's the other thing about Alice—she always knows exactly how to cut right down to the heart of the issue.

Luce releases the shaky breath caught in her chest. "You know we were both in that classroom that late because she wanted to come over to my place to work on the speech team presentation, and I wouldn't let her."

"So? You didn't know you were gonna get caught in a freak accident."

"They never figured out how it started."

"More reason to not mull over it, Luce. Seriously. Harley doesn't blame you either."

"Sometimes I think she does."

Alice's calm face falters. It's not fair to her either, Luce knows. There's no reason to put any of this on her, when it's all Luce and her own bullshit, her childhood conviction that she's to blame for the string of accidents, her own brain playing tricks for her entire life.

Harley really does believe Luce is to blame, though. It's in the way Harley looks at her in the halls sometimes. They're still in half the same extracurriculars. Luce knows that Harley cares, even though she skips half her classes and smokes on campus when she can get away with it. She only ever skips the ones she could pass in her sleep. Last week at band, Harley was tuning the ensemble because she's stubborn enough to take the challenge of being first oboe, and she looked right at Luce when she did it, gaze level. It's not accusatory. Just—Harley looks at her without the same venomous contempt that she used to, and that's the weird part. More sinister, somehow. Like her clear-eyed gaze is all the accusation in the world she needs. Like it's Luce's fault because it's *always* been her fault, and Harley's the only one in the world who knows.

"Do you want to leave?" Alice asks, finally.

Luce purses her lips. "No," she decides, mind made up on the spot. "No, actually. Let's go back out there. I'll be fine."

There's no point in feeling sorry for herself, right? Alice doesn't need to know the way she can still feel the fire in her veins sometimes, when she's so angry at herself it hurts to breathe. Alice doesn't need to know about the way she wants to scream and laugh both when it gets too loud in her own head. Maybe what she needs is some music to drown it out, a good Halloween fright. Maybe something else can haunt her for tonight.

"You sure?"

Luce climbs to her feet, plants them solid in the ground. "C'mon," she says. "Before I change my mind."

Alice cackles and jumps up. “All right, Miss Lucy. Let’s fucking go.”

“Bye, Jiyong,” Luce calls, giggling, as they march arm in arm back into the rowdy mix.

It’s as loud as it was earlier when they get to the living room. Alice is more graceful—she tugs Luce through the mess with ease. Or maybe it’s that as the host, everyone actually gives her the respect to part enough to let them through. Alice pulls her by the hand into the throng, leads her into the dance. Truth be told, it’s more swaying with the group than anything else, but Luce tips her head back and laughs, lets the music bleed into her and replace all the churning inside with its own pulse. Dances like she has nowhere else to be. Doesn’t matter if she accidentally backs into Jacob from math class, drunk off his ass. Doesn’t matter if she steps on Alice’s toes; Alice doesn’t mind.

Someone is playing a loud EDM remix of “Monster Mash,” and for some reason, Luce finds this the most hilarious thing ever. She shakes her hair out, loosens her ponytail. Before long, her hoodie is soaked in sweat, her skin warmed over.

“Better now?” Alice shouts in her ear.

“Yeah!” Luce shouts back. “This is great, actually!”

Maybe she should’ve known better than to tempt fate.

There’s a lull, the song overhead changing to something more midtempo, mellow. Makes Luce nostalgic for eighth-grade school dances, when the Ed Sheeran would start up and people would pair off one by one to slow dance awkwardly—the only way middle schoolers knew how. She giggles again, reaching out fully intending to drag Alice into one, but someone else grabs her hand before she can.

Instantly, bile floods her mouth. Harley's dark blue nails are sharp against her palm. Luce thinks her orange juice is about to make its way back up, stain the shimmery little dress that's plastered to Harley's body.

"Hey," Harley says, like they're friends. Her voice is low, husky, like she's spent the entire night shouting. Painfully intimate. Like they know each other like that.

Luce gulps. "Um," she says.

Harley smiles beatifically, like she doesn't know what effect she's inducing. Like she doesn't always know, because it's always the effect. "You ran away from me," she says plainly. Her other hand snakes around Luce's waist, pulls her properly into the dance.

"I—had to go find Alice," Luce tries.

Harley cants her head. When Luce follows her gaze, she sees Alice pushing Eugene Kim nearly into an expensive-looking plant, definitely shoving her tongue down his throat. Well, then. "I did find her," Luce says defensively, "before."

"Looks like she doesn't need you to look after her right now," Harley says easily.

Luce tries to back away, but Harley only follows, until they're pressed in the corner of the room somehow, tucked in next to the Suns' expensive display bookshelf that has somehow not been wrecked.

Harley's eyes flicker. She's wearing contacts. There's a thin rim of frosty blue around her dark irises. "You, on the other hand."

"Shut up," Luce finds herself saying.

Harley doesn't even need to laugh.

It's like she's her stupid self all over again, when confronted with the truth of Harley in front of her. Something about her always so easily riled up, incendiary. "What do you want?" Luce asks.

"I want to dance with you," Harley says easily. She looks eerie, peering out of the dark. The party lights like this over her face creating kaleidoscope shadows. She's solid underneath Luce's hands—her fingers curled in Luce's, her body, hips pressed close—but why does she seem like smoke? Like she could slip away, any moment? Luce knows she's holding Harley's hand tight enough that it must hurt. Harley's expression doesn't even falter.

"You—" Luce starts, doesn't know how to finish.

Harley inclines her head. "Me."

"Are you mad at me?" Luce finally says. She always feels like an idiot around Harley, so might as well be blunt about it. No games, right?

A flash of teeth—Harley's incisors are so sharp, Luce thinks she's wearing fangs for a brief second. "Why would I be mad at you?"

"Because—"

"Because you nearly killed us both?"

Luce's fingernails are digging into Harley's flesh. Surely that hurts her. She isn't pulling away. "That's *not* what happened."

"Isn't it?"

The music changes again, bass thumping through the air and into Luce's bones. Harley stays close, draws closer, even. Peers up at Luce through the spidery shadow of her lashes.

"No," Luce says through gritted teeth.

"Hm," says Harley. "Okay."

"Okay? Is that all you're going to say?"

Harley's hand has wound itself closer to the hem of Luce's hoodie. She can feel the ghost of her nails at her hip, tracing the skin. Luce wants to crawl inside herself. She wants to turn herself inside out. She wants to take Harley's wrist and wrench it away, and she wants to let Harley carve her open with that too-sharp nail, slice her belly button to sternum, find what lies beneath. Surely Harley knows, can see it. Understands something about Luce that she doesn't know herself. Why else would she still be here, like this?

She doesn't have to say a word to get Luce's nerves lit up. She smiles for real, then, her lips twisting up. Teeth sharp—for real, not an illusion. "Did you want me to say something else?" She tilts her head, suddenly innocent again, mercurial. "I can say whatever you want me to say, Luce."

Something about her name in Harley's voice—almost sweet, almost gentle, too intimate—makes Luce so angry it hurts.

She flips them, easy. She's taller than Harley by nearly a head. It's simple to use the hand that Harley grabbed to push her against the wall. Harley stretches her fingers properly into Luce's hoodie, like a test.

"I want you to leave me alone."

Harley laughs lightly. "Do you really?"

Luce hesitates. Harley takes that opportunity to lean up from where Luce has her caged in, brings their faces close enough that her nose nudges up against Luce's. Makeup mesmerizing, like a lightning bolt across her face. Is it only the light, or are her eyes glowing? A terrible disquiet catches Luce by the heart, a network film of hesitation.

"Luce," Harley says again, like silk, like ice in Luce's veins.

"Fuck off."

"I don't want to."

Luce kisses her first.

Harley kisses back with teeth. It hurts. She draws blood. She kisses like the wild creature she is. She digs her claws into Harley's skin, pinpricks of pain at her ribs. Luce tangles a hand into Harley's hair, pulls. Harley hisses in her mouth, grins again. Tugs her close, hips to hips.

Luce's blood is boiling. Luce's skin is alight. The heat is so close to the surface of her, it wants out. Luce wants—

"Holy shit!"

"Is that a—"

"—Fire!"

Luce stumbles back, gasping. Smoke curls in the air. Right beside them, the fancy bookcase is aflame, licking up into the ceiling, sooty black already. She doesn't know how she missed it—now that she sees, the heat is oppressive, circling.

"Shit," Luce gasps. Turns her head.

Harley is still smiling at her, unmoving. "Jesus," Luce cries, reaching out to grasp her by the wrist. "C'mon, we need to go."

"Are you still sure?" Harley asks. Her mouth is a gaping wound. Luce wants to kiss it again. "Still think it wasn't your fault?"

"That's—" Luce shakes her head, backing up more, more, anything to get away from Harley and her sullen mouth, her glowing eyes, her conviction. "That's not true. That's not fucking true."

The fire leaps higher. People are screaming now. Luce is

breathing in a face full of smoke with every passing second. Harley stays right where she is, and if Luce blinks, she can see the same visage, all those months ago, Harley caught aflame, her arm in the blaze, the line of her body twisting away into the fire.

Harley smiles, wide. Shows her teeth—no, Luce wasn't hallucinating. Harley bares her fangs, eyes ghoulish, body shimmering. Dragon of the hills, come to play with her prey. She looms, bigger than her presence. "Do you believe in fate?" she asks, her voice a hiss in the dark. "Did you think you and I would end any other way?"

"I have no idea what you're saying," Luce says, but there's a rock in her gut, and her fingers are aching, twitching, remembering.

Harley takes a step back, leaning against the wall like there isn't smoke whipping across her face. Luce shakes her head. She doesn't understand.

She does the only thing she knows: she runs.

The house is a blur around her. She finds the crowd, follows it, and manages to make it all the way to the front foyer before the mass of people is too thick to move forward. Someone slams into her from behind and Luce falls to her knees, forehead knocked against the bannister. She reaches forward, crawls. Her tongue tastes like metal.

"Shit, Luce!" Alice's voice is a godsend, like it always is. Her hand appears again in front of Luce's face, always here when she needs it.

Luce could cry. "Alice," she sobs.

"Get up, get up," Alice says, reaching in to literally haul Luce upright. "What the hell happened?"

"I don't know," Luce says, even though some part of her understands it, the burning certainty in Harley's eyes: *I did this*, she wants to say, but she can't get the words out properly, *I did this, I made this happen*. She kissed Harley, and the world ended. She flexes her fingers, caught in Alice's.

"Okay, I really want to know if you're okay," Alice says, talking a mile a minute, "but we have to fucking get out of here right now holy shit Lucy, oh my god."

They're stuck pressed to the stairs, too many people trying to shove out the front door in front of them and not enough space. Luce's vision is blurry with tears. "Fuck," she says, trying to shove through but getting pushed back.

"Shit," Alice exhales. "God!"

"I know, I know."

Alice suddenly halts, standing stock-still instead of trying to push through with Luce. "Wait," she says, "the fucking lizard. Luce. Luce!"

"Seriously?" Luce yells. "You're thinking of the lizard right now?"

Alice whirls around, her face streaked with soot, caked across the bridge of her nose like it's already a mourning mask. Above their heads, the high chandelier creaks, a long crack running through the ceiling suddenly. The crowd below shrieks collectively, showered in plaster dust. Everyone pushes harder, but the front door is a bottleneck, trapping them all. Luce watches as the foyer lights sway and creak.

"Luce, I can't let Julia's pet lizard *die in a house fire*!" Alice practically shrieks, hysterical. Her breathing hitches, tears spilling. "She loves that thing! She'll kill me!"

"Shh," Luce says, smoothing a clumsy hand over Alice's hair, not having the heart to try and tell her that the lizard is, well. It's not looking good for any of them right now. "It's okay. Alice, it's okay."

Alice sobs.

Luce hears shattering glass. Watches the inevitable crash with some form of detached acceptance. The foyer collapses. How did they get here so quickly? Alice sounds so far away when she screams, again, before everything is—all at once—quiet.

⁂

She wakes up alone in the middle of the living room.

There's still smoke lingering in the air, the bookshelf charred, but the world around her is washed out, not quite there. Luce pushes herself upright, blinks down at her hands, unsure if she's still real.

She looks up.

Scratch that—not alone, never alone.

Harley Tam sits perched on the edge of the pool table, legs dangling. She wears ashes like eyeshadow. Her socks are smudgy, and Luce realizes with a start that she looks like the way she did in that classroom, hair half-charred, uniform in tatters, flames still casually licking up one arm where the dragon would be, breathing fire in its place. She sucks in her cheeks, leans back.

"You're lucky the blue moon makes it easier to fuck with reality," Harley comments lightly.

"What the fuck is happening?"

Harley hums. "Didn't you hear what I said? We're in limbo."

"Am I dead?"

"No," Harley says, snorting. "But, man, you really fucked up this time, didn't you?"

Luce grits her teeth. "Shut up."

"Did anyone know?" Harley asks like she's genuinely curious. "Your little arson problem, that is."

"It's never on *purpose*."

"Does that really make a difference?"

"Yes," Luce bites out before she presses her lips tighter together, quiet in her lack of self-defense. Luce wants to fall to her knees. Beg forgiveness at Harley's feet. Harley, who is looking down at her with something akin to pity in her gaze.

"When I was five, I nearly killed my younger brother," Harley says. "He pissed me off somehow, stole one of my snacks or something. I grabbed his arm, and when I let go, it was frozen. Completely. Like he'd spent the night outside in the snow, but only his arm. It took him years to get the feeling back properly. He still drops shit sometimes, fucked-up nerve endings."

Her voice is so flat, icy. In this lighting—the party still going around them without any of the people—she tilts her head, and Luce sees antlers. Sees the shimmering mass of scales, except she's not wearing makeup, so Luce thinks that if she reached out, she could touch them and feel the ridges.

"What are you saying?" Luce asks.

"When I was fourteen I made our entire backyard freeze over. My dad broke his hip because he stepped out without realizing he was right on black ice. Do you remember that snow storm in the middle of July last semester?"

Luce nods, hesitant. She knows where this is going, but she doesn't want to hear it.

Harley's smile this time is a death mask, a predator on the prowl. There's something inextricably mournful in her eyes. "I got a bad mark on my AP Bio final," she says dryly. "You beat me by a solid ten percent. It was kind of a shitty day."

"None of this makes any sense," Luce says desperately.

"Oh, shut up, Lucy," Harley says. "You know exactly what I'm talking about. Because you and I are the same, aren't we?"

"Fine," Luce spits out, ignoring the widening smile on Harley's face at her concession, "but what does that have to do with anything? What the fuck does any of this *mean*?"

"Have you ever heard of the story of Nezha and the Dragon King?"

Luce startles. "What?"

Harley scoffs. "C'mon, don't tell me you didn't pay attention in Chinese school."

"No," Luce says, "I know what that is. Just—" She stutters and has to clamp her hands into fists again to stop the frustrated confusion from bubbling into anger. Luce has to be so good about her temper. It makes her so tired most of the time. "What does that have to do with anything?"

"Tell me the story," Harley says.

"Um," says Luce. "I don't really remember; it's been a long time—"

"Nezha is born of chaos and fire," Harley says. She nods her head toward Luce, like that means anything. "A boy—but that's malleable, of course—who brings omens to his parents. He kills the Dragon King's son"—she presses a hand to her own breast, like *that* means anything—"either in combat or unfairly, and the Dragon King seeks revenge—insists that Nezha repent." Harley reaches back, grabs solidly onto the pool cue, flips it in one hand easily. "With his own life. On his father's sword."

Luce's mouth is dry. "You're crazy."

Harley's mouth is full of teeth. "Lucy," she says flat and sweet, "I'm dead. You killed me."

It hits like a punch in the gut.

Because, of course, something in Luce has always known, this entire time.

The image again, flashing in her mind: Harley lost to the flames, Harley's mouth open in a terrible scream. Maybe no one else but her could see the truth, but this is what Harley has been since she came out of the fire. When Harley moves, it's with the fluidity of something other than human. She surges forward in a rush, her body collapsing and coalescing, and in that moment, Luce can see what she is: a ghost, a dead-eyed thing, an ancient thing. She was right, earlier—dragon girl, bursting at the seams of her humanity.

She veers close to Luce, nose to nose. Unchanged from where Luce left her in the classroom, dead. "Touch me, Luce," she murmurs, baring her throat.

Luce is easy. She knows this. She's angry enough to comply, one hand coming up to grasp Harley's neck. Fingers on skin. Harley isn't cold, but her skin is ashen, unresponsive. No pulse. Luce wants to shove her back, but a slithering terror has sunk into her veins, and she can't move.

"See?" Harley says, her voice still sugary, cloying. She's beautiful. "It's okay, Lucy," she breathes, "I don't blame you. That's the truth, since it's been eating you up alive, I can tell. You woke me up. I realized what it was all about when I died. I *remembered.*

We're the story, reborn. That's why you're fire and I'm ice. We were always meant to find each other like this. You were always meant to kill me."

Saliva gathers in Luce's mouth. "Stop that," she says weakly. "No." She's not stupid. She knows what Harley means.

Harley nods her head, feverishly eager. She snaps the pool cue in two with a clawed hand, presents it to Luce with a flourish. "There is no Dragon King," she says slyly, lips lifting in a smirk. "Just me. And I want my revenge."

"You think you can sweet-talk me into believing your insane theory?" Luce's eyes skitter off the sharp end of the pool cue, alluringly jagged.

"Don't you want to remember too?"

Luce's body is too tight to hold her. She's felt full to bursting her whole life, not quite right. Maybe this is why the fire comes so easily. She's scared, but Harley's taunt hooks into something deep inside her, some yearning that she never had a name for.

Maybe Harley can sense this. She puts her fingers on Luce's jaw, tugs her face down gently. "I know you, Lucy," she murmurs. "You're so angry all the time. That's why we used to hate each other, right? You wanted everything I had, and you hated it."

"I hate you," Luce tries.

"No," Harley says, "you need me."

This time, Harley is the one who kisses her. This time, the kiss tastes like ash instead of blood. Harley's nails dig into Luce's jaw, and the touch is pain and also freedom. Something crumples inside of Luce. The heat flickers underneath her skin, but Harley's mouth is cool, a balm. Kissing her is like drinking ice water, slithering down her throat. It's like relief. It's like Harley is the answer to the question she's been asking her entire life.

When Harley presses the solid column of the broken cue to her palm, Luce takes it.

Holds it to her throat.

Closes her eyes.

⁂

"Luce! Luce! Hello? Are you coming to the party tonight?"

Luce gasps, her hand flying to her neck. Solid, intact. No blood in her throat. Lungs expanding easy.

"Hey," Alice says hesitantly, one hand held out, "are you okay?"

She looks around, eyes wild. Students are milling around in the hallway. Alice has her messenger bag slung over one shoulder, looking at Luce with barely concealed concern. She glances around the hall. It's daytime. It's daytime, and it's Halloween, and Alice is asking her to come to the party.

"Yeah," she says hesitantly, "of course." Then, wildly, "Hey, does Julia still have that lizard?"

Alice gives her a weird look. "Yeah? He's camped out in her room. I need to find somewhere better to put him because she's making me look after him while she's away, but honestly, he gives me the creeps, so."

"Can I see? Later tonight?"

"So long as you come to my party," Alice says, half laughing, nudging Luce's shoulder.

It's all the same.

No fire, no smoke. Alice alive and well.

But.

Across the hall, there she is. Harley, with her hair silvered, her tattoo a flickering, sinister reminder running down her arm. She meets Luce's eyes. No contacts, but the blue lingers. Something hot and fierce jumps in Luce's throat, and Luce knows she's different now. She remembers. They're standing in the school hallway, but they're also standing across from each other over an ancient river. Luce remembers the feeling of armor on her shoulders, the bow and arrow supple in her hands. The dragon, across from her—silvery scales like Harley's hair, laced in electric blue. Millennia of cycles, finding each other and fighting each other all over again. She feels the weight of something ancient pressed to her pulse. The fire feels like hers now. The look in Harley's eyes more of a challenge than ever.

Harley smiles. *See you there, Lucy,* she mouths.

ANNA

Shelly Page

Tonight happens once in a blue moon. Literally. The second full moon this month peeks out from puffy gray clouds, its frame milky white and promising. The muggy swamp heat and the likelihood of rain haven't kept many people home. Danger flickers in the air like fireflies. Devils, zombies, and vampires stalk the streets of New Orleans, emitting high-pitched squeals that raise the hairs on the back of my neck.

"You're coming to Sara's party tonight, right?" The tinny sound of my girlfriend's voice through the phone draws my gaze from the window and back to the scarcely furnished living room where I sit alone on a couch just shy of uncomfortable.

"Oh. I, uh, took a last-minute babysitting job."

Dani releases a stilted puff of air at my response. I can practically see the downward tug of her lips, though she's across town getting ready.

I continue quickly. "The family's paying me double what I'd usually charge for two kids on account of it being Halloween. I don't even have to take them trick-or-treating since one kid is sick. I can turn the lights off and let them eat from the candy bowl while they watch movies until bedtime. It's easy money. I couldn't say no."

"I mean . . . you *could* have." Dani drags out the words, sporting her frustration. "I've been talking about this party for weeks. I thought we'd spend tonight dancing with our friends, drinking jungle juice, and making out, but you're cuddled up with some snotty-nosed kids."

"It's a full moon tonight. If I'm staying in anyway, I might as well make some money." My words knock clumsily against each other, none of them actually getting to the heart of the matter.

"Really, Elise? The full moon excuse *again*?"

"It isn't an excuse. The Rougarou—"

"Is just a story! There's no such thing as werewolves or any of that supernatural stuff your grandma told you about."

Maw grew up south of here in Terrebonne Parish, where stories like Le Feu Follet and the Rougarou are as well known as Disney princesses. When I was three, my parents dropped me off at her house and never returned. Every night for years she'd tell me Cajun folktales to chase away my loneliness and prepare me for nights like this one.

I rub at the pressure building behind my eyes. "Well, I believe in those stories. Not everything is black and white."

Dani and I have different understandings of danger. She doesn't believe in ghosts, but she does believe in assholes. She keeps an old softball bat in the trunk of her car and pepper spray on a key chain. I keep a dime fastened around my neck to ward off evil.

"This isn't about the stories. You always have a reason why you can't hang out with me," she complains.

My grip tightens on my phone. "That's not true."

"Then why have we hardly seen each other this month?" She says it like a challenge, and I picture her lithe arms crossed, full mouth pinched, and shapely brows knitted together. It's an expression that used to annoy me when we first met, but thinking about it now softens me.

I sink further into the couch. "We just went pumpkin-picking."

"That was three weeks ago," she replies. "And only after you canceled on going to the haunted house because there was a full moon—"

"There's been two this month," I remind her. "It's not the rarity you'd think, but that the second one falls on Halloween *is* rare. I don't know, it feels like a bad omen."

"So what about last weekend when you said no to the screening of *Scream*?"

"It was in a *cemetery*."

"And now you're babysitting instead of going to Sara's party with me," she finishes with a huff.

I pluck lint off my fuzzy socks, my fingers stiff with nerves. "Is the party really that important to you?"

Dani exhales slowly. "This isn't about the party. It's about you finding every reason to avoid me. It's you not trusting me enough to tell me what's going on. . . . Did I do something wrong?"

I curl an arm around my waist to stop the cold feeling blooming there. It doesn't help. "No. You're perfect," I reply honestly. "Nothing's going on. I just don't like Halloween."

The silence rings in my ears like tinnitus after a concert. Dani doesn't believe me, and I don't blame her. I have been distant lately.

The quiet on the phone makes me conscious of how quiet it is in the house, which is not good where ten-year-old twins are concerned.

"I've gotta go, but I promise to call you later, okay?" I don't want to end our conversation on a bad note, but I need to check on the kids.

"Fine," she replies coolly.

Guilt is a sinking stone in my belly, and I feel heavy as I hang up and crawl off the couch. I listen for laughter, for crying, or for something breaking as I walk around the unfamiliar house.

"Girls?"

Upstairs, I poke my head into their room. It looks like a bag of purple dye exploded. Toys and clothes are strewn everywhere, but there's no sign of the twins. In fact, every room on the second floor is empty.

"Girls? If you're hiding, come out. We can watch *Coco*, and I'll make pop—"

A muffled scream sends my heart slamming into my ribs. I jerk my head toward the sound, my eyes landing on a hatch pulled flush against the ceiling. The woven cord sways, like it's been used recently, and a yellow plastic stool sits just below it. I jump for the cord, and the door clicks opens. With it, a set of stairs unfold. Another scream sounds, this one much clearer.

"Kayla? Emma?" My voice quakes as I yell into the dark.

"Elise?"

My shoulders sag at the soft sound of my name. As fast as I can, I clamber up the stairs, my socks slipping on the metal rungs. Breathless, I hoist myself over the edge and sprawl out on my stomach. I nudge a clump of curls out of my face, push my wire-framed glasses up on my nose, then get a good look around.

The attic is a dimly lit hellhole.

Boxes line the sloping unfinished walls. Dust clings to the exposed ceiling beams, the wooden floorboards, and just about every visible surface. Black moths flutter near the naked light bulbs, hungry for their warmth. Flies collect along the baseboards and listlessly flap their broken wings. The air is thick enough to see and cloying with abandonment.

And yet . . . the room doesn't look like any attic I've ever seen. It's more of a child's playroom.

Near me sits a dilapidated dollhouse next to a rocking horse with cobwebbed holes for eyes. I spot a faded rubber ball, a knitted blanket with the name ANNA in white letters, three creepy-looking dolls, and a flaking chessboard.

Sitting on an ornate rug in the center of it all are two pigtailed girls in pumpkin-colored pajamas, their brown skin ashen in the jaundiced light as they survey a decrepit Ouija board. Even from where I'm still sprawled, I can tell it's not the kind you buy at Party City. It's intricately crafted. The wood is stained umber. Each corner has a black, hand-painted moon and skull. The planchette, a smooth triangle with a dingy glass eye in the center, rests on the word *No.*

On instinct, I touch the dime around my neck. My voice is higher than usual when I ask, "What are you doing?"

Emma, wide-eyed and caught, yells, "Kayla found it! She said we should play a game." She sniffles loudly, and it's then that I notice she looks clammy. I wonder if I should take her temperature.

Her parents said she's been sick on and off since they moved in a month ago. Allergies or something.

Kayla sticks a hand on her hip and flashes Emma a look that could scare a demon. "*You* found instructions online."

"So? *You* summoned the ghost."

Ghost? Nope. No way. "Enough," I say before a fight starts. "Why are y'all even up here?"

Kayla shrugs. "We were curious."

"Dad told us not to go into the attic. We wanted to see why," Emma adds.

Of course they did. I glance around again. Nothing seems dangerous, just . . . weird. "Did he say why you weren't allowed up here?"

"No," Kayla says as she shuffles around me and toward the hatch.

"And the Ouija board?" I ask.

She points at a loose floorboard next to the dusty rocking horse with no eyes. "Found it hidden in there."

Okay, kids these days have no fear. Lucky for us, I was raised on a healthy dose of it. "All right, go downstairs and stay out of here, or I'll tell your parents you tried to hold a séance on Halloween."

Kayla climbs over the edge of the hatch and scrambles down the ladder. She lands on the soft carpet with a thud. "It's just a game!"

"Ouija boards aren't *games*," I say as I help Emma down. "Haven't you seen any scary movies?"

"Not really," Emma replies as she moves to stand next to her sister. "We're ten."

I drop into the hallway, then dust off my T-shirt and loose-fitting jeans. I close the hatch firmly behind me and check it twice. But what Emma said about summoning a ghost keeps circling my brain. I need to know. "Did it work? The Ouija board . . ."

The girls stare at each other, their round eyes saying more than words could. Something made them scream.

Emma sniffs. "The piece started to move."

"But only after we asked a bunch of questions," Kayla says.

I think of the planchette sitting on the word *No*. "What question made it move?"

Emma looks at Kayla before responding. "I asked if it was a good spirit."

I laugh, more out of shock than amusement, but neither girl smiles. Emma glares at the ceiling before hurrying downstairs. Her sister is hot on her heels.

Goose bumps sprout along my arms as I linger, staring at the attic door. I touch the dime around my neck again before tearing my gaze away and joining the twins.

⁂

I am not crying. I'm not. There's just something in my eye, and it happens to be at the moment where Coco remembers her papa. I don't know why my glasses are fogging up.

"What's wrong with your face?" Kayla asks, scrunching her own like I've just admitted I hate chocolate.

"Nothing! What's wrong with yours?" Kayla rolls her eyes at my terrible comeback. "I'm gonna make another bag of popcorn," I announce, before she can pick on me some more or the movie gets sadder.

I've turned the lights off to keep trick-or-treaters at bay, so I use the faint glow of the TV and the three autumn-scented candles I lit to make my way from the couch to the kitchen. So far, only two kids didn't get the memo, banging their greedy hands on the door like we owed them money.

I flip on the light switch, preparing to find the popcorn box on the table where I left it, but what I find sends me reeling back so hard, I smash my elbow against the wall behind me. My hands tremble as I rub uselessly at the pain.

Not popcorn, but a hand-painted Ouija board sits in the center of the table, the planchette still hovering on the word *No.*

My heart strains against my rib cage and my breath wheezes out in bursts. I can almost hear a whispered, *No. I'm not a good spirit.* I can almost feel the tickle of breath against the shell of my ear. Can almost smell something damp and rotten like grave dirt seeping through the vents.

I run back to the living room with as much grace as a newborn deer and plant my feet in front of the TV. I have to fold my arms to stop their shaking.

"Hey!" Kayla whines. She and her sister are right where I left them on the couch.

"Who went back into the attic? Was it you, Kayla?" I flash her a no-nonsense glare I learned from Maw.

"What? No! I've been watching the movie with you and Emma!"

Emma tilts her head, studying me. "We haven't left the couch."

I pinch the bridge of my nose. Right. Yeah. We've been watching *Coco.* So who moved the Ouija board?

"What's wrong?" Kayla asks, her voice absent of its usual haughtiness.

My tongue is thick in my mouth. "Nothing. I'll be back."

I leave the girls in the living room, their eyes burning holes into my back, and return to the kitchen. The Ouija board is gone. A Pop Secret box sits in its place, perfectly positioned in the center of the table.

My stomach knots. I'm seeing things. I have to be. My nerves about the blue moon are making my mind play tricks on me.

Ignoring the way my hands quiver, I snatch a bag of popcorn out of the box and stick it in the microwave. I tap my foot in time with the music from the movie and try to keep calm. My thoughts merry-go-round between the full moon, the Ouija board, and Dani.

"Is the popcorn ready?"

I spin around. Kayla leans against the doorframe with her arms crossed. Her expression is somewhere between concerned and amused. Emma stands placidly behind her.

I look back at the microwave and blink hard. The popcorn's finished, but I didn't even hear it pop, let alone the microwave beep. I shake my head, trying to clear away my confusion and loosen my overcrowded thoughts.

"The movie's over," Emma says. She pulls a tissue out of her pocket and blows her nose. "Can we watch something else?"

"Um. Yeah. Whatever you want." My voice is far away and strange, like a gurgle underwater. I feel as unmoored as I sound.

One bag of buttery popcorn later, I'm squished between the girls and a scratchy pillow watching *Monster House*. I try to pay attention, but I keep thinking about the Ouija board and what it could mean. It gnaws at my focus like a hungry dog until eventually, I give up all pretense of watching the film.

"Your family's new to the neighborhood, right?" I manage to

keep the edge out of my voice. "Do you know anything about the house?" I look around, searching for cracks in its facade. Strangeness tends to leave a calling card. I don't find anything.

Emma shakes her head. "Dad said it was a steal."

"That means it was cheap," Kayla clarifies.

"I know what it means," I tell her.

All the houses in this part of town are old but freshly renovated. Ancient bones wearing new clothes. I wouldn't be surprised if one was haunted. Why else would a nice house like this be priced cheaply? Thinking back on it, the house was vacant for a long time before the girls moved in. I don't live in this neighborhood, but I do pass by to babysit, and I haven't noticed the house occupied until now.

I start to ask if they've noticed anything weird about the place, but the question is swallowed by the stretched groan of a floorboard above us. We whip our heads toward the sound.

"What was that?" Emma asks, inching closer to me on the couch.

I turn the TV volume down and listen.

Thump. Thump. Thump.

The noise overhead travels from one spot to the next. Rhythmic and even. Like a pulse.

"Someone's upstairs," Kayla whispers. All her vowels are soft and dragging. She sounds like the scared kid she is, and that startles me almost as much as the noise.

My legs shake when I stand. Emma grabs on to my wrist, her fingers squeezing frantically. Her pupils are so dilated that her eyes are nearly black.

"It's just the wind," I say. "You probably left a window open. I'll check. Stay here."

I want to believe what I'm saying but there's always a chance it wasn't the wind. Maw taught me not to assume anything.

I inhale deeply, let the air bloat my lungs and steel my nerves. My feet are leaden as I climb the stairs, socks scraping against the shaggy carpet. The hallway is a dark tunnel into nothing as I reach for the light switch and flick. A stale glow illuminates the empty hallway. I heave a sigh of relief. I need to relax. Dani will laugh when I tell her what's been going on tonight. She'll blame it on movies, overactive imaginations, and this old, dark house.

"Elise?" one of the girls calls from downstairs.

"Everything's fine! There's nothing to be afraid—"

With a crack, the light burns out, plunging the hallway into a darkness so consuming, it feels like being buried alive. My fingers feel like they're made of cotton as I fumble for my phone. When I find it, I hold the screen until the flashlight function blinks to life, then wield it like a weapon aimed directly into the dark.

There, hovering in midair like black fog, is the ghostly outline of a girl.

I run so fast, I trip down the stairs and nearly land on my ankle. I launch into the living room, clutching my chest. Hands pinch and pull at my arms. I scream. Two matching faces peer up at me, their features yawned wide with fear.

Just the girls.

"What happened?" Emma asks. Her voice is barely above a whisper.

"I saw a ghost," I reply just as quietly.

I've never seen one before, and for that I'm thankful. She was something straight out of Maw's stories. Only worse. A girl in an old-fashioned nightdress, a seaweed mass of long black hair and darkness where a face should be. A chill settled in my bones just looking at her, and I knew then what she'd said was true.

She is not a good spirit.

I toss my shoulders back and clear my throat. "We need to leave." I've seen enough horror movies to know that staying in the house when something weird is going on only ends with everyone dead, especially for three Black girls like us. No one's dying on my watch. "Get your coats and shoes on. We're going trick-or-treating after all."

To their credit, the twins move quickly, and we're all buttoned up and ready to go not three minutes later. I'll text their parents to explain once we're outside. Once we're safe.

"But we're not wearing costumes," Emma complains as I usher her and Kayla toward the door.

"That's okay. I'm not wearing one either. We can still trick-or-treat. We just need to get out of here." I unlock the door and pull. It doesn't budge.

Strange.

I try again, harder this time, so hard the frame rattles, but the door never moves. It's stuck like the wood is swollen.

I inhale through my teeth. Fine. There are other exits, like the big bay window near the couch. I tear open the curtains and pause. My reflection is wild, curly black hair springing around a flattened brow and scrunched nose. My glasses are askew. My lips are chapped. I'm terrified, and I look it.

I try the window, pulling until my arms strain. It doesn't give an inch. Stuck, same as the door.

Outside, a group of teens wearing matching angel costumes stand on the sidewalk. I bang my hand against the glass so hard, it hurts. They don't turn their heads. Neither do the dads pushing a baby stroller laced with fake cobwebs behind them. The house sits too far back from the sidewalk, and the night is too loud and thrilling for anyone to notice me.

"What's happening? Why aren't we leaving?" Emma has come to stand behind me, sounding and looking a lot calmer than she should.

"Stay here."

I try the back door and the kitchen window. Both sealed. In a moment of desperation, I lunge for the kitchen stool and hurl it at the window. It bounces off the glass like a rubber ball. The frame doesn't even shake.

No. No. *No.*

I suck in empty breaths that do nothing to slow my climbing heart rate. I can't say the words that are spinning around my head, egging on the fear I'm trying to keep at bay. I can't say them, but I hear them all the same.

We're trapped.

Panic drags its slimy fingers across my skin until I'm so keyed up, I might combust. I can't even attempt to formulate a plan.

Recently, when I get like this, only one person has been able to help me.

Dani answers on the third ring, and thank god even ghosts have limits to their power. It's so loud on the other end of the phone. Lil Nas X blasts through the speakers, and laughter echoes between the beat. "Hello?" Dani yells.

"Dani! Hey! I, uh—I know you're at the party and you're probably still mad at me about earlier, but I really needed to hear your voice." I tap my blunt nails against my phone and start to pace.

"What's going on?" Her voice is strained. The echo of her earlier question makes all the reasons I've pushed her away feel immaterial now.

"I'm scared. *So* scared."

She inhales soundly. A door opens and closes, and the background noise dims to a distant hum. "Of what?" she asks carefully.

"Of us. Of my feelings for you. Of the ghost tormenting me and the kids."

"Wait, what—"

"I love you," I blurt out. And there it is. The true reason I've been pulling away. Those three words have been the elephant in the room for months. Even though I've felt their truth, I haven't gathered the courage to tell Dani until now. What if she doesn't feel the same way? Worse, what if she does but ends up leaving me anyway, same as my parents?

Dani doesn't respond right away, and I worry I was right to be afraid. I *am* alone in this feeling. But then she makes a soft sound in the back of her throat and replies, "I love you too."

My chest expands until I think it might burst. "You do?"

"Yeah. A lot. I wasn't sure if you did. You never talk about your feelings," she says.

"Oh." I wish I could see her. Tuck one of her purple braids behind her ear and kiss her. "That stops now. I promise."

"Good. Now, what's this about a ghost?" she asks, steering me back on track.

I glance over my shoulder to see the girls watching me closely. "A ghost has me and the twins trapped inside the house." I try the door once more, just in case, but it doesn't budge.

A second of silence passes before Dani says, "A *ghost*? You know what, it doesn't matter. I'm coming over. What's the address?"

"No!" I blurt out. It isn't safe for her here, and four trapped girls is worse than three. "It's okay. I'll figure this out. Thanks for calming me down." Just talking to her has my panic dissipating and my head clearing.

"Sure, but if something's going on, you should call the police and the kids' parents," Dani says.

"I will. I'll call them now."

"Good. Call me after."

"Okay."

When we hang up, I feel lighter than I have in months. I spin around, ready to keep the kids close while I call the police, but I'm alone.

A quick glance at the ceiling, then I'm darting upstairs, taking the steps two at a time. The yellow stool sits in the middle of the hallway, and I snap my attention to the attic hatch. The cord swings and swings.

At once, all the doors fly open, then slam shut. The hallway light bulb shatters, and glass rains down on my head. I bite back a scream.

The ghost is trying to scare me, or stall me, or both. I won't be stopped, even if my legs have turned into jelly. Pieces of glass crack beneath my shoes as I stumble forward. I grab the swinging cord and sink to my knees, letting my body weight release the stairs.

It's a struggle to pull myself into the attic with all the adrenaline rattling my bones, but I make it. The hatch slams closed after me. I want to sag against the cold dusty floor and catch my breath, but my muscles are too taut. My eyes strain, trying their hardest to adjust to the dark.

The ghost is here. She has to be. The twins too. And to think I had a plan. To think we'd be safe. I could laugh.

I push myself to my feet, grasping for courage I don't have. Finally, the room comes into focus. A slice of moonlight from the dingy skylight is enough to make out the twins and another, taller figure. The summoned spirit.

"Let them go!" I yell.

The ghost glides forward. She isn't as blank-faced as I'd first believed. She has bottomless holes for eyes and a gap for a mouth, like a spill of ink across paper. Light slithers through her pores, paling her skin until it's blue and translucent. Piercing collarbones frame a gold necklace engraved with the letter A. I wonder if the blanket with the name *Anna* belonged to her.

The girl hovers in front of me like a dark cloud. She slants her head and stretches her mouth until it's a chasm swallowing half her face. I would scream if I could, but my throat is closed.

"Leave her alone!" Kayla darts in front of me, squaring her

shoulders and puffing out her chest. She balls her hands into tiny fists. She's so small. How does she fit all that fight inside of her?

Seeing her next to me fuels me into action. I yank her to my side and fashion my body into a shield. "Emma, come over here. It's okay." I outstretch my hand, but she doesn't move. "Emma, come on!"

The ghost girl—Anna, maybe—makes a bloodcurdling sound. A devil's laugh.

"What do you want?" There is venom in my voice now and a slow-building fire in my veins.

When the ghost speaks for the first time, she sounds disjointed and airy, like a deflating balloon on a hot summer day. "To be free." She drops her gaze to the Ouija board still sitting on the ornate rug in the center of the room. "Another must take my place."

Emma. My realization is the opening Kayla uses to slip through my fingers. She tugs on her sister's arm, yelling for her to run, but Emma is in a trance. She doesn't react. Doesn't seem to hear her at all.

It's with startling clarity that I understand this ghost isn't going to let us go. Not until she gets what she wants. As a babysitter, it's my job to keep the kids safe. I can't let her have Emma.

I calculate the distance between Emma and the ghost and try to estimate how fast I can reach her. If I can scoop her into my arms, maybe we can make a run for it.

I barely manage two steps before my body jerks to a stop. An invisible hand latches on to my throat and squeezes. Anna has her arm outstretched, fingers unnaturally long and pale. She curls them, and I wheeze.

I raise my hands, scrambling for purchase on something that's not there. The world grows fuzzy around the edges. I have only an ounce of air left in my lungs, but it's enough.

"You need one of us, right? Let the girls go . . . you can have me."

Kayla whimpers. Anna inclines her head again, and I get lost in those ink splatters she has for eyes.

She glides forward until she's inches from my face. A blast of cold air washes over me. Then, a fingernail drags down my cheek. The attic flashes a blinding white before darkness falls. For a moment, I wonder if I'm dead. If the ghost has finally swallowed me whole.

Then muted light swells around me. The world has slipped into grayscale. The twins are gone. The dust is gone. I'm alone until the attic door opens. A man with a stern face and dark eyes throws a slim girl into the room and slams the hatch closed after her. She bangs on the door, yells and cries, but the man never returns.

I call out to her several times, but she doesn't respond. She doesn't seem to notice me at all. When she finally turns around, my breath catches. It's her. Anna. I recognize the bleached white nightgown and the dark hair hanging in waves to her waist. Except now she has a face. She's young despite her lonely eyes, delicate cheeks, and chapped lips. No light slips through her skin. She's as solid as the floor beneath me, and I realize that wherever or *whenever* we are, she's still alive.

Time passes slowly. Sunlight drags across the floor, fades into moonlight, then back again. All the while, Anna remains. Alone.

She holds her stomach and paces, her bare feet heavy on the

floorboards. *Thump. Thump. Thump.* My skin pricks with goose bumps at the familiar sound.

Once she's practically worn a path in the floor, she kneels. She shoves one of the boards in front of her and the end pops up, revealing the perfect hiding place. The Ouija board is still old, but not decrepit like it is now, when she brings it out. She runs a tentative hand along the wooden frame before resting it on the planchette.

"Can you hear me?" she whispers.

Nothing happens at first, and the quiet is suffocating. Then the planchette moves, jerking across the board in a jagged line.

"Good," she replies. "I thought about your offer, and I'm ready now." She hangs her head. "He isn't coming back. Not this time. I'm ready for you to help me."

I'm stone-still, desperate not to miss anything.

The board jolts as another girl—a *ghost*—wearing an even older-looking dress than Anna's materializes right out of the wood. Her skin is thin and luminous, like she's swallowed the moon. She holds out her hand and a crooked smile stretches across her black lips. "Come with me. You don't have to be alone or afraid anymore. No one will hurt you again."

Anna nods, hope brightening the dark corners of her face. I know that feeling. I know the bone-deep loneliness that comes with being abandoned and the fear that it'll keep happening no matter what you do. Maw did her best to dampen it with folktales, but Anna's alone.

As soon as she touches the outstretched hand, there's a violent flash, and I watch in horror as a ball of light slips out of Anna's body and sinks into the Ouija board. Then a dim swirling mass fills the husk of the girl left behind.

Darkness rises up to meet me as the memory ends. The world returns in splotches of browns and blues. Someone's shaking me.

"Elise, wake up!"

That voice. I know it. "Dani?" I open my eyes just in time to see her tilt her head back and catch unshed tears. She's dressed like Max Chapman in *A League of Their Own*, her braids hidden beneath a blue baseball cap and her slight frame swimming in a gray jersey. I must look a mess in comparison, but I stopped being embarrassed around her months ago. "What are you doing here?" I ask hoarsely.

"You never called me back! I got worried!" She levels her gaze. Tension hides in the tight slope of her shoulders. "The front door was unlocked. And I heard screaming coming from upstairs. I found you and the twins up here. And a . . ." Her words fade out as she shakes her head.

I know what she saw. I look around, but Anna's gone. The Ouija board is smashed to pieces near my feet, a familiar softball bat lying next to it. The ghost's hold over us is gone.

I sit up, my head spinning in more ways than one. "You came." Dani doesn't believe in the supernatural, but she does believe in me, and that's all I ever needed.

Her hands squeeze my shoulders as those tears she's been trying to hold back finally fall. "Of course I did. You needed me."

"How'd you find me?"

"You said I was paranoid for adding you to Find My Friends,

but it saved your life. That and my bat." She wipes her eyes. "What happened?"

"The ghost, Anna, showed me how she was mistreated. How a man left her up here, probably many times before, with only a ghost for company. She was withering away. And the ghost promised Anna that she didn't have to be alone anymore . . . but she lied."

All Anna wanted was for the pain to end. Instead, she was manipulated into trading one prison for another. Anna was just as lonely in death as she was in life, and she was going to subject me to the same fate just to be free.

Dani frowns. "Well, you were unconscious when I found you. Scared me half to death."

"Elise saved us," Kayla says. She's sitting across from me, and when our gazes meet, she smiles shyly. "For the record, you're the best babysitter we've ever had. Are we the best kids you've babysat?"

My mouth drops open. "Seriously? You unleashed a spirit trapped inside a Ouija board! I nearly died! No offense, but I'm never babysitting you or anyone else again."

Kayla rolls her eyes, and Dani drops her head onto my shoulder. I let the weight of it ground me. She knows how much I care about her, and I know she cares about me. She risked her life coming to my rescue like a knight with a Louisville Slugger instead of a sword.

Emma shifts closer to me. "Thank you," she whispers.

I turn so I can look at her properly. When I do, my entire body locks up like I'm back in Anna's grasp.

Emma looks almost the same: frizzy pigtails and round cheeks. But her skin is no longer clammy with sickness, and her eyes are all wrong—two bottomless holes swallowing all the light. And when she smiles, her mouth is stretched and crooked and dark.

A spill of black ink on paper.

HEY THERE, DEMONS

Tara Sim

There were three things Noah Kohli hated more than anything:

1. *That his family had to move to a strange town for his junior year of high school, separating him from the few friends he'd made back home;*
2. *That he was frequently asked to babysit his little sister, who wasn't even his* full *sister but instead the product of his dad's second marriage; and*
3. *The poltergeist in their new house.*

It had taken him a long time to even *think* the word *poltergeist*, but after sleepless nights of researching on his laptop under the covers, he couldn't think of what else could be haunting his family. It was bad enough they'd had to move here for Rebecca's new job; what made it even worse were the slamming doors, things disappearing and ending up in weird spots, and ominous knocking in the middle of the night.

"It's probably just Nina knocking on the wall between your

rooms," Rebecca had said one morning when Noah had complained about how little sleep he'd gotten. "She's four. She's restless." Nina, face covered in strawberry jam, had made a pointed screech.

"But the knocking isn't even coming from that wall," he'd argued, only to see his dad give him the single raised eyebrow that meant *Quit it.* Noah got along with Rebecca well enough, but he'd be the first to admit their relationship wasn't spectacular. Maybe that was why he tended to look at his baby sister with such dread: a living, shrieking reminder that his mom was ten years gone, and this was the new normal.

Only living here wasn't exactly turning out to be *normal.*

"Recurrent spontaneous psychokinesis," he muttered as he scrolled through an article titled "The 7 Most Prominent Signs of Poltergeist Activity." "What the hell does that even mean?"

The signs matched up, though. When he was in a bad mood, the lights and screens around him flickered. Every so often there was an odd smell, like cigar smoke, although no one in his family smoked. Creepy and unsettling, sure, but not exactly dangerous.

Then they all woke up one morning to Nina screaming and sobbing. When they rushed to her room, Noah had balked at the sight of three small, red lines scratched into her chubby arm.

The situation was getting out of hand, and neither his dad nor Rebecca believed him when he brought up the idea of a poltergeist. In fact, his dad looked at him with concern.

"I know the move must have stressed you out," his dad said. "It's not easy getting used to a new place, a new school. Maybe if you made some friends—"

"This isn't about me making friends," Noah shot back. He had no desire to go through the hassle, and besides, he was terrible at it. It was far easier to hide away in the library or an unused classroom instead of being the loner kid no one liked.

Noah was an excellent hider. Whenever the front doorbell rang, he kept out of sight and pretended no one was home. When the phone rang and it wasn't his dad, he didn't answer. And when the poltergeist attacks increased, he retreated to bed and waited them out. (Sometimes, if their parents were out, he was forced to bring Nina with him and keep her entertained with cartoons on his laptop.) Things were just . . . easier that way.

Still, something had to be done.

"I can't hire a pastor," he mumbled to himself as he looked up *best way to get rid of a poltergeist* on his phone. The window in his room was open, letting in a late October breeze. "Or consult a Bible, since we don't have one. We're not even Christian . . ." Or at least, he didn't think so. Rebecca was firmly agnostic, and his dad's side was Sikh. "Burn sage? How does that even work?"

His thumb hovered over a related article. It was called "How to Use Geomancy and the Earth's Energy to Rid Negative Spirits." Figuring it couldn't hurt, he tapped it and proceeded to chew on his thumbnail while he read about a strange field of paranormal study. It detailed how to rearrange furniture and use meditation to bring harmony to the house, and he was about to chalk it up to nonsense when he caught something toward the end.

"A rare cosmic event may help in these matters," he read out loud, "such as an eclipse. When channeling the earth's good energy through this event, doorways may be opened through dimensions in which the negative energy is cleansed."

He wasn't entirely sure what that meant, but it tickled his memory. Some kids at school had been talking about how this weekend—Halloween weekend—was going to have something called a *blue moon*. It was supposedly super rare, and the fact that it was happening on Halloween made it even more special.

That definitely sounded like a "rare cosmic event."

Behind him, his bedroom window suddenly made a loud *bang*. He jumped and spun around. There was a long crack running through the glass, but nothing had hit it from the outside.

It had happened from the inside.

Shivering, Noah gripped his phone tighter.

Halloween. One way or another, he was going to get rid of this poltergeist for good.

"Are you sure you'll be all right?" his dad said for the tenth time. He and Rebecca were heading to a Halloween party across town that one of Rebecca's coworkers was hosting, and they wanted to go to "make a good impression." His dad had half-heartedly put on a pair of light-up devil horns, which poked up now through the same thick, curly hair Noah had inherited. Rebecca had put in the effort to throw together a witchy outfit.

"We'll be fine," Noah lied while Nina pushed at his legs. When his parents left and he sat on Nina's bed to read her the same story three times—"Again!" she ordered like a little bedridden tyrant—his heart raced at the thought of what he was planning to do tonight.

Finally, *finally*, Nina drifted off to sleep and he crept downstairs. His parents had filled a bowl with candy for trick-or-treaters, which he put outside the front door before turning off all the lights. Then he collected salt from the kitchen, Nina's sidewalk chalk, and some of Rebecca's crystals she insisted would "heal the energy of the house."

"I guess they're going to come in handy after all," Noah muttered as he unlocked the door to the basement and went down the short flight of stairs. There wasn't much down there, just the boxes they hadn't yet managed to unpack. When he flipped the light switch on, it flickered in warning.

Noah swallowed. He was *not* going to hide. He wasn't.

He had to do this, and tonight was his only chance.

Earlier, he had peeked out the window at the blue moon. It was beautiful, full and round and ethereal. Of course all the pictures he tried to take on his phone turned out terrible, even with the hack he'd read about how to take nighttime photos.

Taking deep breaths, he grabbed a purple chalk stick and drew the geometric design he'd taken a screenshot of: a circle with strange symbols that were from alchemy or something like that. Then he made a circle of salt around that and put Rebecca's crystals around the symbols.

"Okay," he breathed, scrubbing his hair out of his face. "This is good. This is fine. This is normal."

An unpleasant odor assaulted him, like the cigar smoke mixed with rotten eggs. He choked and held his hoodie sleeve to his nose and mouth.

"You aren't welcome here," he said as firmly as he could. He knelt at the head of the circle. "So . . . get the hell out."

For a moment, nothing happened. His shoulders hunched in embarrassment. What was he *doing?* Did he really think some creepy magic would take care of the poltergeist? What if it wasn't even a poltergeist at all, and it really *was* in his head—

Noah gasped when the circle began to glow. It was the same color as the moon outside, a pale, eerie blue. Noah scrambled to his feet and backed away, hitting the wall. The lights flickered so hard that they blew, the bulbs shattering and raining glass.

"G-get out!" he yelled through chattering teeth. "Blue moon, or . . . or whatever energy I'm calling on, *please* help me get this thing out of my house!"

The circle glowed brighter. Noah couldn't look at it directly anymore and flung up his arms to shield his eyes, the horrible odor getting stronger.

And then came a low, growling laugh.

Noah's stomach swooped. Could poltergeists laugh?

The light dimmed, and slowly he lowered his arms. He had to blink several times to make out what he was seeing in the dim glow of the circle.

A figure stood within the ring of salt. It was about as tall as him, humanoid, but . . . wrong.

"Interesting," came that low voice again, coming from the shadowy figure. "I definitely sense a presence here. And it is *not* happy with you."

Noah opened his mouth, but all that came out was a faint squeak. He shuffled behind a stack of boxes, peering out while he fumbled with his phone.

"A-are you the one who's been doing all this?" he demanded, thumbing open the flashlight app. When he flashed it onto the figure, he nearly dropped his phone.

The figure narrowed its eyes at the light, hissing slightly. From the shadows it could have been mistaken for a human teenager, and at first glance it fooled him too; it had pale brown skin, dark hair, two arms, two legs, black clothes (or were those shadows?). For a moment Noah wondered if it was wearing devil horns like the pair his dad had worn to the party. Then he spotted the amber hue of its slitted eyes.

This . . . was not a poltergeist.

"Oh no," Noah whimpered. "Oh god, oh no, I . . . I summoned a *demon?*"

The demon grinned, revealing two sharp canines. Fangs.

"You said you needed help." The demon cast a glance up at the broken lights. "Pesky little spirit you have on your hands, huh?"

"I . . . wait. *You* are going to help me get rid of the poltergeist?" Noah demanded. He wondered if this was a fever dream. Maybe the fun-sized candy bar he'd eaten earlier had been spiked.

"Sure. Nothing better to do." The demon frowned at the line of salt. "But this needs to go. Not a fan. Also, I need an offering." It held out a hand, beckoning impatiently like Nina did when she wanted something.

It was said so matter-of-factly that Noah found himself nodding before wildly shaking his head. "Wha—no, no way, I've read the plots of enough horror movies to know that's a terrible idea. You're not taking my soul."

The demon's nose wrinkled. "Why would I want your soul, of all things? Probably tastes like lemons. I *hate* lemons."

This was rapidly making less and less sense. Noah pinched the bridge of his nose and counted to ten. "What sort of offering do you want, then? We've got, uh . . . candy?"

The demon picked up one of Rebecca's crystals between two long talons, turning it this way and that, before letting it drop. "No. I don't know what I want yet. Let me out and I'll see what you've got."

Noah was going to refuse when he realized the horrible odor was gone. Was the poltergeist scared of the demon? He couldn't decide if this was a good thing or a bad thing.

"On one condition," Noah said, utterly serious. "You can't go near my sister. You can't have her, or anything of hers. Deal?"

"Why would I want a *child?*" the demon muttered. "Disgusting. But sure, deal."

This seemed to go against what Noah typically knew about demons via popular media. But then again, what did he have to lose? Other than his soul.

Reluctantly, Noah wiped away some of the salt, breaking the circle. The demon laughed and Noah tensed, afraid he'd made a terrible mistake. But the demon only hopped out of the circle with two arms raised skyward.

"Freedom! Okay, show me something more interesting," the demon demanded. "This place is boring."

Noah's head was spinning. "Can't you take care of the poltergeist first?"

"Nope." The demon wagged a long, taloned finger in his face. "Offering first."

Sighing, Noah ran a hand down his face and trudged to the stairs. "I can't believe I'm doing this."

Upstairs in better lighting, Noah saw the demon's eyes go wide with intrigue. He took a moment to get a better look, too, realizing the demon really *did* look like a teenager, but . . . warped a bit. And . . . oddly handsome?

You cannot *think that a demon is hot,* he scolded himself as the demon began to pick up the various knickknacks Rebecca had placed around the living room. And for that matter . . .

"Hey, uh, what are your pronouns?" Noah asked uncertainly.

"What's that?" the demon asked, scrutinizing a small silver elephant Noah's aunt had gotten him from India.

"Pronouns? You know, like, the words you use to describe yourself? They're usually attached to genders, though not necessarily."

"We don't have those," the demon said idly, throwing the elephant over its shoulder. Noah fumbled to catch it. "What use are genders?"

"No, yeah, I totally get it . . ." Noah placed the elephant back gingerly on the shelf. "But it's, um . . . Wait, I have an idea."

As much as he hated the thought of leaving a hot demon alone in his living room, Noah ran into his dad's office and grabbed some paper and a pen. He ran back out to discover the demon casually pulling the cushions off the couch.

"Stop that!" Noah snapped. "Do you really think you're going to find an offering in the couch?"

The demon shrugged. "I already found some loose change." Then, eyeing the paper that Noah tore into strips, asked, "What are you doing?"

"It's a thing I saw on TikTok where people write down different pronouns or sexualities for their pets," Noah explained as he wrote. "The pets choose a random slip of paper. It's just a joke, but if you don't want to do it . . ."

The demon's strange eyes flashed with curiosity. "I want to do it. Is this how all human genders are assigned?"

"Um . . ." Noah shook his head. "Not really?" He shuffled up the slips of paper on the coffee table, making sure they couldn't be read. "Okay, choose one."

The demon squinted at the slips. One taloned finger hovered over them with far more consideration than Noah had anticipated, until its long nail tapped on one in the middle. Noah flipped it over. It read *he/him*.

"Are you okay with this?" Noah asked, handing it to the demon.

"I don't know what it means," the demon admitted. "What are *your* pronouns?"

Noah stifled the strangled laughter that rose up his throat. He couldn't believe he'd been asked that question by a *demon* when most *humans* didn't even bother.

"These ones," he answered, tapping the same slip.

The demon's eyes sparkled again. "Then I'll use these."

Suddenly, the slip went up in flames. Noah yelped, but the paper quickly turned to harmless ash.

"I just cleaned the table," Noah mourned.

The demon stood up, so fast and fluid that Noah stumbled backward. "I'm bored again," he announced.

"I'm . . . sorry? If you're bored, then can you *please* deal with this polter—"

"I hear something." The demon went to the window and pulled back the drapes. "Out there."

"That's probably trick-or-treaters."

"Children," the demon grumbled with a shiver. "No, it's something else. Something *loud*."

Noah blinked, then remembered what he'd overheard in the library last week: there was a Halloween party being held tonight at Henry McKay's house, which was down the street.

"That's just a stupid party. It—"

"I want to go."

"No, no, *absolutely* not. I don't do parties, especially not with *dem*—hey!"

But the demon was already hurrying out the door. Noah quickly weighed *leave my little sister alone for a few minutes* against *let a demon loose on the town* and, choosing the greater evil, swore and followed after. He made sure to close and lock the front door behind him.

Outside, the blue moon cast a pale light on the humble suburban street. There were far less trick-or-treaters here than there would have been back home; he spotted maybe only three kids with their parents walking down the sidewalks.

"Th-this is *not* a good idea," Noah stammered as he followed behind the demon. "Besides, you look—"

The demon stopped suddenly and spun around. Noah choked on his words.

He had *shifted*. His horns were gone, leaving only tousled brown hair, and his eyes had become normal brown. There were even freckles splattered across his face.

Cute, Noah thought amid a fresh wave of panic, then shoved it far, far down.

"Illusion." The demon pointed at his human face, grinning. Even his teeth were normal. "Pretty good, huh?"

"Y-yeah, it's . . ." *Cute,* he thought again, and flushed painfully. "But you can't just stroll into a random party. You don't even go to the school."

"Eh." The demon waved his hand dismissively and continued on. Noah struggled to keep up. "If you have enough confidence, you can get away with a lot."

Noah wondered if that was true. As someone with approximately negative one hundred charisma points, he didn't quite believe it.

But as they approached Henry McKay's house, music throbbing behind the windows that lit up with changing lights, no one on the lawn stopped them. Some gave Noah second glances, and he tried to hide in his hoodie.

Please forget you saw me, he pleaded.

"Oh, yeah," the demon gushed once they walked through the open door and were flooded on all sides by bass-heavy music. "*This* is the quintessential human experience."

"Is it?" Noah rather preferred watching anime in bed. This was . . . unnecessarily loud. And there were so many *people,* all crushed together with red Solo cups and making out and . . . yeah, he definitely smelled weed. "Okay, you've seen it, time to go."

"But we just got here!" The demon was actually *pouting* at him. His unfortunate hotness made Noah's knees grow weak at his impeccably executed puppy dog eyes and jutting lower lip.

"You . . ." Noah forcefully cleared his throat. "You don't even have a *name.*"

"I have a name," the demon grumbled, kicking away an empty cup.

"What? Then why haven't you told me what it is?"

"Because our kind don't typically hand them out. Unless," the demon said with a spreading grin, "you give me yours first."

"Oh. Uh, sure. I'm Noah."

The demon mouthed the name quietly—or maybe it was drowned by the music. *No-ah.* Noah's neck grew uncomfortably hot.

"I'm Kodiziah," the demon said. Although the way he said it, there was a faint rumbling that seemed to come with the name, as if speaking it out loud could call down lightning and thunder.

"That might be a mouthful for some folks," Noah said. "Can I call you Kody?"

The demon's eyes widened with glee. "Yes! A human nickname!"

Someone passed by and did a double take. "Are you new?" she asked the demon, voice pitched high over the music.

"I am Kody!" he answered loudly, making her jerk back.

"Cool?"

Noah dropped his head into his hands. More than anything he wanted to wait outside while Kody got whatever this was out of his system, but he couldn't in good conscience let a demon run amok at a party.

However, when he lifted his head, Kody was gone. Noah wheezed.

"No, no, no!" He looked around wildly. The demon may not have wanted children as an offering, but did he have the same reservations about high schoolers?

Noah elbowed his way through the throng of dancers. Some

of them swore and some tried to get him to dance, but Noah wriggled away like a fish and called for the demon.

"Kody?" he yelled. The music had gotten even louder, a throbbing pressure between his ears. "Crap . . ."

"Hey, aren't you Noah?"

He spun around. The one who'd spoken was a girl he recognized from school, who shared a couple classes with him and sent him polite smiles whenever they passed in the hallways. Although most of the kids here weren't wearing costumes, she'd done some dramatic, colorful makeup to look zombified. He was pretty sure her name was Natalie.

"H-hi," he stammered. "Yeah? Sorry."

She made a confused face. "Why are you apologizing?"

For the mere awkwardness of my very being, he thought somberly.

"I wasn't invited to this party," he admitted, then winced.

To his surprise, she laughed. "Me either! But my friends convinced me to crash, so here I am." Noah was pretty sure he'd seen Natalie with some of the music department kids at school. "We might leave, though, and go to Max's instead. Have you been? They have the *best* chocolate shakes."

"I haven't, no."

"Wanna come with us?"

Discomfort scorched through his chest. Natalie didn't seem like she was flirting or doing that thing mean people did sometimes where they pretended to be nice only to embarrass you later. She seemed . . . sincere. Friendly.

But Noah had decided he didn't need to make friends. It was easier to hide away, to rely only on himself.

What if his family had to move again?

"I . . ." His mouth was dry. "Maybe some other time? My—my friend, I lost him in the crowd . . ."

Natalie nodded. "Okay, yeah. Just message me on Insta if you want to join."

Noah didn't know how to tell her he didn't have an account. He was about to open his mouth for some excuse when his gaze slid past her, and he choked.

He'd found Kody. The demon had managed to climb onto Henry McKay's dining room table and was dancing. Not the awkward flailing or grinding the others were doing, but honest-to-god *dancing*. As others cheered him on, Kody did a move where he spun on his back that made Noah feel dizzy just watching it.

"I gotta go," he said before running from Natalie and toward the table. "Kody!"

"Dude, this guy's *wild*," said someone beside him. "Is he from the school across town?"

"No idea," said someone else. "I've never seen him before."

Kody looked to be having the time of his life—his eternal, demonic life—and was therefore miffed when Noah reached out to grab his leg.

"Get *down!*" Noah said between gritted teeth.

"No," Kody answered. He broke free and continued to dance, even pulling someone from the crowd up onto the table with him, who shrieked with laughter. Noah shrank back, the others pressing in too close, eyeing him and sneering.

He began to shake. Breaths coming in short, hurried pants, Noah turned and ran.

He found the first closet he could and shoved himself inside.

In the dark, he tried to catch his breath, away from the loud noises and strangers' gazes. His eyes prickled, and even as his swelling panic began to ease, a new one took its place: the poltergeist was still in his home. And his only way of getting it out was currently too drunk on attention to do anything.

After a minute, the door whisked open. Noah started as Kody shoved into the closet with him and closed the door, casting them in darkness.

"Hi," Kody said. "You left."

They were awfully close. Noah sensed the heat coming off of Kody's body and swallowed. The demon wasn't even out of breath. "You were dancing."

"I was. It was fun." He sensed more than saw Kody tilt his head. "You should have danced with me."

Noah shook his head fervently. "No way."

"Why not?"

He thought about dancing with the strangers outside, and his insides squirmed. But when he thought about dancing with Kody, they squirmed in a slightly different way.

"I don't know how," Noah mumbled.

"I can teach you."

Kody grabbed his hips, and Noah gasped. They were *way* too close now, close enough that Kody could surely hear how hard his heart was pounding.

"There's so much human activity here," Kody murmured, almost to himself. "So much noise and movement and heat."

Noah struggled to swallow. "Is that what drew you here?"

"Mm. But mostly, when you're stuck in an interdimensional

rift in the cosmos, you just want to have fun once in a while. You know?"

Noah very much did not know. He shifted in Kody's grasp. "I don't like parties," he admitted.

Kody tilted his head again. It was very close to Noah's. "What do you like?"

"I like . . ." *You,* his stupid brain supplied, but he shoved it down. "Watching stuff on my laptop. Reading. Playing video games." He thought about Natalie's offer, and his voice lowered. "Milkshakes."

"We should do those things, then."

Noah's heart was going to thunder out of his chest. Kody didn't smell like brimstone or sulfur; he smelled like rainfall and summer nights, like sunlight on water. Noah was a little dizzy with it, especially as they swayed closer.

But the pleasantness of the scent reminded him of the awful odors the poltergeist brought with it. Noah started back.

"N-Nina," he whispered. "My sister's back at the house all alone, and the poltergeist . . ."

Kody's eyes flashed amber in the dark closet. "Let's take care of it, then."

They hurried out of the closet, and Noah nearly had a heart attack. Kody's illusion had been shed, revealing his demon self.

"Cool costume!" someone called as they sped away. Noah tripped over a laugh.

Kody grabbed his hand as they ran down the street back to Noah's house, fingers entwined. The moon was so large overhead, bearing down like a watchful eye.

"Looks like my parents aren't home yet," Noah panted when they tumbled through the front door. Other than Kody's previous mess, the house didn't seem touched. "Okay, let's go downstairs and—"

A high-pitched, familiar scream made his blood run cold.

"Nina!" he shouted. He went to open the door to the basement, but it was stuck. He pounded on it. "*Nina!*"

"Stand back," Kody said. Noah did, and Kody's eyes flashed bright yellow before the door was thrown off its hinges.

Rather than bemoaning how he was going to explain *that* to his parents, Noah nearly fell down the stairs in his haste to reach the basement. "Nina?!"

His baby sister was floating above the circle Noah had made earlier that night. She was bawling furiously, her face scrunched up and streaked with tears. When she saw Noah, she reached out her arms to him desperately.

"Noah!" she cried, and it sent pain arcing through his chest.

He rushed forward to grab her but was pushed back by some invisible force around the circle. It was glowing a malevolent red, sending little shocks through the floor as the walls groaned around them.

Noah didn't know what to do. He took a step back, then another, even as his sister sobbed and reached for him.

Are you going to hide like you always do? he thought with disgust.

He curled his hands into fists. *No.* He was going to fix this problem, one way or another.

"What do we do?" he asked Kody, who studied the circle calmly.

"The spirit got in because the salt circle was scored," the demon explained.

"So this—this happened because I let you out?"

"Yes." Kody turned to give him a mischievous smile, and Noah's chest fluttered. "But that was part of the plan."

For a moment Noah despaired that the demon and the poltergeist were working together. Then he realized what Kody meant.

Noah had broken the circle to let something out. And also to let something *in*.

"I'll distract it," Kody said. "You fix the circle."

Noah nodded. The demon snarled, revealing his fangs as his eyes filled with red. The ceiling above him cracked, and a box was flung toward him, but Kody easily dodged and sent a plume of fire toward the circle.

"Don't hurt my sister!" Noah shouted as he fell to his knees and quickly shoved the salt back into place. When he did, the red glow faded back to blue. The whole house shuddered with the poltergeist's wrath, and Noah yelped as three unseen claws scratched across his face. Drops of blood fell to the floor outside the circle.

"Noah!" Kody snarled again and held out his hand, looking like he was Force-choking someone Darth Vader–style. Nina screamed while whatever had hold of her hissed and fought, the pipes within the walls creaking.

"How do we get my sister out?" Noah demanded as the circle quickly brightened, the way it had before Kody had appeared. "Kody? *Kody!*"

A deep, guttural roar filled the house. Noah shielded his eyes, unable to crawl forward into the circle, repelled by whatever energy was sucking the poltergeist through.

Then came a deathly silence. Noah dropped his hand and blinked in the darkness. There was no sign of Nina.

"N-Nina," he croaked. His throat tightened, and his eyes grew hot.

"Noah . . ." Kody put a hand on his shoulder, but Noah shrugged it off.

"Did you really *sacrifice my sister* to—"

"Noah!" Kody held up his hands, amber eyes gleaming in the dark. "She's safe upstairs, asleep. Or, well, she was. Pretty sure that woke her up."

Noah stared at him, pulse racing. "What?"

"Illusions." Kody wiggled his fingers, little fireworks shooting from their tips. "Remember?"

Noah's jaw dropped. The Nina he had seen in the circle, the one the poltergeist had taken hostage . . .

"She wasn't real," the demon confirmed.

Swearing, Noah rushed back into the house. Nina was standing at the top of the stairs that led to their bedrooms, her eyes wide and her mouth wobbling.

"Noah?" she whimpered. "What happened?"

He raced up the stairs and scooped her up into his arms. She squeaked but returned the hug, uncharacteristically quiet as he shook and held her.

"It's okay," he breathed. "It's okay, I was just . . . playing a game. With a friend."

He looked over his shoulder and found Kody at the bottom of the stairs, watching them with curiosity. Thankfully, he'd put his human disguise back on.

"Hello, human child," Kody said solemnly.

Nina giggled. It took a while, and he had to come up with an excuse about why he was hurt, but Noah finally got her back into bed before he came back downstairs and collapsed onto the couch.

"That was the single most terrifying experience of my life," Noah groaned, pressing a paper towel to the scratches on his cheek. He narrowed his eyes at Kody, who'd decided the best way to sit on the armchair was to perch on the back of it. "Wait. But you didn't take an offering beforehand. Is this the part where you cackle and steal my soul?"

Kody rolled his still-human eyes. "I *told* you, souls taste nasty. Besides, I got my offering."

Noah slowly sat up. "You did? When?" He looked around the room suspiciously.

The demon nodded to the coffee table. The slips of paper were still there, as well as the small pile of ashes.

Noah recalled how the paper had gone up in flames. "You . . . you chose an offering of *pronouns*?"

"I like these pronouns," Kody said with a sniff. Then he jumped from the armchair to the couch, jostling Noah. "And I like human things. Good thing I'm stuck here, huh?"

Noah's eyes widened. "Stuck?"

"One entity goes in, one goes out," Kody explained, moving his finger through the air. "Your poltergeist is gone. But now you have *me*, which is a much better deal."

"B-but . . ." Noah's heart sped up again. "If you're stuck here, that means you . . . You'd have to go to *school*, and . . ."

Noah thought about it: going to school with Kody, not having to hide in the library anymore, letting the demon pull him out of his comfort zone. Laughing, joking, dancing. Going out for milkshakes.

Kody grinned, as if reading his mind. Noah helplessly grinned back. For once, he wasn't afraid.

In the span of one night, he'd defeated a poltergeist and fallen for a demon. He could do anything.

SAVE ME FROM MYSELF

Ayida Shonibar

Content warning: suicidal ideation, death

Are you there, Kali Maa? It's me, Mona.

Paraphrasing the great Judy Blume probably isn't what Mom meant when she reminded me to ask for a divine blessing earlier today. But after a lifetime of unanswered pleas, I don't expect the wording of my internal dialogue—well, more like monologue at this point—to improve my luck during this year's Kali Pujo festival.

Nobody cares what I think. Not my unimpressed teachers, nor their fave straight A student Nadine, and definitely not my father, whom we haven't heard from since Mom left him. Why should the primordial goddess of death and rebirth be any different?

I could disappear this very instant, and nothing in this whole fucking universe would bat an eye.

So when the sun starts to set and the brass statue of the fierce deity in our living room cabinet sticks out a bloodred tongue in her signature demon-slaying pose, I write it off as a figment of my imagination. My four-hour sleep schedule blurs my vision sometimes. Occupational hazard of being a seventeen-year-old with way too many thoughts.

Then something reverberates through my mind.

What do you seek?

It's not *words,* exactly. There's no particular language to it. More like an abstract idea sprouting out of nowhere. Something shapeless for me to parse out and interpret.

Oh, goody. More shit my brain wants to overwhelm me with.

This is not your brain.

If I'm perceiving it, it's definitely in my brain. Even with my C in biology, I know that much.

In *your brain does not mean* from *your brain.*

What's the freaking difference?

Could the brain of an unenlightened mortal conceive of this?

A rushing sound crowds my ears. For a moment, my retinas are filled with darkness and sparks of light. It's vast and cold and chaotic, and even for that brief second, I can't keep up.

Divine intervention in action.

Air snags in my lungs, and I wheeze. This is actually happening. I . . . think I might be seeing the whole fucking universe. The one that wouldn't change an iota if I were to vanish.

You wish to stop existing.

Heat floods my face. *I didn't say that.*

I'm very careful never to say it. I'm enough of a problem for Mom already, on top of her long shifts at the restaurant and the sideways glances from some of the other South Asian families when she shows up to functions as my single mother.

She works hard for our modest but comfortable life. The last thing I'd want her to think is that I'm not grateful.

The doorbell rings. Mom leads her friend, one of the neighborhood's nice aunties, into the living room. She's brought my favorite cashew sweets for Diwali, which is also celebrated the same day we dedicate to Kali Pujo.

When I turn to grab a katli from her tray, the two adults freeze in their tracks.

"Mona, what happened to your face?" Geeta Aunty exclaims.

I check the vomit-colored wax I've shaped into demonic spikes along my otherwise sandy-brown cheekbones. In the glass cabinet's reflection, I inspect the congealed blood on the tips—fake this time, since Mom freaked out when I showed up for the school's annual party in ninth grade with 100 percent authentic chicken innards from the restaurant she works at.

Today, my outside resembles the way I feel within. I'm monstrous all the way through. And for once, I'm going to win a big freaking prize for it.

There's a reason Halloween is my favorite time of year. Nobody can read the crushing doubt in my gawking brown eyes or catch me self-consciously pushing my chin-length black hair over my too-big ears. My awkward, stocky posture disappears into someone else's figure until there's nothing left remaining of me but my spirit. If only I could slip so easily out of my skin the other 364 days. Be something that isn't Mona, but better.

"It's for the school Halloween party," I say. "You know, the costume contest?"

For the first time in my experience, Kali Pujo in the Bengali calendar falls on October 31. The same date as Halloween. A once-in-a-two-moons kind of thing.

Which makes it once in several decades, actually—Mom said the last time this happened was the black moon year she was born, eons before she moved away from Kolkata or paid any attention to Halloween. So in a way, this is a first for the two of us.

The parties will continue into the next day, a whole season of celebration. But both are festivals of night, of blessings or curses that unfold in the dark. A double holiday for the cycle of death and life. The rare occasion, apparently, for me to commune with a deity. Auspicious, I think. Or maybe bad luck.

Mom not-so-subtly represses a shudder. "Every year you go looking like some wicked rakkhosh straight out of Kali Maa's legendary battle. And you never win. Why not try something prettier? Like a princess. Or fairy!"

It's my turn to shiver. Plenty of people can pull off the beautifully cinched waistlines and find tiaras that flatter their faces. I'm not one of them. "They don't feel good on me." To be fair, little does. "It would be pretending to be someone I'm not."

"Isn't that why you do this?"

"Halloween costumes are supposed to be unsettling," I insist. My plain gray tunic serves a purpose—it keeps the focus on the inhuman tusks protruding from my face. And the sharp talons on my fingers and the spiky faux fur scarf wrapped around my neck evoke the sort of terror that comes from facing down a ferocious animal. After all, confronting your worst fears and ugly truths is the entire point of Halloween. People like golden girl

Nadine and her charming boyfriend, Gaurav, might disapprove of my gruesome outfits, but it's the one occasion I can express myself without judgment. "I lost before because I didn't put in enough effort."

This time, my painstaking special effects makeup and handcrafted cardboard armor glue-gunned to my top will bag me the trophy—and the coveted $250 gift card that comes with it. The supplies cost me a pretty penny, but the return on investment will be more than worth it.

The front door chimes again. Mom's eyes widen and dart to the kitchen exit.

My stomach clenches in shame. She's embarrassed for her other guests to see me like this. *You're a disappointment again. Her gathering's ruined. They're better off without you.*

The only thing more terrifying than leaving the whole fucking universe unchanged in my absence is upgrading it instead.

"I'll go the back way," I reassure her, shoving down tears that would spoil my red-painted eye sockets, and slip into the alley where we take out the trash.

If you desire to be taken out, that can be arranged.

I try to ignore the intrusive thought. It isn't the first. And it certainly won't be the last.

As the final rays of sun dip behind the horizon, the second moon of the month takes up its quiet reign in the dark sky. Shadows creep across the pavement. It seems like a trick of the waning light, at first. Until my own shadow does something weird.

I pause to consider it. For a fleeting moment, I swear it keeps moving along the road, nothing binding the dark shape of me to my body anymore.

But then I blink, and it's back where it's supposed to be. I start to walk again, faster this time.

⁂

The school building teems with students and chaperones by early evening. My phone vibrates as I follow the ominous organ playlist booming through campus. I pull up a message from Gaurav, Geeta Aunty's son.

where you at?

costume competition filling up fast

Mom introduced the two of us after Geeta Aunty's family moved in down the street last year. Since then, he's made a point of volunteering to be my class partner when nobody else will and sitting at my lonely little lunch table. He's the ultimate Goody Two-shoes grown-ups adore, and I'm one of his pitiful charity cases.

Well, not just grown-ups, I guess. Nadine sure likes spending time with him.

Whenever Gaurav and I have something to do together at school or at his house, she often shows up as well. It's not just for homework assignments—this past spring, she joined our families to play Holi and chased me around Gaurav's garden with a fistful of turquoise powder.

The two of them always whisper and giggle when they think I'm not looking. Nudging each other and exchanging winks. It's clearly because they're dating. Either that, or they're having a sly laugh at my expense. They don't ever talk to me, the third wheel, about it, though—since we're not actually friends, I suppose. I did almost ask Gaurav about their relationship once but chickened out at the thought of him making fun of my interest in their personal lives.

If they wanted me to be part of their circle, they would've included me in their secrets. I can take a hint. I'm not going to force my way in.

I find Gaurav waving at me from near the judges' table, dressed in a beige sheet. "Ghost of a brown person," he responds to my questioning look. "Also, Baba didn't want me ruining the white linens."

He's draped the cloth over his head so the hem brushes his ankles, slapped a belt around his waist, and cut uneven holes for his eyes, nose, mouth, and arms. The whole thing couldn't have taken more than five minutes to pull together. Yet somehow, Gaurav looks suddenly transparent, a full person fading into oblivion under my disbelieving stare.

The feeble string lamps hanging across the school walls must be making me see things. Their tiny bulbs are the only things keeping out the heavy night. I give my head a quick shake; thankfully, Gaurav returns to his fully solid appearance.

He's not alone. A cluster of contenders itching to get their painted or gloved or furry hands on the prize money waits in the dimly lit hallway. Although simple, the decorations around us honor the Halloween vibe. Bat-shaped streamers dangle from walls. Orange and black balloons bob by the ceiling.

I join the end of the line with Gaurav. And I stop short when I see who we're standing beside.

"What's up, Mona?" Nadine says with her annoyingly perfect

grin. It's obviously fake, since she has zero reason to be smiling at me.

My sarcastic reply dies on my tongue as I take in her costume. Her dress is stunning, true to her usual style. A floor-length slip gown with streaks of gold over a gray base. Sunlight breaking through clouds.

But it's her face that steals the words out of my mouth. Done up in her standard elegant look, her thick lashes and glossed lips are framed by box braids swept loosely into a half bun. A zipper traces over her dark bronze skin and splits open at her cheek. Between the diverging sides, an explosion of bright colors and glitter look like pretty, kaleidoscopic insides bursting out of her skull. A work of art.

Figures that Nadine's hypothetical brains, very much unlike mine, would look like *that*.

Gaurav breaks my awkward silence. "Our turn."

I snap my mouth shut. Getting frequently dazzled by Nadine is one of the side effects of hanging around her boyfriend. You'd think I'd be used to it by now.

Nadine winks at me, getting in one final provocation before spinning around to submit her costume for consideration.

I roll my eyes. If she thinks her taunts will scare me away from the contest, she's dead wrong. This isn't math class, where she throws me smug looks before offering the teacher solutions to problems she knows I don't have the answers for. My costume might not draw admiring gazes like hers does, but I worked hard on it.

I'm going to win.

After we all throw our hats into the ring, we try our hand at some of the other games. They come with small prizes, but none as substantial as the costume competition. The three of us suck at pinning the tail on the werewolf and shuffleboard with pumpkin discs, but Gaurav does well at candy cornhole.

He gives the devil-shaped key chain he wins to me instead of his girlfriend, Nadine, probably so I'll tell Geeta Aunty about her generous son, and he can score brownie points with the South Asian network. The trinket is pretty cute, so I don't mind doing it.

When the clocks strike nine, it's time for the costume judges to announce their decision. "And the winner is . . ."

I push through the crowd, ready to claim my voucher. My heart pounds in anticipation. Normally, I loathe being the center of attention, but my two seconds in the spotlight with my horrific getup will be worth it.

"Nadine Williams!"

I jerk to a stop. Cheers erupt around me.

In front of the main cafeteria window, where the judges wait, Nadine glows. The brightest star against an inky sky. As if this evening hasn't been bizarre enough already, the very paint on her cheek swirls into impossible motion while I watch incredulously from the sidelines. It's like the warmth of these people's affection actually changes her physical existence.

That could never be me.

Everyone wants to see their queen up there. And she does look regal as she beams while collecting my prize.

A chill runs down my spine. When I borrowed money for costume supplies from Mom, it was with the promise I'd pay her back by the end of the month.

I can't face her now. There's no way I'm going home after this.

I tear my gaze away from Nadine and stumble into the gym. It's been turned into a haunted labyrinth, barricaded with desks and track-and-field hurdles. A cheap smoke machine coughs fog into the dark room.

Of course they chose Nadine. Her face art looks so amazing, it practically came to life. The dress, beautiful. And she's flawless in it.

Me . . . I'm all flaws in a trench coat. I look like one of the monsters Kali Maa vanquishes and whose defeat people celebrate for centuries. I was out of my mind to think anybody would validate the mess I am, Halloween or not.

You could have me destroy your demons. On this one eve, I might oblige mortal yearnings.

The wax spikes crumble off my face and into my trembling fingers. I toss them in the trash. I *am* my own demon.

Do you consent to my assistance?

The voice in my head is seductive. A clever trick. I no longer have the will to fight it, not when there's nowhere for me to go, no one I can face. I'm drowning, water filling my lungs and choking me from the guts out. The hand that wraps around my neck at this point is surely a mercy.

So I give in.

Okay. Do it.

The words ring as if I've said them aloud. It's one of those things you can't take back, even without a witness to overhear.

I wait for Kali to smite me like she promised.

A hand closes over my wrist.

I whirl around.

Nadine freaking Williams has followed me into the haunted house. Even in the flickering red light, she looks lovely.

"What could you possibly want from me?" I growl. She's chosen the worst possible time to show up, moments before a goddess is penciled in to strike me down.

She tosses a braid over her shoulder, unfazed by my bitterness. "I thought we could check out this maze together."

I stare at her incredulously. "Why would we do that?"

She bites her lip and releases me. "Well, only if you want."

"Where's your boyfriend?"

She blinks. "You mean Gaurav?"

My eyes fall on the trophy clutched in her hand. Blood rushes to my head. "I'll escort you out of here on one condition. If you give me the prize."

Her gaze follows mine. "You want my trophy?"

"I want the money."

Nadine's expression clears. "Okay."

"Wait, just like that?"

"Sure."

"My company's not worth two hundred and fifty dollars." I scowl. "Don't do me any favors."

She smirks. "Oh, I'm good with the trade."

"There has to be something else you want."

"All right." Her eyes meet mine, the laughter fading. "If you insist, I'll accept one more thing in exchange."

"And what's that?"

"A kiss."

My heart plummets in my chest. This is an attempt to humiliate me, I'm certain. To revel in the absurdity of someone like me making a move on someone like her. A twisted entertainment, one more joke for her and Gaurav to chuckle over together.

But wrapped up in all her glory, Nadine doesn't realize a fundamental truth about me: I've got nothing to lose.

"Fine."

The corner of her mouth lifts. "Fine."

Gritting my teeth, I draw closer. She leans in, dragging out this charade. Her long lashes flutter closed. She looks perfect in mockery too.

My pulse skyrockets. The instant before our lips touch, I can't tell whether I hate myself because I wish I could be her, or if it's something else I want.

Be her, then.

The world spins. This bitter night squeezes me in its vise grip. Shadows and colors tip out of place like they've been doing all evening. I barely register the sensation of Nadine's skin on mine. The smoke and screams in the background disorient me. This *would* be the sort of morbid place I'd have my first kiss. Lost to some ridiculous dare.

She pulls away abruptly, which isn't unexpected. It still stings.

I run. Through the darkness, tripping past volunteers who jump out in garish masks. My neck is hot. Sweat slicks my palms. It's almost ten o'clock. I search desperately for the way out of school.

Someone raven-haired and chiseled blocks my path. "Hey! I've been looking everywhere for you." It's Gaurav. "Congrats on the win, by the way."

"What are you on about?" Maybe this is another prank Nadine put him up to, perfectly timed to rub my loss in. I, for one, am not amused.

"Told you your dress would go well with your makeup," he barrels on. "You had nothing to worry about. Gold and rainbows bursting forth—it's the perfect canvas to represent your true self. Even if the judges don't know the story behind it."

He's so full of it. I'm not even *wearing* a dress.

Yet when I glance down, Nadine's gown fills my vision. The gray underlayer beneath the golden satin looks almost like the color of my tunic, but that's where the similarity ends. Even stranger, Nadine's trophy is in my hand.

My fingers pat my face gingerly and feel the zipper stuck onto it.

This is her.

I'm Nadine.

"Excuse me," I squeak, and bolt back to the haunted house.

A simple misunderstanding. It's been an emotional day. The quickest way to calm my frazzled mind is to set my eyes on the *real* Nadine, who's obviously not me, and put this confusion to rest once and for all. Easy peasy.

When I retrace my steps to where we kissed, there's a body lying on the floor. Its mask is collapsing and ill-fitted breastplate torn. Kids skirt around it like it's another prop set out to scare them. I can see where they'd get the idea, what with the grotesque costume it's wearing.

But it's me. Mona.

Only I'm not inside anymore.

It is as you wanted.

What is *this? Why am I still here?* My mouth tastes sour. *Why am I* her?

You had this sole night to choose your fate. I complied with the path you most desired.

Something clenches in my stomach. My prone form lies there, a shell abandoned. Even by me. I could walk away right now, let them find Mona and spread the news. Start a new life as golden girl Nadine and never look back.

A thrill shoots through me. What a glow-up. Kali has a point; it's a blessing in literal disguise.

I start to turn away.

But then I think of the teachers calling Mom. Of her driving to school in a frenzy, only to find *this* on arrival.

Heaving a sigh, I stoop to prod Mona's—*my*—artificially bloody cheek. A cropped haircut in dire need of a trim frames my round face. It's disconcerting to see myself from the outside. A relief, but still weird. I'm glad I have the option of looking away whenever I want to now.

I brace a hand against Mona's waist and wrap her limp arm around my neck. I'll drop her off quietly in her bed. Mom will think she passed peacefully asleep. All will be well.

I drag Mona out of the gym. The corridors are lighter, and some people give me strange stares as I pass them with what looks like the life-sized corpse of a demon slung over my shoulder.

It's tough work. When I move to wipe sweat off my brow, a smudge of rainbow streaks along my wrist. I wince. It feels wrong to remove anything drawn on by Nadine's hand. I've stolen her appearance, but the truth is, I'll never be her.

To my gaze, she's always looked perfect.

But that's because she's been herself. *She's* what's perfect.

And I'm already ruining it. Nadine's beauty isn't a costume. Nobody else can be her.

For every action, there must be an opposite and equal reaction.

Sorry, did I ask for a physics lesson?

It is metaphysical. If you move one soul, you must remove another. Death turns to rebirth, and life to death. All matter, all existence, evolves and devolves in a cycle.

An icy trickle of fear chases me down the hallway. My consciousness poisoned Mona first, and now it's destroying Nadine. The longer I take over her life, the more damage I'll be doing. Besides her impeccable dress sense, she's at the top of our class and beloved by everyone.

What happens when my C-level biology skills drag down her grade point average? Or my bad temper spoils her romance with Gaurav?

My stomach turns. I'm a literal curse. Nadine doesn't deserve this.

No one does.

Put her back as she was. Reverse it and get rid of only me.

You must will it thus.

I do. I want to undo it right now.

You do not want it enough.

Of course I do.

All I have done is realize your wish. It is up to you alone to dissolve it—so long as you do it by the ultimate hour of this eve.

You mean past midnight, there's no going back?

"Mona?"

I pick up my pace when the familiar voice comes from behind. But Gaurav the ever-persistent boyfriend doesn't give up. "Hey, what's wrong with her, Nadine?"

"Nothing," I say quickly. "I'm taking her home."

"Do you know where she lives? Here, let me help." Before I can stop him, he takes Mona's other arm. The makeshift ghost costume slides out of place, his head poking completely through the crooked mouth hole. His expression falls when he gets a good look at Mona's blank, sallow face. "Maybe we should go to the hospital. What happened?"

"It's fine, really."

"How can you say that? We're not doctors. Seriously, I think she needs help."

Frustration wells inside me, hot and acidic. "What do you care? You only tolerate her to appease Geeta Aunty."

His head jerks in my direction. "That's not true at all."

"Oh yeah? Then why'd you give her that demon key chain you won?"

"Because it matches her costume! I thought she'd appreciate it." He stares like he's never seen anything quite like me before. Which he probably hasn't.

"There's no fucking way you give a damn what she appreciates."

"I do, actually." His voice goes cold, nothing like his usually lighthearted demeanor. "She's my friend."

My throat tightens suddenly, and I have to fight the inexplicable urge to cry. His reaction makes it seem like what I said about Mona—about *me*—isn't okay. Yet these thoughts have run wild in my head for years, unopposed. No one has objected to them before. Nobody's argued for the right to call themselves my friend.

"We should let her mom decide what to do," I say thickly.

"Fine."

A thick blanket of clouds blocks all natural illumination, leaving only intermittent pools of lamplight. But I still feel the moon hiding in plain sight, knowing our every move, connecting to us through the darkness.

We walk silently down the blocks to my—Mona's—house. Leaves drift to the ground around us, reds and yellows and browns kissing our hair, crunching beneath our feet. It's the autumn cycle, the slow demise of this year making room for the next. October's first moon giving way to a second one. Kali's flow of destruction and creation, time and change, that touches everything. Everyone.

I steer us toward the back door and remove the key from Mona's hidden jacket pocket. Gaurav's little demon attachment sways from the chain.

"Where are you going?" Gaurav asks. "We should ring the bell and talk to her mom."

Oh, right.

Oh, *no.*

Gaurav reaches for the front door. But I can't show up in front of her like this, with her lifeless daughter in tow.

A familiar ache builds in my chest. I don't want to watch her expression sour again because of me.

I stretch past Mona's limp figure and grab Gaurav's half-extended arm. He has no idea what he's gotten himself into. If he would only do as I say, we could stay on top of the situation.

I need him to listen to me. Right now. Before he does something irreversible like I did.

Take him instead, if you want. But you have little time left to make your decision.

My grasp on Mona slips, and her body slides forward. Even now, she's literal dead weight. Gaurav lurches to catch her, and in the commotion, the three of us tumble like a house of cards. Somewhere in this human sandwich, his mouth ends up squashed against mine.

It's the least glamorous kiss this side of the century.

The overcast sky above us whirls. In there, somewhere, the moon watches me spiral. I sprawl to the side, unsteady on my suddenly larger hands and feet.

A pair of arms shoves me back. "Mona?"

I untangle my limbs from Nadine's with as much dignity as I can muster. Which isn't a lot, given my legs are caught up in Gaurav's bedsheet-slash-lost-spirit robe. Her amber eyes glint with suspicion. Does she know what I did?

"I thought you were Mona. We were just—" She glances around, absorbing our surroundings. "What is this place, Gaurav?"

She's talking to *me*. Because Mona's still-unmoving body is lying on the grass.

I'm torn between relief that Nadine hasn't disappeared into the ether and terror that Gaurav—my self-declared friend—will. Because of me.

This isn't what I asked for.

It must have been, for you to have manifested it in this manner.

You're distorting my intentions.

Or perhaps you are too indecisive.

But Nadine returned.

You vacated her body.

So where's Gaurav?

I have explained the cost of displacing souls. One had to pay in order to move the two of you.

"Oh my goodness," Nadine exclaims, bending over the husk that was once me. "Is that Mona? I swear, I was just with her."

She's certainly committed to her prank, continuing to feign interest in my situation when she probably just wants to know what happened following our little encounter in the haunted house. I suppose I've cheated her out of my embarrassing meltdown after the kiss. She lined up all the pieces only to be denied her prize. That's an experience I can relate to tonight.

I clear my throat, hoping to distract her with Gaurav's romantic wiles. "Never mind her. We're together now, right? It'll be fine."

She doesn't budge. Instead, she takes Mona's hand in hers. "I do mind, though. You know how I feel about her."

Our eyes meet, and something electric crackles in the air between us. "No." Late-night mist ghosts over my skin. I shiver. "Why don't you tell me how you feel about me?"

I don't realize the slip of my tongue until she replies, "You're my best friend."

"And what's Mona to you?" My mouth is dry. "A punch line? Something for you to laugh at?"

A crease of confusion appears between her brows. My fingers curl into themselves, face burning under the heat of her scrutiny. I wish she'd stop studying me like one of her A+ homework tasks.

"I'm your boyfriend," I blurt out foolishly to break the unbearable tension.

Nadine reels back. "Shut up. That's not funny."

"I wasn't—"

"You're the second person to say that today." She turns away, wringing her hands. "You, of all people. Are you telling me I'm not queer enough?"

Her words leave me breathless. "Sorry, wait, I didn't know," I squeeze out. "Earlier, when you said . . ."

She spins back around, eyes shining. It's a punch to my gut. I've made her cry. I'm the worst scum on this planet—

"I need to talk to her," Nadine says. "We left things unfinished, and I don't want her to get the wrong idea." She eyes me warily. "Like you seem to be getting."

I want to scream. It's not Nadine and Gaurav's romance I'm wrecking, it's their best friendship. I'm hurting them both. Forcing my way into somebody else's identity doesn't change my corrosive touch. It doesn't entitle me to their talents or the love they've nurtured for years of their lives.

If anything, it's me losing the people I have in mine.

In my undeserving hands, it's all crumbling to dust. And things so precious should be preserved, not crushed.

"Nadine, I have to confess something," I say. "You can't blame Gaurav for my behavior. I'm—Mona."

I wait for her to yell or slap me, my face taut with apprehension. Instead, a muscle tics in her own jaw. "If this is your bogus way of avoiding responsibility—"

"We kissed." The words come out quiet, but from the way

her brow furrows, I know she hears me. "In the haunted house. Because you dared me to. And then you—passed out."

She doesn't move, neither away nor closer. I don't know why she won't simply turn her back on this mess. On *me*.

After blinking rapidly for several seconds, she finally speaks in a hoarse voice. "Say more."

I explain what happened after our kiss and why she missed part of the evening. She lets out a choked sound at my description of the transference and definitely sighs—in exasperation?—when I recount Gaurav's totally shocking friendship declaration. I leave out the part about Kali Maa's involvement for now, unsure how to quickly convey the manifestation of a spiritual entity I've shared with only Mom my whole life.

When I finish, I steal a sideways look at Nadine, having avoided her eyes during the entire discussion. "Do you hate me?"

"Is that what you think?" Nadine twists to face me. "That I constructed this elaborate and childish plan to show you up with a kiss, of all things, because I can't stand your guts?"

I blink at her. "Well, isn't it?"

"Since I'm oh-so-perfect, as you describe me, you can't possibly imagine me wanting to pursue anything else with you."

"What about all those times in class when you gloated about getting the answers right?"

"Mona." Nadine shakes her head. "I was trying to impress you."

My heart begins to pound unnecessarily hard, afraid I might

think unrealistic thoughts, or give in to dangerous hopes. It's a nervous organ. "It worked."

"Oh, did it?" She smirks. "You've clearly proven I'm not flawless. Since apparently my flirting skills are abysmal."

I cough, sputtering on air. Nadine pats my back, making the hair rise on my skin.

Except, it's not really my skin. If I were in mine, I could have this conversation with her face-to-*real*-face.

"Do you have anything to say to me?" Nadine shifts on the grass. "Now that I've bared my soul to you, I mean."

She's sitting very close to me. Her perfume lingers on my breath. When she slides her hand into mine, all I have to do to cross the narrow space between our lips is lean down and—

I jump back. *That was way too close.*

"Don't worry, I won't bite," she giggles.

I run my hand through Gaurav's curly hair. His displaced ghost sheet feels uncomfortably tight around my throat. "If I kiss you, I might replace you again."

The smile drops off her face. "What does that mean?"

"If I'm not myself by midnight, it'll be at the cost of Gaurav." I swallow thickly. "Or you."

Nadine draws away from me, wrapping her arms around her torso. "Then let's put you back where you belong."

We hoist Mona's body—*my* body—upright so that it's propped against the wall of the house. It looks like it might be taking a mythical nap, waiting to be roused by true love's kiss.

I crouch beside it and peck myself quickly on the lips.

An owl hoots overhead. My watch beeps to signal the eleventh hour of the night. The lights of an upstairs window—Mom must be in my empty bedroom—flicker on. Her friends seem to have left already.

Nothing else happens.

You do not will it from the depths of your soul.

Sweat pricks the back of my neck. Kali tells me what I've always known—my mind is weak. If I can't return things to the way they're meant to be, I'll lose Gaurav.

And Mom will lose me.

⁂

The demon makeup on my body's face is cracked. Golden skin peeks through the gaps. It looks different from an outside perspective, more like a disintegrating piece of armor than a costume mask.

Nadine and I sneak through the kitchen, up the stairs, and manage to fold the unmoving figure of Mona under my duvet. It's half an hour before twelve, and I'm out of ideas.

"Maybe I should leave a note," I say. The body has been delivered, yet I hesitate to leave. If I'd known this afternoon would be my last interaction with Mom, I would've said a lot more. Like *thank you*. And *I love you*.

"I doubt you can do this shit show justice with two lines on a Post-it."

The sound of approaching footsteps in the hallway sends us scrambling to hide. Nadine lunges for the closet while I dive under the bed.

"Asleep already?" Mom murmurs. She busies herself tidying my already spotless desk.

When she turns off the lamp and douses the room in darkness,

I can't see her anymore. Maybe this is what finally gives me the courage to speak.

"I'm sorry," I whisper, masking Gaurav's voice, "for not being stronger."

Mom pauses by the doorway, halfway out of the room. "I think you're very strong, Mona."

I peek my head out from beneath the bed frame to get a better look, creeping like a monster from a child's storybook. "Are you sure? Because I feel pretty feeble right now."

She turns back to the bed, thinking it's the Mona tucked inside speaking to her. "I know you have a hard time. And I wish things were easier for you." She bends down, bringing her face close to my body. "It takes a great amount of strength to hang in when it gets rough."

"It does?" My voice is small.

"Every Pujo, I tell you to seek Kali Maa's favor and protection. Do you know why?"

"No. Why?"

"If you truly mean it, she's able to listen to your prayer on the eve of her festival. I asked for my blessing once, and she gave me you. I always remember to thank her for it when she can hear me."

I bite back a huff of surprise. Does Kali speak with Mom too? Could her wish have pulled my soul from the end of a previous life to the beginning of this one—for her? I wonder how many other calls the deity answers in a single night.

Mom's fingers push back the baby hairs from my temples, as they've done countless times before. Outside, the clouds start to lift. "I'm so proud to have you as my daughter."

Warmth floods through me, and I understand. It's a blessing to be loved.

To love.

"You're all I want." Mom brushes her lips softly over my body's forehead. "Exactly as you are."

It's a powerful kiss. One of those things you can't take back. She pours her entire soul into it.

The room tilts around me, tipping me out of Gaurav's form and up into mine. Under the bed, I hear the gasp of him returning to consciousness. He's too loud—I worry Mom will freak out when she notices his scandalous hiding place.

I rush to tell her it's okay, that he's only there to help me. But Mom isn't leaning over my bedside anymore.

I peer over the edge of my covers.

Her thick black hair fans over the carpeted floor like a dark halo. She lies there, unblinking, for two heartbeats before I surge to my feet, tripping over blankets in my haste to reach her.

"Wake up, Mom," I sob, pressing kiss after kiss to her face.

She doesn't move.

I race down the stairs, ignoring Nadine's and Gaurav's shouts behind me. Kali's statue is exactly where I saw it this afternoon. I rattle the cabinet and offer her fresh handfuls of hibiscus flowers the way I've seen Mom do, begging her to hear me as she heard Mom, to *do something.*

Are you there, Kali Maa? It's me, Mona.

No answer.

Through the front window, a sliver of moon appears between the trees. When I glance at the clock on the adjacent wall, it reads five minutes past midnight.

KNICKKNACK

Ryan Douglass

Living near a haunted mansion is cooler in theory than in practice. For as long as I can remember, the owners of that ginormous Eldritch property down the street from me have rented out the bed quarters as "Haunted Stay Rooms" or used them as a tourist attraction. The mansion was already home to a mysterious family homicide before the clown moved in. And then came Knickknack—a drifter and the only one weird enough to take the murder house off the market.

Knickknack was a clown who performed live magic and stunts at children's birthday parties in the 1970s. No one knew who he was—only that he went home to that big house all by himself when his jobs were done. The contrast between his seclusion and his very "on" career made him something of a joke among gossipy teens. He'd promote his services on picket signs around town, but nobody ever knew his true identity. They said he was a clown 24/7. He never took the makeup off.

Knickknack met his tragic fate one morning in 1972. He was at a birthday party, doing a backflip on a mini trampoline when a wicked kid named Tommy Smith moved the trampoline out from under him. Knickknack panicked, came down mid-rotation, and landed on his neck, breaking it. He died in a circle of shocked little kids.

I don't believe in urban legends. I've been an adult since I was a child. My parents are interesting in the sense they never truly grew up. I was managing Dad's alcohol addiction and Mom's cryptic affairs with her personal trainer before I could multiply. They've damn near admitted my little brother was an accident and seem to be counting the days until I move out of this house. I keep my emotions and opinions close to the vest because I'm expected to be the man of my house.

But I'd be lying if I said I didn't sometimes wonder about Knickknack and the truth of his story. There's the fact that every kid that was at that party, including Tommy, mysteriously disappeared in the following years. And I do catch fleeting silhouettes in the windows of that Victorian home even when it's empty of visitors. It's a few houses down, but I can see it from my room. Allgood Road slopes up at the end of the street, and the mansion watches over us like a titan from a long-lost realm, fixed to the ground for eternity. His former bedroom peeks out through the gaunt trees, and the glass becomes especially bright when a blue moon rolls around.

Mom and Dad took off to Vegas for Halloween, which, inconveniently, is when the ghost of Knickknack does his dirty business of kidnapping wayward children. I'm stuck in the house with my kid brother, Carl. The kid lives for chaos, like summoning evil and sticking chewed gum into strangers' pockets. I'm convinced our parents go on vacation so much just to make him my problem instead of theirs.

He's watching a movie downstairs, and I'm in the middle of an online *Galaga* tournament with my virtual friends, who are really my only friends, aside from Leo. Something about living on Allgood Road makes kids in Forest Heights want to alienate themselves from your neck of the woods, and by extension, from you.

As I'm shooting away at enemy starships, a text pops up on my phone.

Leo:

You coming tonight?

Me:

Can't. Stuck babysitting, remember?

Leo:

Damn. So much for making your move on Larissa.

Mid-reply, I wonder how much stronger my friendship with Leo would be if he knew I didn't like girls. One time we were in his garage drinking wine leftover from his sister's graduation party, and he let slip that if he was drunk enough, he might consider letting a guy go down on him. It was the most interesting conversation we've ever had.

"Are you texting with your boyfriend?" comes a voice from the door.

I jump and drop my phone. Standing in the doorway is Carl—all thirtieth percentile for his height. He's got my dad's lopsided face and my mom's tiny wrists. He'd nail a Black retelling of *The*

Little Vampire, given the cape he never takes off and all the extra teeth growing in his gums. I don't think he's gotten a haircut in three years—says the barbers give him the heebie-jeebies. His lightning-shaped hairline and frizzy fro are approaching Mowgli levels of feral boy.

"Why are you not in front of the TV watching your movie, like I said?"

"I've seen it already," Carl answers with a shrug.

"Put on a different one?"

He tilts his head, pondering it a moment. "Hmm. Nah!"

My phone pings again.

Leo:

I doubt I'll have any fun at
this party without you. Bring Carl!

Even though my brother gets on my nerves, I love him too much to bring him to a teen party.

Me:

Or you could come over after
I put my brother to sleep.

Leo:

Private party?

Me:

Why not? Bring beer!

For so long I've been trying to get Leo a little drunk again, on the off chance he'll let slip that the secret feelings I'm nursing for him are reciprocated. What is a private party to a bi-curious guy who absolutely seems gay? I know we're not supposed to assume peoples' sexualities, but he's the one who gets touchy with me, not the other way around.

"Hey, Noah?"

I face my brother in the doorway. "What, Carl?"

He's holding a Ouija board now. No idea where he got that from.

"If you need me, I'll be summoning Knickknack the Clown."

"Something, something, stupid urban legend. Sure!"

Why is this town so obsessed with that silly story? I mean sure, kids disappear from this place every few years or so, but it happens in several secluded New England towns—not just Forest Heights.

I go back to my game, and not two minutes later, something hits the window and startles me out of my chair. I hit the floor hard. Pain explodes in my elbow. Okay, maybe I am a little freaked out. I may have stumbled across the Knickknack message boards on Reddit and tracked his killing record for the past few years. It's okay to peek when you treat it like flash fiction, right?

The moon is very full tonight, it is Halloween, and no one disappeared last year. So that means, if he were real—which he isn't—he'd be on the hunt tonight.

I crawl up to the glass and check it for cracks. Slowly, I use the sill to press my weight up and find my reflection in the window for a second. My hair is like a bush these days. I keep it under a beanie, so it sprouts around my forehead and ears like a corkscrew rush. I look more terrified than I feel, my mouth slightly open, my pupils huge in their dark brown irises. Strange to see so much raw emotion on my face, which I've trained to appear apathetic, impassive.

Then the front lawn comes into view. Standing on the grass is not Knickknack but the guy who's always here for me when I need him. Leo.

I open the window and take a good look at the boy who charmed the pants off me in middle school and has had a grip on me since. He's wearing a toga, which is half hanging off his muscular shoulder. I can't even see his shorts underneath it—just the quads and calves he's built up from a lifetime of work on his dad's construction sites. His head is square-ish, like a brick, his nose is round, and his complexion is sandy brown. A gentle Puerto Rican giant with a heart of gold.

"You gonna let me in the front, or do I have to scale the window like Romeo?" he asks.

"Hold on," I say. "My *Galaga* tournament is still going—I'll get back to you."

"Hey, loser? If you don't let me in, I'm gonna TP your house."

I smile all the way out of my room and down the stairs.

As I let him in, Carl screams from the living room, "I knew your boyfriend was coming over!"

"Ignore him," I tell Leo, as I lead him upstairs.

But Leo is laughing—he takes jokes like that in stride. "We could be boyfriends."

One thing I really hate about guys who don't claim their sexualities openly is that you're always left to wonder if they mean it when they say gay shit, or if they're just making you, the queer, the butt of a joke.

As soon as we enter my room, Leo falls on the bed, hiking up his gown some. “Nerdy night in on Halloween? Does this mean we’re officially getting old?”

“Two more semesters and we’re legally grown-ups.” I close the door and sit beside him.

“Ugh—I don’t want to think about that.”

“What are you supposed to be, a Greek god?”

Leo rests up on his elbows and catches me in his hazel stare. “Is it working for me?”

I survey his exposed nipple, then the symmetrical form of his face. The mustache he’s formed the beginnings of looks like a caricature of mannishness, but even that tickles my fancy.

“Sort of—I guess.” A shiver runs through me. When he flirts with me, I go so brain-dead, I wouldn’t catch it if drool decided to leak off my bottom lip. “Speaking of the next two semesters . . . you keep mentioning spending the rest of your life in this town and never leaving, and sometimes I can’t tell if you’re joking. Like . . . you don’t really want to spend forever surrounded by neo-Puritans and superstitious zealots, do you?”

Leo takes a breath to respond. “Well . . .”

A scream erupts from downstairs. Bloodcurdling. It shocks and then freezes us both. Then it stops.

“Carl?” I launch from my bedroom, down the hallway, and nearly trip over myself running downstairs.

God, my biggest fear is that I’d somehow lose my brother, despite the stakes of that being so low. I got all googly-eyed and fucked-up, which is why I don’t do emotions much in the first place.

Downstairs, the living room is empty, the window is open, and the curtains are blowing in the wind.

"Carl?" I run to the window. "*CARL!*"

I tuck through the window and run into the front of our lawn. The driveways all down Allgood Road are like concrete deserts—nobody thinks to trick-or-treat here, because even the adults think Knickknack might nab their kids under the strobe of a flickering streetlight. Stark against the darkness is a red *K* on our mailbox that seems to have been etched in glow-in-the-dark paint.

"Knickknack the Clown," Leo says, coming somberly out the door behind me.

"Don't say that. That's one of the dumbest urban legends we have in this town."

"One of the realest, more like," Leo replies, his brows pressed down with concern. He approaches the mailbox and puts his hand on it. The wet redness that bleed onto his fingers confirms that the paint is fresh.

"CARL!" I cup my hands around my mouth to amplify my voice. "CARL!" But it only travels back to me.

Who the fuck took my brother? Who would even want that little gremlin?

"Oh, god . . ." My breath shortens as I start to panic and walk around in circles. "My parents are gonna disown me and then murder me. I have to call the police."

I run upstairs to get my phone, and Leo's footsteps follow not far behind.

In my room, the phone is still lying on the bed, and a text has popped up on my screen.

Don't even think about it. Call the police, and your brother dies.

"Holy fuck—" I drop my phone, and it tumbles toward the doorway.

Leo picks it up as he enters the room, reads it, and his eyes widen. "Yeah, holy fuck."

I cross the room and snatch the phone back. "I have to call the police."

"Don't call the police," Leo says. "Knickknack hates the police. We'll find him."

"You don't really believe in Knickknack the Clown, do you?"

"Of course I do. This is what he does. Either a kid dies or Knickknack receives something from that house each year to memorialize his impact on this town."

"All that only applies to clown enthusiasts—it's not real. It's like believing in Bigfoot."

"Um, Noah? I hate to break the news to you, but it applies to everybody. People have seriously lost loved ones to that monster. Especially if you're living within his realm of terror—and you live like three houses down from the guy."

"Knickknack is dead, Leo."

"Okay, sure. Explain to me how that's gonna help us find out who stole your brother and left a huge *K* on the mailbox?"

"It's called trick-or-treat for a reason. A dumb joke. When I find out who's playing it, I'm going to beat their ass."

A jingle rings out from down the street. It sounds like an ice-cream truck song at first, but then its haunting jingle becomes familiar, like a music box playing all flat notes. It's largely acknowledged as the tune that Knickknack used to use at his parties.

Leo runs to my window, sticks his top half out, and waves the car down. "HEY!"

“What are you doing?” I ask, coming up behind him.

When the car stops in front of my house, inside are two of the most popular kids in school—the types whose parents can afford to give them cars. Brennan Dart, with a 1950s greaser cut, and his girlfriend, Kayla, in a Daphne costume, her feet kicked up on the dashboard and her thick black hair flowing over one shoulder.

Leo runs downstairs to meet them, and I reluctantly follow.

“Big Leo!” Brennan barks, turning down the creepy music as we approach. “You guys on your way to the party?”

I hate how Brennan and Leo are friends now. Brennan shoved frog parts in my ear in middle school biology, then acted like it never happened once we hit high school. He’s so theatrical in his hot-guy-ness, I can’t even take his sex appeal seriously. I can barely tell if the jean jacket he’s rocking tonight is a costume or nightly dress, and I’m pretty sure he’s already started using Botox in his forehead.

“We’re in a major crisis, actually,” Leo says. “Have you seen an eight-year-old kid, about waist-high, running around, maybe in the clutches of an evil clown?”

“What, like, Knickknack?” says Brennan.

“Most likely.”

Brennan slams the wheel in excitement. “Hot diggity DAWG! Just what we were looking for.” He looks at me. “Did you get a text message?”

“Yeah . . .” I mutter. “How did you know?”

“Oh god, it’s happening. Get in, you nerds.”

⁂

I never thought I'd be riding in the back seat of Brennan Dart's car, but I guess anything can happen on Halloween. Forest Heights is about twenty minutes to drive all the way through, before you get to this long shroud of trees that close the town in. We're bound to find Carl. I know we will.

"I've waited for the day I could kick that fucker Knickknack in the teeth for taking my cousin from me," Brennan says. "Ugh . . . five years of searching, and I've still never seen him. Just re-enactors."

"What's the story with this clown again?" I ask. I want to make sure what I know is accurate.

"How many years have you lived in Forest Heights, Noah?" Leo butts in.

"I know, I know, I just . . . I don't believe in stuff like this. I don't like to let it in."

Kayla says, "The deal is some idiot kid who likes to tempt fate invites him back in with a séance or something. Everybody thinks it's a joke until it isn't."

"Carl is not an idiot. He's just . . . a bit off the beaten path? He sounded so scared."

"So you probably don't know how you beat the clown, then, either," Brennan says.

"No?"

"It's possible. Thing about the dark realm Knickknack comes from is that he relies on yearly sacrifices or earthly possessions to increase his power over our realm. Those are what fuse with his energetic form and give him more power."

"The dark realm being . . . Hell?"

"Precisely."

"Either a kid dies or Knickknack receives something from that house each year," Kayla says, her voice almost sedated as she applies lipstick in the fold-down mirror. She seems half-bored by the whole thing, which is fair—even murder stories get tired when you've heard them your whole life. "But he only kills his victims if we don't get him an artifact by midnight."

"The only way to get your brother back is to offer an alternative sacrifice to Knickknack," Brennan adds.

"And . . . how do we find a sacrifice worthy of His Clownliness?" Please don't say what I think you're gonna say.

"You visit the cursed mansion, of course." The car stops suddenly, and I realize we've been cruising down the street only to arrive at the edge of the mansion steps.

"How are we gonna get in?" I ask anyone in the car—they all seem far more prepared for this than me.

"There's a gap in the top-floor window where his room was," Brennan says. "Some kids broke it a few weeks ago messing around on the property."

"Shit, that's probably why he's so mad," Leo says.

I check my phone, and the time stares back at me—10:30. One and a half hours to save Carl before the evil clown makes stew out of his guts.

I get out at the foot of a set of stone stairs leading up into the front yard. Beyond those stairs is a path of cracked stepping stones, overgrown with moss and worms. Man, the house is hideous. Four stories of terror, roofs like sharp nails, windows rounded and plentiful like the eyes of a spider. Never thought I'd get this close to the evil lodging I've been taught to avoid my whole life.

Leo comes to stand by my side, and with him there, standing nearly a whole head above me, the mission feels less daunting.

"Okay," Brennan says from the driver's seat. "Time to retrieve some piece of the killer clown's home and leave it on his grave, and your brother will come back. He won't need him anymore."

"Quick question," I say. "Why are you guys helping us?"

"Because I don't care if you're the nerdiest nerd in all of Forest Heights. When I lost my cousin, it tore me up real bad, and I wouldn't wish it on anybody. Plus, my dad's chief of police. He can't handle another missing kid case. It helps the town's tourism market to have Knickknack be some urban legend, but not when he's causing real damage to children. That's a federal investigation waiting to happen. Just find something in the mansion you can exchange for your brother. We'll keep watch out here."

Leo looks somewhat blank in the face—his lack of fear soothes my worries.

"Okay," I say. "Ready?"

"Ready."

We run up the stairs and crouch across the paving stones, under the hanging moss of Knickknack's old property. A silvery sheen from the moon casts our shadows on grass and bushes. The graves of the mansion's previous tenants sit under some trees in the deep recesses beyond the tire swing. I imagine the pre-Knickknack family as kids spending weekends bumping into the rubbery rim of that thing, slurping plastic-tube Popsicles, no mind to the dark legends they'd form in the future. No mind to the fact that their dad would end up killing them.

The back of the mansion is a giant brick wall with a million dusty windows, one of which is cracked—like a baseball crashed through it. It leads into a room that must be where Knickknack lived.

Crickets chirp like little tambourines as we tiptoe to the latticework leading up the bricks. I start to climb up the hollow wooden squares, ivy catching my fingers and shoes.

"Hey, Noah?" Leo whispers beneath me. "If you fall, your butt will be right on my face."

"Good," I say as I approach the brick ledge outside the room. "Your face'll break my fall."

I step onto the ledge from the lattice, then scale to reach the window, my fingertips the only thing keeping me from a long fall to my death.

"Lord, please protect me," I whisper into my collar as I tiptoe horizontally across, gripping uneven bricks for support. "I know I haven't always done right. But I try."

The wind whips at my hoodie.

"Don't look down, Noah," Leo says.

In the next few seconds, I reach through the hole of the broken window and release the latch. I lift in from the bottom and flop through, releasing a giddy laugh at having made it. Leo steps in after me. This place looks . . . just like any other bedroom would. Sure, the mini trampoline is unconventional, and the clown outfit and curly wig attached to the garment rack evoke thoughts of sleep paralysis demons, but otherwise, anyone could have lived here.

I crawl to the corner, shining my flashlight on a dresser and bed. In the meantime, Leo's every footstep creaks the floor, making it feel like the whole thing could collapse underneath us.

"You're very . . . heavy-footed."

"AAAHHHHH!" Leo screams in response, making me go still. Then he exhales with relief, shining his light on a set of bowling pins on a desk. "Oh. It's just bowling pins. Not giant dildos."

"Leo? What?"

"Nothing—sorry. Find anything good?"

"Working on it." I feel around under the bed, fingertips collecting dust until I find a plastic bag. I scroll over it with the light and find photos inside, of the clown himself, cutting a birthday cake, swinging at a piñata, bouncing on a trampoline.

"Okay," I whisper. "I got it. Happy memories. These should work, right?"

"Why are you whispering? No one's in here. See? HEL-LOOOO!" A wind roars through the room, rattling the photo frames—the house greeting Leo back. ". . . Oh."

"Yeah, let's get out of here." I stand up and stick the photos in my back pocket. "Before we get taken next."

"So you believe now, huh?"

"I have to—at least as long as it takes to find my brother. If this doesn't work, I don't know what I'll do." I rush to the window, Leo hot on my trail. "Somehow the thought of Knickknack being responsible is less scary than some rando human taking him."

I curl out carefully, but my foot slips on the ledge. The photos slip from my pocket as I catch my balance and fall to the ground.

"No!" I reach down for them, my finger slipping off the windowsill.

For a moment I'm falling sideways, holding on to nothing, my head tipping toward the deadly drop. My life flashes before me as a fork of lightning tears through the sky, and the last emotion that passes through my doomed chest is a sense of pride that at least I met my end trying to save Carl.

Then Leo catches my wrist. Up at the window, he grits his teeth, chest and neck bulging under his toga as the clasp breaks loose and flips through the air.

"I gotcha, Noah—hold on." Breath strained, he yanks me through the window.

I slip into his chest and wrap my arms around him. He saved me. I was almost dead, and now my feet are only barely on the ground, my breath sinking into his warm chest. When we break apart, his skin catches the moon like melted caramel, his expression straddles a mixture of panic and relief. The chaos of emotion overruns his face, temples to chin. And suddenly, it's like that bolt of lightning is between us rather than running through the sky.

He jumps forward, grabs my neck, and kisses me.

I push him off, just because I can't believe what's happening. "Leo?"

"Sorry!" He rubs his chest and then his lips, and then his chest again. "I thought that's what you do after a life-threatening moment."

Well, it should be what you do at any moment. I liked it . . . I just can't convince my body to roll with it just yet.

We're both dazed and breathing hard. This night could get absolutely no wackier. It must be the moon's pull on the earth, making something in the air feel bigger than my desires and my fears. Like, the universe is writing the script against my will.

We start kissing again somehow, and I don't even know who

initiates it. But we're pushing our bodies together. I step forward, and he backs up, wrapping me until we slam into the dresser and squeaky toys tumble to the floor.

His hands wrap around a half-opened drawer behind him. "Jesus, Noah."

"Sorry. We shouldn't be doing this."

I pull away. God, I picked the worst night to turn into a slut.

The swirly wallpaper and clown paraphernalia remind me where we are. This place is not ours. It's the clown's. And he has my brother.

I cross the room, catching my breath, and gaze out on the vast backyard. "Okay, we gotta get that bag. Maybe you should go first." I'm still recovering.

"Maybe you should get on my back?" Leo comes toward me, and I lose my focus in his bicep vein. "Or I could carry you."

"Just go, Leo. Gosh."

Minutes later, we dash off the property. I leap across the street and fling Brennan's car door open. Leo comes up from behind and wraps my body in a hug, lifting me a foot off the ground.

"Please put me down."

He drops me and runs around to the other side of Brennan's car, giggling. I jump in the car, and Brennan takes off.

As we screech down the road, I finally catch my breath.

"I almost lost you, Noah," Leo says. He tugs his toga outfit at the chest to let air in. "Please be more careful."

"Thank you for saving my life." I mean it.

Even though I want to live in this moment with him, I'm

already distracted by the party photos that I nearly died trying to save. There was a time when the clown was so happy. And a quick moment took his life unceremoniously. I think I'd be pissed about that too.

We arrive at the cemetery where he's buried minutes later. At the front is a narrow path, framed by trees, with graves poking up from the hills for miles. Brennan pops open his trunk to reveal an assortment of tools: crowbar, baseball bat, tennis racket, and mallet.

"Okay, guys," Brennan says. "A stone house marks the gravesite for Knickknack—you can't miss it. Only thing we have to worry about are the grave defenders."

"The who?" I say.

"They protect his gravesite from sacrificial exchanges," Kayla says, twirling a strand of hair around one finger. "When Knickknack's soul fuses with pieces of his house, it restricts his scope across the waking world to Forest Heights."

"But if he takes a child from Forest Heights," Brennan adds, "he absorbs a human vessel, and his power expands across the waking realm, giving him freer rein and the ability to nab kids from towns far and wide. They're not gonna want you to save your brother because saving him could spell another year of Knickknack's terror in Forest Heights. If you can't save him, Knickknack may forget about this place next year and choose a kid from across the tracks."

"You can't be serious. This sounds like some guy just made it up."

"I'm only ever serious," Brennan says. "Hold your weapons

high, and don't let the axes hit you. OPERATION SAVE THE NERD'S KID BROTHER STARTS NOW!"

Brennan charges into the woods, mallet held high. Leo grabs the baseball bat, Kayla gets the crowbar, and I'm left holding the rickety tennis racket. Some kind of hero.

As we wind through the trees of the cemetery, it dawns on me that this could really be the end. Maybe superstitions aren't so fake and I have to kill my ego some to confront the world as it exists around me. I can't stop thinking about kissing Leo, what that means amid this nightmare, and—

A whistling goes by my ear, fast, like an arrow. I turn to find a throwing axe embedded in the tree bark right next to me. About fifty feet ahead stands a man in a hospital gown, face painted with a clownish smile. Half his frame is outlined by the moon, and the other half is shrouded in shadow. He's gearing up to throw another axe.

"You approach the grave," the man hisses, "you're dead."

Leo screams, "RUN!"

So, we run, losing Brennan and Kayla in the meantime. I lose my direction in the darkness and fall headfirst into a ditch. When I recover, spitting out soil, I end up shoulder to shoulder with Leo against a mound of dirt. He fell in with me.

"You okay?" he asks, brushing dirt off my shoulders.

"Town lore has gotten out of control," I say through hitched breaths. "I mean, regardless of whether Knickknack's powers grow through child victims or lost artifacts, we shouldn't be killing each other over it."

"You can say that again."

"I'll be damned if these freak clown enthusiasts come at me with some moral position about sacrificing my brother for the greater good. You wouldn't do it, would you? If sacrificing someone you loved meant kicking the threat out of town?"

Leo shrugs. "I mean, we have no proof of how Knickknack operates from beyond the grave. Could be that receiving all the artifacts from his home is finally what puts him to sleep. His legacy is a thing that's impossible to understand and that 4channers have made into something all their own. Sucks your brother was this year's victim, but you know. It happens. I definitely think you should do everything you can to save him, regardless of what the superstition says."

That was perfectly correct. I think I love him. "Um, Leo? I have a confession to make since people are throwing fucking axes at our head for no reason." I take a deep breath and take in his face in the spare moonlight, which comes off more scary than relaxing, because one expression from it has the power to end me. "I . . . I just want to say thank you. For being by my side, even though my parents are freaks who moved us into the creepy side of town. And I get it if you want to stay here in Forest Heights forever and work for your dad, but when I leave, I'll miss you. I'll miss you and Carl and my parents and everybody. I care about you a lot, Leo."

Leo pauses for a while. He's never been judgmental, and I've always known if I expressed the depth of my feelings, there was a chance it would ruin our friendship. Something about this night has me wanting to take a risk, but I can't risk not talking to him anymore, even if I am leaving town soon.

"I really do love our friendship, Noah," Leo says. "There's no one else I'd rather run through these haunted woods and look for their little brother with, other than you. Axes and all. I kissed you because it felt right in the moment."

A little pre-grief stirs in my stomach. Fear of rejection, I guess. That wasn't a very clear confession on the romantic front of our relationship, but maybe what I said wasn't either.

"It was . . . it was nice though, right?" I say, with a slight chuckle.

"Yeah. It was. But we should probably focus on staying alive first so we can save your bro."

"Oh yeah—DUH! Probably."

Leo didn't immediately return my love. Just kissed me in the middle of a haunted room only to leave my heart somewhat cracked. So as we climb out of the ditch and run toward the cursed stone house to leave the pictures in Knickknack's lair, I run the risk of blowing chunks with every step.

But somehow now that I met that courage head-on, I can meet the next challenge too.

The axe-thrower stalks us through the woods, but we're faster than he is, better at dodging, and he's only got two axes. Who even thinks to come out in the woods in a hospital gown in the spirit of releasing a ghost clown's terror?

We dodge the flying axes like *Galaga* starships charging through the sky. And in our dramatic arc through the haunted forest, I manage to avoid becoming chopped meat, owing that mostly to Leo for steering our direction.

Once we climb through the window of the stone house at the gravesite, I'm surprised to find it empty. Inside are some antiques, some trophies, weapons, tools. A living room couch with a duvet.

A television. Like a whole house is being built inside of here, to remind Knickknack of his past life.

And the floor is littered with . . . bones.

"Knickknack, patty whack . . ."

"Doesn't get more matter-of-fact than that," Leo says as he follows me in. "Quick! Leave the photos so we can get Carl down before those fuckers try to kill us again."

"Down?" It's then that I realize my brother is duct-taped to a ceiling fan, spinning in slow circles above us.

"Hey, lovebirds," he says.

"Carl? What in the—who taped you up there?"

"Take a guess, GENIUS."

I bury the pictures under one of the floorboards. I step on Leo's shoulders to get my brother down. I feel a little bad for Knickknack. He grew up without validation. Just like me. And maybe that turns you into a deranged maniac. Or maybe it turns you into a brave father figure who knows how to save the fuck out of your brother when the time comes.

⁂

Leo stays at my house until the dawn breaks. Carl is safe in bed, Ouija board privileges revoked. He said he remembered nothing from the time he summoned Knickknack to the time he woke up taped to that fan, counting the hours until 12:00 A.M.

Back on my bed, I ask Leo, "Can you kiss your best friend and have it not matter?"

"You're still thinking about earlier tonight, aren't you?"

"Um . . . it was a weird night."

"Mad weird. I think there's only one way we can solve the

weirdness of it. You come to the Halloween dance with me next week to commemorate our final fall semester."

I'm . . . speechless. I don't know if I heard correctly. "Dance?"

"I'll need someone to celebrate with. Let me romanticize you."

"Are you joking?" There's this moment where I picture us together, under a disco ball, dancing. It's kind of scary.

"Not at all. I appreciate you. And you're definitely going away next year to be all smart, and I'll be sticking around here forever to work for my dad, probably battling Knickknack until the cows come home. If you're gonna leave me, we should absolutely go on a date. We commemorated Knickknack's fucked-up legacy, now let's commemorate ours."

I can't fight the smile that creeps up on my face as Leo and I face each other and the sun rises outside the window.

"Really?" I ask.

"Absolutely."

I don't know what to say. That the long life span of our friendship culminated in this seems too good to be true. I want him in several ways. I want him to steer me to the parking lot and throw himself on top of me in the back of my car. To dance under string lights outside of a French café. My intrigue about the world and all it could be has definitely stretched larger following the realization that Knickknack is real.

This thing with Leo—it's been my secret for so long that it's hard to even rationalize that it belongs in reality. "I like you, Leo," I say finally. "I've liked you since the eighth grade. And I'm sorry it took being hunted by a demon clown for me to say it."

But maybe being a bride isn't about wearing a dress or being glamorous, any more than putting yourself on the line for your loved ones is about getting the answer you're looking for. It's about naming love when it's there and giving it freely when it exists in you, regardless of the outcome.

"You know what, Noah?" Leo smiles and wraps me in a hug that feels like the culmination of our ten-year friendship locked in an unbreakable embrace. "I like you too. You didn't even believe in the clown, but you still came along for the ride because your brother was in danger. That's love."

I'm flattered to hear him dote on me. But all I can think about is what happened in that mansion.

"Does that mean we can kiss again?"

Leo laughs and plants one on me.

Sometimes, even in towns built on curses, at least once in a blue moon, things turn out okay.

ACKNOWLEDGMENTS

This anthology has been an absolute dream to put together. We are thrilled to be able to bring fresh perspectives to the horror genre. To the contributors: This would not exist without your words. Thank you for trusting us with your stories.

Shelly: To Alex, for agreeing to edit with me and being amazing throughout this entire process! To Mom, you are a force of nature. You were the first person to tell me I could do this. Thank you for believing in me. To Alaya, your patience with me is unmatched. Thanks for always listening. To my amazing agent, Rebecca Podos, for your time, help, and enthusiasm for this project! To Tiffany, for the opportunity and for shaping this collection into something truly special. And to the friends who've supported me throughout this journey: thanks for the hype!

Alex: To Shelly, for having this brilliant idea in the first place—all of this is because of you! To Hannah Fergesen, thank you for your endless support. To Tiffany and everyone at Wednesday Books for making this possible. To Sara and the rest of the Fairchildren for always believing. To Justine—my Salt Friend and hype squad. And finally, to Chris for being the Shaniac to my Boogara, and to Artemis and Baby Bright Star for being the best cats ever.

To the entire Wednesday Books team: Olga Grlic, jacket designer; Austin Adams, marketing; Eric Meyer, managing editor;

Carla Benton, production editor; Lena Shekhter, production manager; Alyssa Gammello, publicist; Kelly South, publicity assistant; Devan Norman, text designer; Cassie Gutman, copy editor; and Soleil Paz, mechanical designer, thank you for turning this anthology into a reality!

And finally, to you, dear reader, we thank you for picking up our anthology. Happy Halloween!

ABOUT THE EDITORS

SHELLY PAGE is a YA and MG writer of queer stories making her editorial debut with *Night of the Living Queers*. She was raised in Chicago, maintains a long-distance love affair with New York, and currently resides in Los Angeles. By day, she's a practicing attorney representing homeless LGBTQ+ youth of color. By night, she's planning ways to scare her readers while simultaneously awakening their inner gay. She's an oil painter, a lover of autumn, and possibly the only lesbian who doesn't own a cat. She can be found online at shellypage.com or on Twitter @shelly_p_writes.

ALEX BROWN loves rooting for the final girl—especially if she's a monster. Alex has a short story in the instant Indie Bestselling YA folk horror anthology *The Gathering Dark*. Alex is also the co-creator of *The Bridge*, a narrative fiction podcast that's had over one million downloads to date! Alex's sapphic YA horror-comedy debut, *Damned If You Do*, will be published by Page Street Kids in fall 2023. Alex lives in Los Angeles with her partner and their two very chaotic cats. *Night of the Living Queers* is her editorial debut. As far as she knows, she hasn't summoned an Eldritch God who loves pizza . . . yet.

ABOUT THE CONTRIBUTORS

KALYNN BAYRON is the *New York Times* and Indie bestselling author of the YA fantasy novels *Cinderella Is Dead* and *This Poison Heart*. Her latest works include the YA fantasy *This Wicked Fate* and the middle-grade paranormal adventure *The Vanquishers*. She is a CILIP Carnegie Medal nominee, a two-time Cybils Award nominee, and the recipient of the 2022 Randall Kenan Prize for Black LGBTQ Fiction. She is a classically trained vocalist and musical theater enthusiast. When she's not writing, you can find her watching scary movies and spending time with her family.

RYAN DOUGLASS (HE/THEY) is a freelance writer, poet, and *New York Times* bestselling author of *The Taking of Jake Livingston*. His work on media representation has appeared in *HuffPost*, *Atlanta Black Star*, Everyday Feminism, Nerdy POC, and LGBTQ Nation. He was born and raised in Atlanta, Georgia, where he currently resides.

SARA FARIZAN (SHE/HER) is the award-winning author of the young adult novels *Dead Flip*, *Here to Stay*, *Tell Me Again How a Crush Should Feel*, and the Lambda Literary Award–winning *If You Could Be Mine*, which was named one of *Time* magazine's 100 Best YA Books of All Time. She has short stories in the anthologies *Fresh Ink*, *All Out*, *The Radical Element*, *Hungry*

Hearts, *Come On In*, *Fools in Love*, and the upcoming *Out of Our League*. She also writes middle-grade books, like the DC Comics graphic novel *My Buddy, Killer Croc* and *Opportunity Knocks* from Scholastic. Visit sarafarizan.com if you dare! MUAHAHAHAHA!

MAYA GITTELMAN is a queer nonbinary Fil-Am and Jewish writer. Their work centers queer, trans, anti-imperialist liberation, joy, ache, and love. She reviews genre fiction for Tordotcom, and their cultural criticism has been published in *The Body Is Not an Apology*, among other publications. Formerly the events and special projects manager at a Manhattan branch of Barnes & Noble, she is currently at work on a novel.

From a young age, when he wrote his first story at six about kindergartners being eaten by a bear, **KOSOKO JACKSON** has always loved stories. Now he writes them. He is the author of several YA novels starring Black queer protagonists, including his debut, *Yesterday Is History*, and *Survive the Dome*. When not trying to decide how to best torture his characters next, he can be found playing with his golden retriever, Artemis, trying to hit his one-hundred-movies-a-year goal, or playing video games (badly). Visit Kosoko online at kosokojackson.com, on Instagram @kosokojackson, or on Twitter @KosokoJackson.

EM X. LIU is a writer and biochemistry graduate who is fascinated by stories of artificial intelligence and Shakespeare in equal measure. Chronically cold-blooded, Em nevertheless resides in Toronto, Canada.

VANESSA MONTALBAN is the author of *A Tall Dark Trouble*, her upcoming YA fantasy debut. She's a first-generation graduate from the University of Central Florida where she received her bachelor's in creative writing with summa cum laude honors. Fueled by the magic of espresso, Vanessa channels her wanderlust for far-off worlds into writing fantasy and romance for teens.

AYIDA SHONIBAR (SHE/THEY) grew up as an Indian-Bengali immigrant in Europe and currently works as a scientist in North America. Their writing received national recognition in the Scholastic Art and Writing Awards, was selected for the We Need Diverse Books and Desi KidLit mentorship programs, and is featured in multiple short fiction publications.

TARA SIM is the author of *The City of Dusk*, the Scavenge the Stars duology, and the Timekeeper trilogy. She can typically be found wandering the wilds of the Bay Area in California. When she's not chasing cats or lurking in bookstores, she writes books about magic, murder, and mayhem. Follow her on Twitter @EachStarAWorld, and check out her website for fun extras at tarasim.com.

TRANG THANH TRAN writes speculative stories with big emotions about food, belonging, and the Vietnamese diaspora. When not writing, they can be found overcaffeinating on iced coffee and watching zombie movies. *She Is a Haunting* is their debut novel. Connect with them on Twitter @nvtran or their website trangthanhtran.com.

REBECCA KIM WELLS writes books full of magic and fury (and often dragons). Her debut novel *Shatter the Sky* was a New England

Book Award finalist, a Bisexual Book Award winner, an ALA Rainbow Book List title, an Indies Introduce title, and a Kids' Indie Next Pick. She is also the author of *Storm the Earth* and New England Book Award finalist *Briar Girls*, published by Simon & Schuster Books for Young Readers. If she were a hobbit, she would undoubtedly be a Took.